MW01280098

Wolfwarrior

by
Bryan Foster

Bloomington, IN Milton Keynes, UK

authorHOUSE

AuthorHouse™
1663 Liberty Drive, Suite 200
Bloomington, IN 47403
www.authorhouse.com
Phone: 1-800-839-8640

AuthorHouse™ UK Ltd.
500 Avebury Boulevard
Central Milton Keynes, MK9 2BE
www.authorhouse.co.uk
Phone: 08001974150

First published by AuthorHouse 3/29/2006

ISBN: 1-4259-1089-0 (sc)
ISBN: 1-4259-1090-4 (dj)

Printed in the United States of America
Bloomington, Indiana

This book is printed on acid-free paper.

Preface

Wolves

It was a dank, dark evening. Clouds covered the moon and there was very little light. The air hung heavy with the day's rains and the water that was lying still in puddles on the ground. Crickets sang in the dark and somewhere toward the cover of the wood, a wolf bayed in search of something. Little else stirred.

He came out of the wood line into a field. Standing taller than most, long blond hair in damp streaks down his back and in his face. His black cloak was dry. The sigil on his back, black on black but still discernable in this low light, was of a wolf. It was trimmed in red. His sword was belted to his right side and a belt knife was cinched to his left. The hilts of both gleamed with the same sigil. His gauntlets gleamed silver in what little light they could gather, as did his boots. He moved like a shadow and seemed to have all the consistency of one.

He walked up to the lone ranch house. As he entered, he removed his weapons, took off his gauntlets, and sat down to take off his boots. He made no move to remove his cloak. He let out a sigh as he sat. In the light of house, you could see his gauntlets, boots, and sword were all stained with blood. He sighed again at the sight. Then he stood up and walked from the sitting room to the kitchen. At the kitchen table sat three other men all dressed similar to the man, cloak and matching sigil, but with different color cloaks. They paid no mind as the man sat at the table. There was one chair empty.

He looked at all three, and finally spoke "It is done"

To his right sat a man with a blue cloak. He turned and faced the man in black. "With that task complete, what shall we turn our attention to now?"

The man in black turned to him. "What do we need to attend? Can we not just rest?"

Across from the man in black sat a man with a green cloak. He addressed the table and spoke to no particular person. "You know better than to ask of that. We are always with task."

Facing him, again the man in black asked "But why is it so? Under what rule do we labor?"

To his left sat a man in a brown cloak. He too spoke to the air, not facing the man in black. "It is always that the wolf is vigilant, never stagnate. To what shall we attend now?"

Sighing again, the man in black stood from the table. Three sets of eyes followed his movements as he made to remove his cloak. All three seated gasped audibly.

"It is forbidden!" said the blue.

"Do not continue!" said the green.

"You are wolf!" said the brown.

"I am tired," said the man in black simply. "I want to rest. It is past time for rest." He pulled the cloak down over his shoulders. Strapped to his back was a sling device with two small blades cocked over each shoulder and pointed toward the men seated on either side of him. The blades fired and punctured an eye of the seated men. They went in far enough that each blade touched the intended's brain, killing them instantly. Up his right sleeve and hidden in his cloak was a smaller sling device. He activated it with a flick of his wrist and the man who was seated across from him clutched his neck before slumping onto the table. He shrugged the cloak back on to his back and sighed again.

"I will rest. It is past time. But I will continue. The wolf will not be stagnant. Just sleeping." He rose and turned to leave. "Goodnight my friends."

Chapter 1

Gregor

"So this is Alden Hall? Beautiful."

A young man walked into the foyer of a large castle in amazement. Around him were beautiful tapestries, beneath him a marble floor. The hallway before him was lined on either side by standing suits of armor. At the end of the hall was a mural painted on the stone of a black-clad soldier with no armor riding directly into the midst of a raging battle. The man in the mural was a handsome one, even through a snarling face with long blond hair hanging in it. He had a black wolf sigil on his back.

The young man is dressed well, in a red silk waistcoat and dark blue breeches. He also is wearing a red cape with a sigil on the back of a gold crown circled by three moons. Hazel eyes and a head full of red

1

hair round out his features. Even in his amazement, the young man, who appears to be in his early twenties, maintains an air of aristocracy and haughtiness.

He is led down the corridor by a handsome woman in her middle years wearing dark gray livery. She had introduced herself, but already the young man has forgotten her name. She leads him to a staircase near the mural and directs him up it. "At the top of the stairs, turn to your right. The second door on the left side of the hall is where you seek to be. I will lead you no further."

"Thank you," the young man said. He reached the top of the stairs and was faced with another picture of the man in the mural. This time, standing on a clear green field, the man was perfectly groomed and smiling. He really was a handsome man. The hallway was much busier than the foyer, with people of all different types walking quickly and with purpose. Some were dressed in the same livery as the woman from downstairs, some in light chain-mail armor with a similar wolf sigil as the man in the mural was wearing, only a different color. Some in light cloaks with a wolf sigil on the back walked by as well.

The young man reached the door that he was looking for and knocked loudly. "Enter," was the response from behind the door. He walked in to find a man sitting at a desk with a pile of papers in front of him. Three walls of the office were covered in maps, the fourth with a bookcase that was stacked from floor to ceiling with books and scrolls.

"My name is Gregor Holden. I am prince of Kanderfain. I am also Defender of the Realm. I have spent nine years with the *ahin dak* of Horton Bay, as well as studying at the Horton Bay Academy for five years. I now come to Alden Hall to train with Master Pagen Defalorn."

"Cocky little plig aren't you?" the man behind the desk asked, chuckling

Gregor reddened. "I beg your pardon?"

"No need to beg boy, you're supposed to be a prince."

Gregor's face reddened deeper. "And just who might you be sir?"

"My name is Enric Berdard, and I am the special student administer. Now, lets see," Enric riffled through some of the stack of paper on his desk, "Aha…Gregor Holden, decorated by the Horton Bay *ahin dak* Karl Brien, named an *ahin dak* in Kanderfain. Studied under Alexander Blade at Horton Bay academy to be *sul ahin dak* and learned different strategy." Enric paused and his eyebrows raised. "Says here lad that you lead a double life on a forbidden planet? That true?"

"Yes sir. I was born on the planet known only as Earth in the Milky Way galaxy, Sol system. It is very difficult to disappear from the planet permanently. So I have mastered the slide technique and I travel from planet to planet unaided."

Enric looked up at Gregor, "A slider eh? What are your rank and position on this forbidden planet?"

"I am just a citizen."

"Not royalty?"

"No sir.

Enric went back to the sheet. He looked up suddenly and glared at the boy before him. "Says you want Himanoco training. No one trains Himanoco anymore. Choose something else."

"No sir. In fact, Kenor Anor trained under Defalorn as well. I wish to follow in his footsteps. Master Defalorn is said to be one of if not the greatest Himanoco instructor living. He also is taking students. I wish to sign up."

"What makes you think you have the credentials to be Himanoco? *Ahin dak* on one planet doth hardly a Himanoco make." Enric said sarcastically

"I have come to learn." Gregor said simply. "I will be Himanoco."

"Well, for that training, there isn't much that I can do for you. You will be at the mercy of the master. To get to Master Defalorn's quarters, simply find out what the Blackwolf is hiding."

"Hiding?"

"I'm sure you have seen the murals on the wall. After Himanoco the forsaken killed his brother wolves, he set up different learning facilities to help to train people in the ancient arts. He founded this hall. Ask him"

Gregor left Enric's quarters and walked back to the mural at the top of the stairs. Himanoco looked straight toward the stairs, and stood as though guarding something with that smile. *Guarding something,* Gregor thought. *Maybe hiding something?* Gregor reached out to touch the mural and found that his hand passed right through the wall. The people that still remained in the hallway took no notice. He walked straight through the mural into another corridor. There were three doors on each side of the hallway and a door at the end. Gregor could see a sign marked, **Defalorn.**

Gregor walked to the end of the corridor and knocked on another door. Again, the response was "Enter"

Gregor found an office very similar to the one he had just left with the exception that it was not one room but two. The door to the other room was closed. The man behind the desk was older, in his later middle years. Gregor estimated his age to be sixty. He was bald but for the hair that circled the crown of his head, as most bald men were. He had a long braid down his back with the hair that still grew. He also had his nose buried in a book and looked up over the top of his reading glasses as Gregor came in.

"My name is Gregor Holden. I have come to train as Himanoco under you Master Defalorn."

"That so?" was the man's only reply.

"Uh...yes sir," Gregor puffed himself up. "I am *ahin dak* and a slider. I think that I would be an asset to the Himanoco clan and I wish to join up."

"You don't say?"

"Uh...," Gregor didn't know how to respond. "What is it that I need to do to register master?"

"First, do you know your history Prince Holden?" Defalorn asked.

"History sir?"

"The story of Himanoco the black and the Wolf Warriors of ancient times."

"Oh yes sir, of course."

"Well, tell me what you know." Defalorn said sternly, setting his book down.

"In times of legend, it is said that five of the greatest warriors in the universe came together to battle any evil and injustice that they could find and to protect the universe at all times. They consisted of Bayer the Strong, Kivkavzed the Hunter, Gingee the Blade, Malada the Gentile and Himanoco the Shadow. Each was found with the trademark color, Bayer in brown, Kivkavzed in green, Gingee in blue, Malada in red, and Himanoco in black.

" After a heated battle at a place referred to as Gerintan, Himanoco and his followers were to have stopped a usurping of the reigning king. It is said to have been one of the bloodiest battles in the history of time and Himanoco suffered no losses. His warriors used blades and magic to dispatch the uprising. He then headed to the assigned meeting house that the wolves always went to when a mission was over and it was time to decide a new task.

"It is said that Himanoco, in a fit of rage, killed his brother wolves. Malada was not there at the time. He then used the buildings and sanctuaries that he already owned to start training academies and this particular building was one of his firsts. After he left, Malada arrived and found the carnage that had happened at the meeting place. She mourned for three months, one for each of her fallen companions.

"It is then said that the only woman wolf, Malada the gentile, became so enraged she hunted down Himanoco and vanquished him. With no other companions, she slumped into sadness. She resigned herself to vanishing from the universe , but she liked the idea of the wolves living on, and found the best dervish of each clan to help to teach the ways of the clan. She then united the clans to spread the power of the wolf throughout time." Gregor finished.

"Excellent. It would appear that you are as learned as a prince of your standing should be." Defalorn returned to his book.

"Sir, does that mean I have enrolled in your training?" Gregor asked, standing at attention.

"No, it means that you are as learned as I expected of you." Defalorn set his book down again and opened one of his desk drawers. He pulled out a small lapel pin in the shape of snarling wolfs head. "This means that you have enrolled in my training. It will start in five weeks of your normal Earth time. We will see how well you do.

"But, before you go," Defalorn continued, "I have a few questions for you. One, why would you want to train in the arts of Himanoco the forsaken when you are so knowledgeable about his history?"

"The reason that Himanoco killed his brother wolves is unknown. It may never be known. It doesn't change the fact that Himanoco was arguably the strongest of the wolves with his abilities in both with weapons and magic. Wolf warriors were defenders. I am a defender of a realm. The history of Himanoco's insurrection shouldn't mar the fact that it is still wolf warrior training and it is difficult wolf warrior training and it produces great warriors."

"That is an acceptable answer." Defalorn said, rubbing his chin thoughtfully. "Question two, it says here that you idolize Kenor Anor. You also know that he was a former student of mine. He now has his own army and is bent on becoming strong enough to lay claim to the title of Blackwolf. Do you wish to become the challenger for the Blackwolf title?"

Gregor looked down at his shoes. He had often dreamed of leaving the job of defender to another and explore the galaxy. He almost felt as though it were a calling, an itch he had to scratch. Defalorn regarded him, watched him struggle with his answer. "No," Gregor said finally, "I seek only to increase my skills and to protect my realm for as long as I live. I want to ensure that it will always be safe, even from other wolves that might come sniffing around our door."

Defalorn didn't appear pleased by the answer. "Well, we shall see. In five weeks, you will report to the Himanoco Tower on the grounds at sunup. You can get a map from Berdard if you need. Do not forget to wear the pin that I gave you or you will not be admitted. You are dismissed."

Gregor left the room and the hall. He stood just outside of the main arch and created a portal so that he could return home. He lived in northern Michigan. It was a house on the lake Michigan shoreline, three stories, with an attached two-car garage. The sun was setting, making one of those "million dollar sunsets" in the sky that his region of Michigan was so famous for. The sky was alive with every shade of orange, blue, and purple imaginable.

The portal or 'slide' Gregor had created opened up to his room, so no one noticed him coming or going. It wasn't that his parents didn't know. They were the king and queen of Kanderfain, sliders themselves. No, Gregor was always careful that no one noticed his comings or goings because it was ingrained into him. As he stepped through the slide, he waved his hands and his clothes changed from his Kanderfain royal garb to a tee shirt and jean shorts.

He lay on his bed with a flop. *Five weeks*, he thought to himself. *What am I going to do for five weeks until I can go to the academy?* He thought back to the years he had spent at Horton Bay on Tankaras. How he had enjoyed Xavier Braddock's lectures. Xavier was the one who told him to pursue Himanoco. Xavier himself was a Himanoco, an adventurer, and had served alongside Kenor. Gregor had envied him since the first moment they met.

For the second time that day, Gregor found himself wishing that he could shirk his duties to Kanderfain and travel abroad for more than just training. He had heard so many legends in his time, warriors who traveled here and there in search of everything from fame and treasure to well, just plain old adventure. Being born a prince, the first-born son, Kanderfain law stated that unless he was the only heir, he would be the Defender of the Realm. What that meant was he would be commander of all of the armies of the land. If he were the only heir, he would be king, but that was unlikely as the people preferred female heirs to ascend. When his younger sister Haley was born, he knew at five years old that his fate was sealed.

As he was thinking this, Haley came bounding into his room in her usual manner. Sighing, he leveled a cool gaze at her. "For being a princess, you should really learn to knock."

"It's because I'm a princess that I don't have to big brother," she responded smartly. At fifteen, Haley is every bit as attractive as her brother and looks older than his twenty. She has auburn hair that she is currently wearing pulled back in a ponytail, but is stunning when it is let loose. Her hazel eyes always seem to be hiding some sort of mischief. She smiles at him sweetly and any man other than a brother would have melted.

"What do you want Haley?"

The smile fades a little. Just a little. "Mom and Dad want to talk to you when you get in. They're downstairs. I was just popping in because I felt you slide home"

Since Haley was three, she and Gregor had a bond formed between them. It is three that royalty on Kanderfain begin to train for what they will later become. Since she was the oldest female heir and was going to be queen, she had a bond with the brother that would be her defender until both were dead. That bond never ceased to irk Gregor just a little, as though his sister always had her eye on him.

Gregor got up and shoved his sister as he walked past her. She yelped and moved to shove back but Gregor danced away and headed for the stairs. "Go play in your own room," he called back to her.

He knew that she didn't "play" anymore, but he was a big brother and like all big brothers, he had to irritate his little sister anyway that he could. As he headed down to the family room, his younger brother Alexander was coming in the front door. Alex had just turned twelve last month. His hair was darker than Haley and Gregor, and his eyes were greener. Otherwise though, he looked just like his siblings; a distinction he had already grown tired of hearing.

"Hey Greggie, Mom and Dad are looking for you"

"I know, Haley already told me." Gregor regarded his brother. He was covered in dirt and his shirt was torn. " What have you been doing."

Alex had a tell tale sheepish look whenever he had been doing something that he shouldn't be doing, and that look was spread across his face now. "Nothing," he replied.

"Uh-huh, right" Gregor said with a grin on his face. "Good thing Mom and Dad already want to talk to me. That'll give you time to run upstairs and clean up eh?" Alex was regarding his shoes, his ears tipped in red. "Go on, hurry up. I'll stall for you as long as I can"

Alex returned Gregor's grin. "Thanks Greggie, I owe you one." Alex shot past his brother and ran up the stairs.

"You owe me several," Gregor called after him, "but who's keeping count?" Gregor rounded the corner through the foyer and headed into the dining room. With a long, oak table, the dining room had become the meeting headquarters in the Holden family. Whenever any of the children were summoned to their parents, that was always where they were expected to go.

Arthur Holden was already seated at the head of the table when Gregor arrived. A handsome man still today, Arthur was well into middle years. He had a youthful face, and except for the graying of his beard and a few streaks of gray in his hair, he appeared much younger than he was. It was often discussed that if Arthur were to shave his beard, he and Gregor would have passed more for brothers than for father and son. His green eyes, sometimes appearing to be able to pierce armor with a stare, looked thoughtfully at his son

"Marion, Greg is here. You wanna come in here?"

"Be right there Art, be right there."

"Have a seat son," Arthur said, motioning to the chair at the foot of the table. "Was it your sister or brother who caught you for us?"

"Haley," Gregor said taking his seat. "She felt me through the bond."

"Oh, I always forget about the bond" Marion said as she wafted into the room. Gregor rose as she entered and she waved him down reflexively. She took the chair to the left of her husband. "We really don't need to tell Alexander when we can just sick your sister on your heels." Marion smiled at Gregor. She was every bit as beautiful as Arthur was handsome, her age hardly reflected in her looks. Her hair was the color of fire, full and braided halfway down her back. Her brown eyes showed the same shine as her children.

There was levity in her voice, but the seating positions were deliberate. If Gregor had been summoned to an audience with the king and queen at Gavenmoor, the Holden's castle on Kanderfain, the situation would have been the same and Gregor recognized that. He knew what was coming next and his hackles began to rise.

"Son," Arthur started, "we ask you here because we are concerned with your continuing training. You are *ahin dak* on our planet. You have made strides and are almost *sul ahin dak*. Your magic surpasses anyone in your family. Why then, do you plan to study for another three years to become Himanoco? You could be *sul ahin dak* in six months."

"Dad, what should it matter? Six months, three years, thirty years. If need be, I'll come running. But Haley isn't queen and I am not defender yet and so I am going to train to my full potential."

"But Greg," Marion started, "Himanoco are so dangerous. It is a forsaken clan whose members have been either swearing loyalty to Kenor Anor or disappearing. Neither of these is an option for you. You could be Gingee, and your magic would just be accepted but never really necessary."

"Mom, I like magic. I have expanded my geomagic to the point where I am almost a licensed practitioner. I have been a licensed slider since I was three. And my summoning and illusion powers are coming along. Master Braddock thinks I could be great. Why don't you?"

"It's not that we don't think you could be great son. We just worry about your allegiance when this is over. Will you swear to the crown or will you swear to the Blackwolf?"

"Dad, I will be the Defender. I was born the Defender and I will die the Defender."

"Are you sure about that son?" Arthur asked accusingly. "Your mother may forget the bond, but I sure haven't. Your sister feels you pull away. She sees your feelings and can feel your anger. That's the problem with having an empath for a sister." Gregor's face turned sour and Arthur held up a hand. "Don't you go blaming her. I had to put my own daughter to the inquiry just to get it drug out of her. I thought the threat would have been enough. That's the problem with having an empath for a mother." Marion shook her head sadly.

Gregor paused for a moment. Hearing his sister was exposed to an Inquisitor and him not feeling it through the bond they shared meant that her empathic powers had grown to where she could reverse the power and disconnect the bond. He may always have acted as though he hated having that nagging bundle of thoughts and emotions in the back of his mind, but knowing now that it could be taken away or "blocked" upset him. He would discuss that later with his sister and he sent that thought through the bond with some force. He couldn't defend her if he couldn't feel her.

Marion brightened at her son. "He feels concern for his sister."

"Good," Arthur said. "That's something. Now tell me Gregor, why should we allow you to partake this training?"

Gregor studied his father for a moment. He had never even considered the fact that he need ask. He had pursued any study he wanted to for so long now that he had just assumed he could follow wherever the path led him. "You should allow me this training because I want it. It is training that we make me stronger. The strongest Defender of the Realm in the history of Kanderfain. It will be beneficial to put down squabbling and uprising. If the queen has the backing of a full Himanoco warrior, who would dare challenger her? And invasion? What kind of an army would a Himanoco warrior have at his disposal? My presence alone could help Kanderfain to avoid battles and usher in a new era of peace. A sort of cold war maneuver."

Arthur considered this for a moment. He looked at his wife and Marion inclined her head slightly, a gesture that Gregor recognized as a confirmation that what he said he felt to be the truth. In essence Gregor did believe what he said, but it wasn't the only reason that he was going to train Himanoco. The part that he left out was that he wanted to invade other lands in the name of Kanderfain. If he couldn't seek out adventure, he would create some of his own.

"Alright son, I concede for now. You can have your training. But I have five weeks before it starts to poke holes in your story. If they exist, I'll find them."

"I have no fear of my father's sword." Gregor said formally as he rose. "By your leave."

Arthur shot Gregor a hard look for the formality in his action while they were in the Michigan house and not the castle. "You may go," he said simply.

Alexander came bounding back down the stairs. Marion caught a glimpse of him as he headed into the family room to watch some television. "Alex, weren't you wearing a blue shirt when you went out this morning?"

Gregor heard little else of his mother chasing Alexander. He headed back upstairs to find Haley. She was still in his room, waiting patiently at his desk. She knew what he wanted from the bond; it had felt like someone hit her when Gregor sent that through.

"So, you can block out the bond?" he asked.

"I can block emotion. You never lost touch with me." Haley responded indignantly. Then she moved her eyes away from his face and looked at the floor. "I wouldn't have been able to hide the pain if the inquisitor really had started in on me, so I spilled my guts." She looked back at him, "I didn't want to tell! I'm sorry!" Tears started to well up in her eyes. "Why didn't you tell me? I will be queen and I could release you from you obligation."

Gregor sighed. "I'm sorry Haley. I really am. I don't really want to leave you. I would worry too much about you to leave your protection in anyone else's hands. It's just," Gregor thought for a moment, "don't you sometimes feel trapped by what you are? By what you have to become? Don't you sometimes wonder if the grass really is any greener on the other side? God, sometime I am so envious of Alex! He may have our expectations to live up to, but not our destiny!"

Gregor wiped away the tears in his sister's eyes. "Besides, you couldn't release me even if you did want to. You will be queen, but that won't be strong enough to break that tradition." Gregor smiled at his sister and she managed a watery smile in return. "You don't worry about me or my protection. You leave the protection bit to me little sister, you just work on diplomacy."

Haley left the room and Gregor sat at his desk, pulling out his journal. He wanted to log the events of the day. He was going to train Himanoco. He was going to be like his mentors. Gregor felt it was one of the most exciting days of his life. When he was finished, he set the journal back on the shelf and went to the phone to call his girlfriend.

"Hello?"

"Sam! Hi!"

"Well, you certainly are in a good mood. What's up?"

"I was just calling to see what it is we are going to do today?"

"Well," Samantha paused for a moment, "did you have anything in particular in mind?"

"Seems your in a good mood too," Gregor said, impishly. "Why don't I swing by and we can come up with something, I'm sure."

"Sounds good. See you in a few minutes?"

"Absolutely!" Gregor said enthusiastically and hung up the phone. He and Samantha had been together for three years. He had never told her what he was or what his family was, it was forbidden. This new training was going to be tough on them. He didn't know how long he was going to be away and he had to come up with an excuse as to where he was and why she couldn't get a hold of him.

Worry about that later he thought to himself angrily. *You have a great girl waiting for you, you're going to be one of the strongest warriors in the galaxy, don't start to wallow in that same old self-pity now.*

Whistling, he shut the door to his room and headed to the garage. *Someday, you'll tell her everything. Then we'll see just how much that she loves you. Then again,* he thought with a smile, *not many guys can make a girl a princess!*

And on that thought, he got in his car and drove away.

Chapter 2

Candace

Candace Orthon entered the foyer at Alden Hall with a look of awe on her face. She had just reached eighteen, the minimum age requirement to train as Himanoco, two days ago. Now she was standing in a school founded by Himanoco.

The woman in the dark gray livery took Candace to the staircase at the end of the corridor. Staring at the mural of Himanoco charging into battle, she completely missed what the serving woman was saying. "I'm sorry, could you repeat that please?"

"At the top of the stairs, turn to your right. The second door on the left side of the hall is where you seek to be. I will lead you no further."

"Oh, thank you very much"

Candace went to the door that she was instructed to and knocked. A voice from behind the door called "Enter" so she went in. In the crowded office, a balding man sat at a desk behind a sea of papers. He didn't raise his head as she came in.

"Hello sir. My name is Candace Orthon and I have come here to train as a Himanoco warrior under master Pagan Defalorn. I was instructed by the serving woman downstairs that I was to see you."

"Orthon, you say? Let's see." The man shuffled through the files on his desk and pulled one out triumphantly. "Orthon, a legacy from Baktarus. You will be the fourth generation Himanoco in your family if you can pass the training. Decorated *ahin dak* by Anskin Ross and Casgill Hofver'Cho, both of Baktarus. Licensed conjurer and illusionist by the Cordon Council. How will you traveling back and forth from Baktarus to the academy?"

"I have a slide stone that is keyed in to my room at my families keep. I just need a slider to tune it to a dormitory room here and I can move about at will. I do wish to remain on site for my training though and would not expect to leave the academy very often."

"Not a problem. I will set you up an appointment with one of our sliders. Also," the man pulled an envelope from her file, "I had taken the liberty of already getting you a room in the dormitories. Your room assignment, keys and a map of the grounds are all in this envelope. To get to your instructor, you need figure out what the Blackwolf is hiding."

"Thank you sir," Candace said, saluting the man.

"Don't salute me, I'm just a councilor," the man said with a dismissive wave.

Candace walked back into the busy hallway. She went to the mural of the Blackwolf at the top of the staircase and walked right through. She was familiar with the hidden hallway trick and as an accomplished illusionist, she saw that it was a hidden passage the minute she came up the stairs.

At the end of the short hallway she found the door marked **Defalorn** and knocked. "Enter" was once again the response from the other side of the door and Candace entered to find an office similar to the one she had just left. The man behind the desk seemed distressed over something. He was wiping sweat from his brow and the room was far to cool for heat to be the cause.

"I was sent here to sign up for Himanoco training sir," she said, saluting.

The man behind the desk returned her salute. "I am Master Pagan Defalorn. Who might you be young lady?"

"Apologies sir. My name is Candace Orthon."

"Orthon?" the man asked, his eyebrows going up. "Why, I trained your father, Mitris Orthon! It's hard to believe that his daughter is already old enough to begin the training." Defalorn paused for a moment. "How is your father these days?"

"Well as can be expected sir. He has chosen to renounce Kenor Anor's claim to be the Blackwolf incarnate. He has been ostracized by many of the people he once counted as friends and is having a hard time with the clan. Had it not been tradition in my family, he may not have allowed me to train."

Defalorn scratched his chin thoughtfully. "Well, we all do what we must," he said. "In any event, the training for Himanoco begins in five weeks. This will give you plenty of time to get settled into the dormitory and familiarize yourself with the academy. You will report to Himanoco Tower in the center of the grounds at sunup. Wear this lapel pin or you will not be admitted." He handed her a snarling wolf's head pin. "Dismissed."

Candace saluted again and spun around to leave the office. She walked back down to the foyer and found an out of the way bench so that she could examine the envelope that Berdard had given her and the wolf head pin. The pin was solid silver and glinted menacingly when it caught the light right. It was a symbol to be both feared and respected, although it was typically just feared.

The contents of the envelope were next. First, Candace studied the map. A fifteen-foot stone wall surrounded the entire compound of Alden Hall. Alden Hall was not only the name of the Academy, but also the name of the building she was in. It stood at the north end of the compound, at the only entrance, and served as the administration building. Her dormitory quarters, and all of the dormitory including the Master trainers living quarters, were at the opposite end of the compound from Alden Hall. Also at that end were two different general stores, one for food and the other for battle equipment. The Himanoco Tower stood in the middle of the compound, a circular spire that stretched thirty feet into the air. The other four wolf towers ringed it, each standing just slightly lower in size to Himanoco Tower. On the east perimeter of the compound stood the library, where most of the Malada spent their time and the open ground where you could find the majority of the Bayer, and the Gingee gym. On the west perimeter, the mess hall and four different chapels lined the wall. Outside of the great wall, the entire compound was surrounded by forest, with two small lakes on the north and west sides. The forest also appeared on Candace's map because they were used to help train the Kivkavzed in tracking and survival. Candace noticed that, beside the tower, each different wolf clan had a separate area to themselves but the Himanoco. She didn't dwell on that fact though.

She found her room assignment and found where she had to go on the map. Out in the compound, Candace marveled at the different structures and the different people. There was a bustle in the air as students, masters, and workers alike scurried here and there. Most classes were to begin in a week and registration was only today and tomorrow. Candace had been surprised when Defalorn said that she had five weeks to wait, but she didn't dwell on that fact either. What she did dwell on was Himanoco Tower.

The map did the building little justice. Its own courtyard surrounded the tower and you could see the square-like perimeter created by the other four towers. It was every bit as wide as it was tall. It had no windows and no mortar anywhere that she could see. It appeared to be carved out of one solid piece and was black as pitch. Two large guards, spears in hand, guarded the only entrance at the north face of the building. No one else even seemed to come into this part of the compound, preferring to stay outside the perimeter. Candace noticed that the buzz that she felt when she was walking toward the tower was completely silent. It was an odd sensation and she jogged around the tower so that she could get back in the hustle of the crowd.

Finally, she reached her dormitory. It was a five story brown building. People were moving their items in as she walked up and Candace realized that she didn't have any items with her. *That's all right though,* she thought to herself. *I'll just slide home after I find my room and have someone slide me back with my stuff.* According to her map her room was on the third floor.

When she entered, she was surprised at the layout of the room. It was more like a house and less like a barracks then she had anticipated. The room itself was actually two rooms, the first was a living room, dining room, kitchen combination. There were five plain chairs, a wooden table, and an "L" shaped counter to separate the kitchen from the rest of the room with four stools around it. There was a very small space between the next room that had a lavatory closet and a door that led to the lavatory. She peered inside and saw three sinks, two commodes, two showers, and a door that she assumed led to the room next door. The second part of her room was the bedroom and it had two desks, two sets of bunk beds, two closets and two dressers. There was a young lady already in the room unpacking her things.

She was about five and half feet tall, with long blonde hair and the most striking blue eyes. Slight of build, she gracefully moved about the room, unpacking her things and putting them away neatly. Then she noticed that Candace had come in.

"*Salo pas, ken codatia* Lohane" the girl said smiling.

"I'm sorry," Candace said, confused, "what was that you said?"

The girl held up a finger to signal Candace to wait a moment. She rummaged through a bag on one of the desks and pulled out a small, brown, disk shaped object. She placed the disk on her temple and made a motion at Candace as if she wanted Candace to say something else.

"Hello, my name is Candace Orthon. What's your name?"

The girl paused for a moment and the disk changed color from brown to blue. "I'm sorry," she said. "My name is Lohane. I come from the planet Lovnijk and we speak a different language than is spoken here. I forgot to put on my speak stone before you arrived, that is why we could not understand eachother."

"Oh, I see." Candace said, not really seeing at all. "Well, anyway, it looks like we will be rooming together for the term. This is a great room."

"Yes, it is very nice," Lohane agreed. "And I must say, I am anxious to meet the other people who will be living with us Candace Orthon. I have never been away from my home, much less off of my planet. I am very excited!"

"Me too!" Candace eyed the room. "Well, where should I sleep?"

"Oh, I do not mind where I sleep Candace Orthon. Choose whichever bed you would like."

"Actually, I don't have anything with me right now. I was thinking I would slide home really quickly and be right back. Want to come with me?"

"Where is home Candace Orthon?"

"Lohane, just call me Candace o.k." Lohane shook her head in agreement and smiled. "I come from the planet Baktarus," Candace continued. "I'm Lady Candace there, but you can still just call me Candace."

"Ohh my, another planet. How exciting! Yes, I would love to accompany Candace Or..." Lohane paused, "love to accompany Candace to her home to see her planet. If you could just help me unpack a few things and perhaps we should leave a note for our prospective roommates?"

"Oh sure, absolutely." The two finished unpacking Lohane's things and wrote a note to their, as yet, unknown roommates. "All right, Lohane," Candace said, "I need you to hold on to my cloak, o.k."

"Certainly."

Candace took a small, copper colored stone from one of her waist pouches. She rubbed the stone and a portal opened. When a person slides, it resembles being in a hallway. A door opens with a bright flash of light and you walk in. Everything is dark. Then you picture in your mind where you want to go. The hallway "slides" you to the door that you want, the flash of light returns, and you walk out. In this case, since Candace used her slide stone, the hallway started to shift as soon as she and Lohane walked through the portal.

They emerged in a large bedroom. There was a four poster bed, a large, hand made rug on the floor and a sitting area with three cushy looking chairs. A large chest of drawers and dresser were on the wall near the door and a walk-in closet was across from the two pieces of furniture.

"Well, welcome to Castle Orthon," Candace said with a wave of her arms. "Would you like to take the tour, or do you want to just pack and get out of here?"

"No, let us stay. I would love to see where and how you live."

"You bet. C'mon."

The two left the room and moved through the hallway. Candace's room was on the third floor, so the girls had to make their way down. On the way, they passed a woman in dark green livery with a yellow star on the left breast of her jacket and each shoulder. She brightened when she saw Candace.

"Lady Candace, I thought you had gone off to the academy. What are you doing here?"

"Oh, I needed to pack my things. This is my one of my roommates, Lohane. Lohane, this is Giselle. She is the headmistress of the house." Lohane made a bow to Giselle. Startled, Giselle tried to imitate the motion. Candace just smiled. "Giselle, could you have Rosivich pack my belongings? I would like to take my new friend to Tuscaway proper."

"If my lady thinks that her father will approve a visit to Tuscaway, I will have no problem making sure that her luggage is prepared for her tenure abroad." Giselle regarded Candace sternly as she spoke. Then she nodded curtly and proceeded on her way, directly towards her father's quarters. Candace picked up the pace and Lohane rushed to keep up.

At last, they reached the hall of the castle and headed out the wide double doors that always stood open during the days in this summer heat. As they were headed down the pathway to the village below, a flash of light appeared a few feet in front of the duo and a man strode out. Slightly over six feet tall, he was dressed all in black with a black cloak that fit tightly in the shoulders and flared out just below the knees. His stern face regarded the two suspiciously and his hands planted themselves firmly on his hips.

"*Oy com bliklern* Himanoco!" Lohane cried. Quickly, she made a motion with her hands and a small ball of blue flame streaked towards the man.

A startled look appeared on the man's face and he barely dodged the fireball. Recovering quickly, he leapt into the air, seeming to jump forever. He flipped and twisted until he landed right behind the girls, facing their backs. He scooped up Lohane and held both of her wrists in one of his large hands. She struggled frantically.

"Father, Lohane, please stop!" Candace cried.

Lohane's mouth dropped open. She stopped struggling and stared at her newfound friend.

"*Geko* Lohane. *Den nor* Candace. *Sil no pa. Ken codatia* Mitris," the man said, setting Lohane down. Candace's face was red from embarrassment and worry.

"You know my language! I apologize Candace's father. I should not have reacted so hastily."

"That is quite all right *sylnre*." Mitris said, smiling. Turning to face Candace, his smile quickly faded. "I am dressed and about to leave for a meeting when Mistress Giselle breaks into my quarters to tell me that not only is my daughter in the keep, she is headed for Tuscaway

unescorted with a young lady who has never before been seen with her."
He turned back toward Lohane and smiled. "I must say though, that
was an excellent Blazeball." Back to Candace, "Now, would someone
like to tell me just what is going on here or should I try to deduce it
for myself?"

"Father, I just came back to pack a few things and show off our
wonderful castle and our exciting planet to my roommate at the
academy." Candace forced a smile, prayed that her legs would hold
and that the redness had faded from her face. "I also was going to have
Master Luhagne lock in the coordinates of my room at the academy to
my room at home." That last was not a total lie. Now that she thought
of it, she would have Master Luhagne set those coordinates.

This time, Mitris managed a smile for his daughter. "You were
always a quick thinker Candace. It's one of the things about you I'd like
to take credit for." Mitris sighed. "I really don't have time to go into this
attempted deception. What I suggest is you let Casgill accompany you
two ladies into Tuscaway." Shaking his head, Mitris continued. "You
have to learn, light of my heart, that it really is improper for a woman
of your stature to go riding into town unescorted. Besides, times have
been hard and the people of Tuscaway are not as receptive to aristocrats
as they have in years past, even to the lord of their land and his lady
daughter."

"But father," Candace started indignantly, "I am training to be Himanoco and...," she paused and whispered to Lohane. "Quick what are you training to become at the academy?"

"Malada"

"And Lohane is practically a Malada. I think that we can handle ourselves" Candace finished, crossing her arms across her chest.

"It isn't that I think you incapable of handling yourselves. It is protocol Candace. Now I must leave. Give me no more trouble over this." With that, Mitris made another slash of light and disappeared.

Glumly, Candace motioned for Lohane to follow her. "We have to head over to the backside of the castle, where the training fields are and where Casgill's quarters are."

Lohane followed in amazement. "Candace, are you really going to train to be a Himanoco warrior?"

"Yes. My father is one, my grandfather was one, and my great grandfather was one. It is tradition in my family. Fortunately for me, my father only had a daughter so I get to train. If I had a brother, he would carry on the tradition."

"But Himanoco, it is so dangerous and evil."

"That's an unfair stigma. Himanoco may have turned traitor, but that shouldn't besmirch the fact that he was one of the greatest warriors of all time and one of the most successful in battle. Just because I train to follow his techniques, doesn't mean that I will follow his traits."

"Yes, I see your point. The only reason I say such things is that my planet is ruled by a not so benevolent Himanoco named Rath. I and a few others were smuggled off of my planet to train with the hope that we may be able to overpower Rath and free my planet."

" By Jehan's ears, but that's awful! I can't believe the councils would stand for a wolf warrior ruling a planet in an evil way!" Candace said, aghast.

"But what would they do?" Lohane questioned, a confused look on her face. "He is Himanoco."

"But that doesn't mean he is above the law. Don't you have councils on your planet? People who are in charge in some way?"

"But I told you Candace, Rath is in charge" Lohane said, still not understanding.

"But the people who use magic, aren't there laws against who can and can't use magic? Aren't there groups of people that check the leaders of your planet?"

"Ah I understand. You are speaking of a legislative. I have read of such things in study. But I thought that surely all of these things died out in olden times? Do you mean to say that your planet has such a legislative body?"

"Several actually," Candace said. "The Cordon Council monitors and licenses the majority of the magic users on this planet. The Cho-Dan and the Un-Gat monitor warriors and the different *dak* of the planet. Regali Council monitors trade and makes sure to keep a lid on price gouging."

"But your father said that you own the land, you are aristocrats. You then let other people tell you what to do with your land? You let other people tell you what you can and can't be?" Lohane was still confused.

"It's not that simple." Candace paused. "Can I explain it to you later? We're at Casgills."

"Certainly Candace. I look forward to such a conversation as I am still very confused."

Candace knocked on Casgill's door. The house was a modest country house. It was only one story, with a thatch roof. A large, brooding man with a face that seemed carved of stone answered the door. His complexion was darker than both that of Candace and Mitris. He had darker hair than they did as well. His large, brown eyes seemed to bore through whatever they looked at while still keeping the appearance to be watching in every different direction.

"Lady Candace." His voice rumbled as he spoke. "To what do I owe this pleasure?"

"I would like to show my friend the town of Tuscaway and father has said that I am not permitted to venture into town without proper escort."

"You need a flag bearer?" Casgill's face softened and he seemed amused. "I'm sure that irked your bottom good. Very well mistress, if you and your friend would like, you can wait inside while I put on the proper attire."

Candace blushed slightly at the 'bottom' remark. It was a well known fact that even though Casgill was more than ten years older than her, she had a flaming crush on him when she was his student. "Thank you Casgill, I believe we will wait inside while you get ready."

The inside of the little house reflected the outside. The furnishings were plain. The walls were bare. The windows had no curtains. And the bedroom door was open just enough to see a plain bed and dresser.

Casgill got ready quickly. He led the girls to the stable yard and everyone mounted. After a short ride, they were in Tuscaway. The buildings were tall, but not very extravagant. Signs showed different inns, taverns, tailors, and other item shops. The people that they trio passed on the streets paid little mind to the riders. It was not the first time that they had seen the *ahin dak* or the lady of the land.

"Where is our little party headed to ladies?"

"Master Luhagne's shop. I need to get my slide stone calibrated.'

"Magic rocks? I thought that I had taught you to steer clear of such things."

"I am not just a sword master. I will use magic, as my father does. If you please Casgill," Candace finished, motioning the man forward so that he could lead them to their destination. She waited until he could not hear her and Lohane clearly if they spoke in whispers. "So, what do you think of him? Good looking isn't he?" Candace asked.

"Who do you mean, Casgill?" Lohane said, not whispering at all.

Candace turned bright red again. "Keep your voice down!" she hissed. "Yes, I mean Casgill."

"Oh, he is an interesting man." Lohane whispered this time. "But he is not the type of man that I particularly find attractive. My type is of a slighter build and a more inviting face."

"Here we are ladies," Casgill said, breaking the girls from their conversation. The shop they stood outside of was the grandest on the block. The sign had a man opening a door, and behind the open door was a flood of light.

As the three went inside, they saw a smallish man in his later years behind the counter. He had a long, gray beard that hung down to his belt buckle. He also wore spectacles that were very thick; it was rumored by the local children that the man could burn ants on ground just by looking at them. Of course, some of that may be due to the fact that he was one of the most powerful magic users in all of the land.

"Well, if it isn't Casgill and Candace. Always thought you'd make a fine couple, no matter how different your age." The old man spotted Lohane. "Or wait, is maybe this lovely young specimen your intended, swordsman?"

Candace blushed furiously at the old man's remarks. "Master Luhagne! We have come here today to purchase your services, not discuss our love life!"

"Yep, was right the first time eh?" The old man had come around the counter and he needled Casgill with his elbow at the last remark. "Well then, what can I do for ye this lovely day?"

"My stone will have the coordinates from my last slide. It is my dormitory room at the Alden Hall Academy on Gazikstin. I would like you to calibrate my stone so that I can move freely from my chambers here on this planet to my chambers on that one."

"No problem at all young lady. If I can just see the stone?" Candace handed it over. "Ah yes, here are the coordinates right here." Luhagne closed his bony hand around the stone and it began to glow with an eerie green light. Then it stopped. "You are all set there, m'lady. That will be fifty gold crowns."

"Fifty crowns!" Casgill muttered under his breath. "All for a bunch of magical nonsense."

Candace shot Casgill a withering glance. "Of course Master Luhagne. You will bill the house of Orthon as always?"

"Certainly m'lady. Thank you for your patronage. And don't worry, Casgill will come around eventually."

Blushing again, the trio found themselves back on the street. "Well, Lohane, what do you think of everything?" Candace asked, trying to take her mind off of the brooding figure next to her.

"It is very interesting. Much like Gazikstin with its buildings and structure. Thank you for showing me Candace. Should we not get back to our dormitory room as the rest of our roommates have surely arrived?"

"Oh, sure." Candace was suddenly relieved. "Casgill, do you think you could manage to take our horses back to the stable alone?"

"Pugh, that is no challenge at all for me Candace and you know it! Now, go ahead and use your magic toy and hurry back to your training. Remember, I certified you *ahin dak* so you're a representation of me as much as you show off yourself."

"Let's go!" she grabbed Lohane's arm and they slid to her room at the keep. Giselle was already there with another woman. They appeared to be just finishing with Candace's belongings. "Thank you Giselle, Rosivich." Candace and Lohane grabbed her items from the serving women. "If you will excuse us." The portal opened and the two walked back through to the dormitory at Alden Hall. Candace had never been so excited in her life.

Chapter 3

Ran

Ran walked into Alden Hall proudly, though you wouldn't have been able to tell it. His clothes were so tattered as to be considered rags. He was stooped over and needed the assistance of a cane. Quickly, a well-dressed young guard wearing a recently polished suit of armor on came rushing up to him. "I'm sorry sir, we have no alms to give."

Seemingly to appear from nowhere, a woman in her middle years, dressed in dark gray livery with symbols resembling that of the guard stood at Ran's side. "It is all right. He is expected."

The guard had a puzzled look for a moment and Ran grinned a near toothless grin at him. The guard's face soured slightly, but he returned to his post at the door. Ran allowed himself to be led through the foyer of Alden Hall by the woman to a staircase, sparing himself a glance at her backside. If the woman took any notice, she did not show it. *Not bad for a gal of her age, not bad at all* Ran thought to himself.

When they reached the staircase, she turned. " At the top of the stairs, turn to the right. The second door on the left side of the hall is where you seek to be. I will lead you no further."

"Aww, are you sure lass? You've been a great escort so far," Ran said, smiling his best smile.

She did not return his smile. "Have a good day sir." With that, she was off to attend to the other hundred things that women dressed in livery attend to.

And I didn't even catch her name. Must be slipping in my old age. Ran made his way to the top of the stairs, then to the door that he was directed to. He rasped the door with the head of his cane. "Enter" came the voice from the other side, so in Ran went. The man who sat behind the desk did a double take at Ran.

"Are you sure that you are in the right place sir?" the man asked.

"Sure that this is where the pretty thing downstairs told me to come to." Ran flashed that winning smile, but the man behind the desk wasn't convinced. "Name's Ran Grastle. I've come to be a Himanoco warrior."

At this the man behind the desk began to laugh. "Himanoco? Are you serious? You can barely walk and you want to train in the ways of the forsaken?" The man peeled out more laughter. Ran just stood patiently. "For the sake of argument, let me look and see if I have a file on you mister Grastle." Still chuckling, the man rummaged through the pile of files on his desk. He stopped laughing when he came to Ran's file. He opened it up and his jaw hung open in amazement.

"There is no way that you are the man listed in this file," the man behind the desk stated. "Ran Grastle is *sul ahin dak* as well as *sul calen dak* on Balderia. Three different councils on that planet certify the man in this file to be the planetary leader in illusion, battle magic, and geomagic. Not to mention, this man is supposed to be a certified apothecary and herbologist." The man behind the desk finished with a huff.

"I don't see any reason why I shouldn't be that man. Wouldn't you naturally assume that much knowledge would take a body awhile to amass?"

"But," the man turned back to the file, searching. "I guess that I can agree with that. But what in Jehan's name would possess a man of that much knowledge and varied skills, not to mention your obvious age, to wish to train in the rigors of Himanoco?"

"Why not? What else has an old man to do?"

"Sir, with all due respect to the amount of knowledge you have gained over the years, you are in no condition to train Himanoco. In fact, sir, you aren't in any condition to train as any of the Wolfwarriors. I'm afraid we will have to decline your application."

"I'm sorry, but I would like the master's opinion before I pack in my bags and go home. I'm guessing his office is behind that illusionary mural I saw at the top of the stairs?"

"If you feel that you have to, but I'm sure that he will tell you the same things I am telling you sir."

"Mind if I hand him that file, or will he have a copy of it?"

"Oh, he has a copy of all students who apply for Himanoco training. Master Defalorn is the only Himanoco trainer at this academy; he'll recognize your name for sure with all of those talents you have listed."

"Thank you for your time lad." Ran winked at the man, bowed and left the room. He walked through the mural of Himanoco that was at the top of the staircase and to the door marked **Defalorn**. Again, he rasped on the door with his cane and again, the response from the other side was a simple "Enter". Ran entered.

The man behind this desk had much the same reaction as the one in the other office. "Is there something I can do for you sir?"

"Yes, I'm here to train Himanoco."

The look on Defalorn was incredulous. "I'm sorry. I think that is impossible mister..."

"Grastle. Ran Grastle. And I was invited to apply by you personally Master Defalorn."

The look on Defalorn's face softened. Then he grinned at Ran. "My apologies Master Grastle. My illusion skills are sub-par for my station, I'll readily admit. Is there a particular reason for the appearance?"

Ran made a small wave of his hands and his rags turned into a green waistcoat with gold trimming, dark green breeches, and leather boots that came halfway up his calf. His face changed from that of a haggard, toothless old man to that of a handsome man in his middle years with light brown hair and large brown eyes. His grin was broad at Defalorn, "Actually, I'm disappointed it took my name for you to figure me out. What I am curious about is how the serving woman on the first level could tell who I was or that I belonged here?"

"That must have been Alundra. She is the Head Mistress here and greets all of the Himanoco applicants in that same ominous tone. She wears a necklace that was created by four different Himanoco warriors. It allows her to see through the strongest illusions and provides her with a sort of invisibility by making your eyes pass over her if she doesn't move, and generally makes her job that much more fun around here.

"Well," Defalorn said, changing the subject, "with that display of ability your invitation is duly met. If you are still interested?"

"Oh certainly. I'm sure it will be quite the adventure to be Himanoco. At our age, adventure is still something that can be looked forward too eh?" Ran grinned again.

This time Defalorn didn't return the grin. "Then, you'll need this." He handed Ran a silver wolf's head pin. "Be sure you wear that. Training is in five weeks at the Himanoco Tower here at the academy at sunup. The guards there won't let you in without it and no amount of illusionary skill will get by them either." Defalorn paused for a moment. "I don't remember the file specifying, will you be living on site or will you be sliding between?"

"Actually, when I found out that I would be here on Gazikstin I did a little research and found a lovely princess to woo." Ran waved his arms again and his facial appearance dropped twenty years to appear like a man in his late twenties, early thirties. "I figure she'll find out sooner or later. Mayhap later eh?" He chuckled.

This time, Defalorn grinned back. "I'm sure later. There isn't any sort of council for illusionists on this planet. I'm guessing that you are planning to woo either Princess Vos or Princess Haly, both lovely ladies whose courts don't even have illusionists." Defalorn sighed. "You strike me as a man who has never had a problem finding 'adventure'."

"I had intended Vos. I didn't even know about this Haly, maybe I will have to pay her a visit if things go bad." Ran paused for a moment and stroked his chin, his face returning to his normal age. "Actually, I may just stay here. That Alundra struck me as a woman who knew how to take care of a man, even if she isn't quick to smile." Ran turned to leave. "See you in a few weeks sir," he made a mocking bow movement.

"Now, don't go getting insubordinate. At forty-two, we may only be a few years apart, and you are a learned man who I'm sure hasn't taken orders in a while, but I am still the master and you the student and I demand the proper respect."

"My apologies," Ran said sincerely. "I truly meant no disrespect."

"Good luck to you with the ladies," Defalorn said, relieving the tension. "I will look forward to seeing you again in five weeks."

With that, Ran left the room. He walked back down the stairs to the foyer, pausing for just a moment to see if he could catch a glimpse of Alundra. The serving woman was nowhere to been seen, but that didn't mean that she wasn't near. An unlisted talent of Ran's was the ability to read thoughts and project his own. He was far better at the latter and sent out the thought *perhaps later, Head Mistress, you and I could get to know eachother better than just "here are the stairs"?* With that he left the hall to his horse hitched outside.

Ran was not a slider and it had cost him a pretty penny to get to Gazikstin from Balderia. It would probably cost just as much, if not more to get home unless he made friends with a local slider or a student with the ability. He mounted up and rode out of the main arch. The nearest town over was Halith, and it would take most of the afternoon to get there. *Pugh,* he thought to himself, *I forgot how much I hate horses. Why can't every planet have mastered the art of the combustion engine?*

Riding on, Ran's was left to his thoughts. He spent the afternoon reminiscing about his life. Born the middle of five children, the son of a *culdat,* he had always had a privileged life. At an early age, it was discovered that his potential was like nothing his family had ever known. It seemed that young Ran always knew what you were thinking. He used to scare his nannies by changing the color of his hair and his eyes whenever they turned their backs, making them think that they lost him in a crowd when he was standing right next to them.

Ran chuckled to himself at that thought. *Aye and I was a troublemaker from day one. Thank the gods I got some of the looks in my family too or I would have never gotten out of trouble.* His mind wandered back to the first time he picked up a sword. He had liked it, but liked helping people more. He liked flowers and loved girls for as long as he could remember, so he had started studying plants and giving the sweetest ones to young ladies. But his father had slowed his plant studies. He didn't want his son to grow up weak, especially since Ran only had one brother and he wanted to ensure that there would be strong male heirs to carry on the Grastle name. Ran not only studied sword, but also battle-ax, like his brother Athon. His father's voice rang in his head *You leave those flowers for your sisters. No son of mine is going to be a milk-willed weakling!*

Ran shook his head clear and moved his thoughts along. Flashing ahead to his early teen years, his illusion prowess had grown substantially and so had his hormones. He had already duped a few girls into thinking he was much older than he appeared so that he might steal a kiss or two. Sometimes he would go for a few more. The only problem was that, once he got so preoccupied in the moment, he lost his hold on the illusion and the girl would look down to see the grinning face of a boy where the dashing face of a man had just been. *He he, they would look like they had just kissed a toad instead of a prince.*

His mind stumbled across one instance, when he was fifteen and had wooed a young lady with his own looks, just lied about his age. He was near the point of "consummating" their relationship, a first for him, when her father had come into the room. Smiling, to himself, he could almost hear the screams and shouts as he had dropped from her room, naked as the day he was born with his clothes and sword bundled in his hands. How he had run into the street without bothering to get dressed. Then, as fate would have it, another lovely older lady came by, spotted him, and invited him into her carriage. He ended up finishing the deed that he had set out to do, only with someone else. *Aye, and enjoyed it more than I would have with that young lass, I imagine.*

Half the ride had passed. Ran let his thoughts wander on. He had spent four years in his early twenties studying geomagic and what was known as battle magic. Geomagic was the ability to manipulate the terrain around you, while drawing on the power it held. For instance, the most common geomagic spell on his planet was called "Steelgrass". What it required was that the geo-magician and the intended victim be standing on grass. That was all really. Then the geo-magician would draw power from the grass they were standing on and the grass the victim was standing on would grow, wrap around their ankles, and become unbreakable, effectively holding someone to a certain spot. It was one of the weakest spells, but was useful against multiple assailants. You could hold them in place and either run away, getting a good head start, or defeat a couple before the spell wore off while they were unable to move, making the odds of survival better.

Battle magic, on the other hand, was entirely different. It required the magician to tap into a different power. It went by different names on different planets; source, force, power, energy. But always it was the same. The magicians would draw that power into themselves and then channel it into pure force. It was a perilous practice because it was surprisingly easy to draw on too much and destroy the ability in you. Or worse you could injure yourself and possibly even die. But, for those who gained a mastery of it, battle magic was one of the most powerful and feared types of magic practiced.

Ran remembered the lectures and warnings of his youth. He had paid them no mind and pushed the limits of his abilities almost instantly upon learning how to touch the source. That was what it was called on his planet, the source. His talent had grown quickly and his instructors had attributed it to his powerful mind and ability with illusion. Really, the only reason he had stayed on for four years was because he wanted to learn every possible geomancy spell he could.

By the time he was thirty, he had completed his slow training as a sword and ax grandmaster. He could have been *sul ahin dak* and *sul calen dak* much earlier in life, but he never really had the passion for it. Really, the only reason he had finished at all was to try to please his father, whose health was failing. It had too, Ran remembered. His father's face beamed as his younger son was recognized as one of if not the greatest warrior in Havimire. *Aye, and in fact I was believed to be one of the greatest warriors on the entire planet, even then.* Having spent away his youth chasing women and fighting in taverns, he decided it was time to enlist. His brother had grown to the rank of major in the army and was now retiring to take over as *culdat* of their father's lands. So, to see one more of his father's dying wishes fulfilled, Ran joined the ranks of the Blue Guard of Queen Arletta Greyhawk. The Blue Guard mainly served as retainers, usually in recently conquered cities. The main force, called the Green Guard, would take the city and the Blues would hold it for them so that the entire force could move on and conquer another city. It was the Blue Guard's job to quell uprising and send a message of "no tolerance" to any rebels.

In one such conquered city, at the age of thirty-six, Ran recalled his experiences. Ran himself was old to be at only the rank of "enlistee", and he had a hard time relating to his fellow soldiers. He witnessed first hand the dealings his fellow 'soldiers' had with the people. The Blues had the reputation of a respected outfit, one who maintained the 'glory' of the crown. In reality, they were nothing but a bunch of overpowering bullies who killed mercilessly, many times torturing for the sheer pleasure of it. They would rape and pillage the people, making sure that they were poor and scared until a *culdat* was assigned to the land. Ran could barely stomach it. He also was insubordinate, tending to shirk duties to try to calm people and ease them into the change of rulers. It would usually allow him to make good with some of the local women as well, and Ran always did prefer to be given a woman's charms from the lady willingly then to take it by force. *Old habits die hard* he thought to himself.

Thankfully, his father died before Ran was dishonorably discharged from the army. He remained in the last city he was assigned to and met an apothecary. Ran still enjoyed helping people and he wanted to make amends for the deeds that the army he had served for had done to these people. He agreed to be the assistant to the apothecary and spent three years learning herbology. The *culdat* was assigned to the land, and he kept some of the Blue Guard that was already there behind, convincing them to resign from the service to stay on as "town guard."

They continued their reign of terror on the people of the town with full permission from the *culdat*.

Ran went as far as to appeal to the *magih*, the governing body of the *culdat's*, second only to the monarch, to try to be named *culdat* instead of the one who was in charge. But the lands that he was in were too far from his family's holdings. He was declined three separate times.

Finally, something happened that Ran couldn't ignore. He had recently turned forty, and he was now a licensed apothecary. A woman was brought to his office, badly beaten. That was not entirely unusual, but upon further investigation, Ran realized that the woman, who was mildly retarded, had been pregnant. Word came to Ran that one of the captains of the "town guard", a married man, had kept the woman on his property unknown to his wife. He regarded her as a pet and performed deviant acts upon her. When he found out she was pregnant, he was the one who had beaten her within an inch of her life.

That was all Ran could take. The people of the town were not warriors, they couldn't provide much help to him. But as incensed as Ran was, he didn't need their help. His abilities were far superior to that of the 'town guard' and he killed every one of them he could find, decapitating them and sending their heads to the *culdat* of the land.

When it was discovered who was killing the guard, Ran's brother disavowed him, calling him a traitor. Ran understood why. If they had associated with him, all of the lands of his family would have been stripped. He didn't care. He just wanted to see that poor, helpless girl avenged.

Unfortunately, as is typically the case with acts of vengeance, it backfired. Oh, he certainly did get back at the people that had hurt the girl, but in doing so, he opened the city to a whole batch of new Blue Guard. They moved in with one goal, find the traitor and kill him. Ran had taken a few of the new soldiers out too, before they resorted to hurting innocents to get to him. He agreed to leave the city in peace, so long as the people where shown mercy. *Of course, Defalorn's invite had managed to find me a couple of days before that anyway.* A deal was struck, Ran found a slider, and here he was.

Here he was indeed. The lights of Halith shone brightly in the twilight sky.

Ran smiled, but it wasn't the same smile that he had shared with Defalorn. The mirth was gone. Oh, he knew that tonight, like many other nights, he would find a bed and a young lady to help him keep warm.

But he wouldn't get warm. No, he would not get warm for a long, long time. He was the forsaken son, here to train in the ways of the forsaken. He would lay his head down and he would see that girl's face, hear her cries in the night. He would see the look on the eyes of the men he had killed in anger, how they had feared his blade, his vengeance. His heart would beat cold. He had one more person to kill, but he wanted to do that with flair.

He would have laughed if he had any laughter left inside of him.

Chapter 4

Xesca

Xesca loved how the late afternoon sun shone through the stained glass windows of Alden Hall. She marveled at the structure, the squareness of the room. The suits of armor on the guards and on the stands fascinated her. She herself fascinated the young guards.

Standing just hairs under six feet tall, her skin was a pale green and her hair was jet black. She wore a stunning, bejeweled yellow bodice that pushed and cleaved her rather large bosom. Breeches of the same color yellow clung to every curve of her shapely legs. She wasn't wearing any shoes.

She had noticed the woman over in the corner scowling at the guards when she came in. That woman, dressed in dark gray livery with symbols similar to the guards, came striding over to her now. "Follow me please."

Xesca followed her to a staircase at the end of the long foyer. There hung a great mural of Himanoco the forsaken, charging into a raging battle. She recognized that palace in the background of the mural, she had seen it in some of her history texts. It was the former Palace Hacvixnia. It had stood at a place referred to as Gerintan, a land that no longer existed on her home planet of Ohlia. The woman spoke, "At the top of the stairs, turn to your right. The second door on the left side of the hall is where you seek to be. I will lead you no further."

"Thank you very much for your assistance."

She climbed the stairs, then marveled at the fact there actually were stairs and not lifts. She walked halfway back down the staircase, then came back up slowly to experience the stairs again. She felt a slight tension in her legs. It was absolutely wonderful!

She found the door that she was instructed to and stood outside. The door didn't open. No monitor sounded announcing that she was standing there. Xesca was confused. She stopped a person in the hall, "Excuse me, but how does one open this door?"

The young man she stopped ogled her for a moment, then actually shook his head as if to deny something. "You just turn the knob," he said, surprised.

"Knob?"

"You know," he pointed to a brass, circular object near the center left side of the door, "the knob."

Xesca bent down to take a closer look. Her planet had no knobs and she had never read of one in any of her studies. The young man stared at her backside before shaking his head again and returning to what it was he was doing before Xesca stopped him. "Thank you," she said, turning around only to find the man gone.

"Hmm, that seems strange. Not to wait to be thanked" Xesca said to no one in particular. She grasped the knob firmly and twisted. It moved! But the door still did not open.

"Hello?" A voice called from behind the door. "Is there something I can do for you?"

"Yes, I am trying to get in but cannot seem to."

"The door isn't locked. Just turn the knob."

"I tried that," Xesca said, becoming exasperated. "Nothing happened."

"Well, did you pull on the door after you turned the knob?"

"Oh I see," she grasped the knob again and turned. Then she pulled the door open. Smiling, she walked into the room. "I should have deduced that. This planet already seems fascinated by manual labor, with no lifts and no monitors for the door. I should have guessed that there would have been more to opening the door than just turning the knob."

"You have to be Xesca," the man behind the desk said. He regarded her. "We're going to have to get you some different clothes. It's a wonder you haven't started a riot out there in the hallway."

Xesca looked down at her clothes. They were the most expensive and most proper she had. She was hurt that the man thought differently.

"Xesca, daughter of Queklian, you come to us at the ripe young age of three hundred and sixty-one. You have reached *ahin dak* status on your planet, as well as being a battle magic master and an accomplished slider. A learned young lady, you have studied battle tactics under such decorated tacticians as Alexander Blade at the Horton Bay Academy and Havinmire Cazness of the Academy at Sluf-du-lak. Now you come to our academy to train in the ways of Himanoco. Seems kind of strange, a Ohlian looking to become Himanoco after all he did to your people."

"Ahh, but from a strategists point of view it makes perfect sense. What better way to anticipate your enemy's tactics than to train the same way he did? My planet is very aware that Blackwolf cubs still are in the universe. We also have heard of Kenor Anor and his plans to revive the power of the Blackwolf in himself. We are not fooled easily and will not bow to that heel again." Xesca grew heated at the last comment.

"Commendable, certainly. And according to the file, you will be living in the dormitories here at the academy?"

"Yes sir, that is correct."

"Well, then you will be needing this," he handed her an envelope. "Inside is a map of the grounds, a room assignment and key. To get to Master Defalorn's quarters, you'll want to find out what the Blackwolf is hiding."

"What the Blackwolf is hiding?"

"I'll give you more of a clue dear, since you have no experience with illusion. At the top of these stairs, you saw the mural of Himanoco. He was a master of illusion, perhaps the greatest in history. Go to that mural, check it over, poke and prod it if you need to."

"Thank you very muck."

"Much" Berdard said.

"Yes, that too." Xesca left the room with far less difficulty than she had entering it. She went back to the top of the staircase and looked at the mural. She was amazed that someone so unattractive could have been so revered, while being reviled at the same time. Himanoco wore a grin that said to Xesca, *I know something you don't know.* Xesca hated not knowing anything. She made to kick the mural and her foot passed right through the wall.

Xesca was aghast. A wall that was not a wall? *How can that be?* She reached out with her hand to touch Himanoco's face and her hand went through the wall. *Well, it is not limited to just feet.* She stood back from the wall and put her hands on her hips, emulating Himanoco's stance. Nothing. Yelling, she ran at the wall and passed right through.

Xesca found herself in another hallway. Amazed, she got her bearings and saw that the door at the end of the hallway was marked **Defalorn.** She went to it and opened it the way she had the door from the previous hallway.

The man behind the desk gave a start. "Excuse me miss, but in polite circles one knocks before they enter a room," he said sternly.

"Oh, the little man from before mentioned nothing of knocks. What is a knocks?" Xesca asked, confused.

"It is of little importance now Xesca. Please, if you will be seated?"

"Thank you Master Defalorn. Tell me, how did you know who I was on sight? Have we met before?"

"No, it is just that I hand pick all of my students and you are the only Ohlian. It wasn't that difficult."

"I see. Well, when do we start?"

"Hold on now. I want to just check a few things before we get you enlisted. First of all, you are young for your people. Most of the people on your planet live well into their two thousands. My question is how one such as you was permitted even to apply to be Himanoco, much less allowed to come when your application was accepted."

"Well, it is true that most people on my planet don't start to train to become any type of warrior before their thousandth cycle. But I have always shown talent. Sliding on my planet is rare, and in me the talent was stronger at two hundred then for most people in their fifteen hundreds.

"I have a zest for knowledge and interest in war. My superiors allowed me access to two different wolf academies, to study tactics. I had sword training as well. I'm sure you remember the battle at Gerintan. Our sword skill, which we were so proud of, had failed horribly at the hands of Himanoco and his clan. Since then, our armies have been trained by as many Gingee wolves as we could hire, as history told us Gingee was the only man alive who bested Himanoco with a weapon.

"Now I come to learn the Himanoco arts. I will take this knowledge back to my home planet and maybe even pass the knowledge along if it is permissible." Xesca paused for a moment. "Is it permissible?"

"Only if you reach the rank of master, which, and I don't mean to brag, is very difficult to attain." Defalorn thought over what Xesca had told him, then asked, "So in essence, what you hope to do is make a Himanoco army for your planet's defense and your superiors decided if they sent someone who was young, perhaps they could train many warriors over the years?"

"Actually yes, that is exactly what was hoped. If I may ask another question of you sir, how long did you train to reach the rank of Himanoco master?"

"I was made a master after twelve years of training."

"But then, you realize our point. Twelve 'years' as you call them, while being almost a fifth of your average life span, is only seconds in the life a Ohlian. My mission is clear. Bring back knowledge of the forsaken so that we will be ready if he ever decides to return."

"I do see your point, and I acknowledge both you and your superiors for devising such a plan. What I wonder now is, why was it over twenty thousand years in the making?"

"Again, that is only ten generations for us. In most cases, three generations of your kind are in existence at the same time, for us, usually seven. When you think in that term, it's not that long."

"You do have a point there m'lady. Well, you've answered all of my questions to my satisfaction. This is for you." Defalorn handed her the wolf's head pin. "Be wearing that pin in five weeks. Come to the Himanoco tower on the grounds of this academy at sunup. Dismissed."

Xesca regarded the pin intently before moving. The symbol had been synonymous with everything that was feared on her planet for so long that it still held some fear to her. But she pinned it to her bodice anyway, stood up and left the office. She went to the main foyer of the hall and paused. She caught the same guard's eye she had caught when she came in, but this time, the minute he saw her pin he averted his eyes. It appeared that this sigil held some fear to these people almost as much as her own people.

She made her way to the courtyard and marveled again at the structures. They were just so much different than what she was used to. The shape, the structure, the lack of magical use, it was all amazing. She followed the path to the center of the grounds, where the five towers stood. Xesca pulled out her map and eyed up the other towers. It was well past mid afternoon and there were very few people in and around the grounds, so she was free to wander about without too much resistance.

Gingee, Bayer, Kivkavzed, and Malada were all here. They had sent that weapon of destruction to her planet. It was still unclear why. Many believed that they thought there was some secret to her peoples longevity. Others thought it was for the magical techniques that her people had incorporated into every day life. For whatever reason, her people, while having some army to speak of, had been peaceful for over thirty thousand years. They were unprepared for the ferocity of Himanoco and were ravaged by the wolves.

She found herself standing before Himanoco tower and she caught her breath. This was a building that she would have found at home. It was smooth, seamless, and had no windows. It was as dark as night and she knew that she should feel some urge to get away, and she was surprised when she didn't. *The pin,* she thought to herself, *I'll wager that it is the pin that is blocking the power.* She removed the snarling wolf head from her bodice and, sure enough, she immediately felt the overpowering urge to get back to the perimeter formed by the other four towers.

Well, he did learn something of our ways when he was on our planet. It is too bad he did not learn peace. Xesca shook her head sadly. Himanoco had wrought so much death in his lifetime.

Xesca walked on, to the dormitory that she was assigned to. She found her room and knocked this time before she entered. A plump young lady in a flowing red blouse with light red breeches answered the door. She regarded Xesca. "Yes, is there something that I can do for you?" she asked.

"Yes, according to this, I live here for this term."

"Oh my," the girl said, her face brightening, "You didn't have to knock! Didn't they give you a key?"

"Well, yes, but," Xesca stuttered. This was all so confusing to her. "I was told that it was polite to knock?"

"Oh it is," the plump girl said. "But it isn't necessary to knock on the door where you live."

"I see. I will try to remember that."

"Well," the girl said smiling, "are you going to stand there for the rest of the day or are you coming in?"

"Certainly, I will be coming in." Now it was Xesca's turn to regard the girl strangely. "What kind of question was that? Was it not obvious by my knock that I wished to be granted entrance?"

"I'm sorry," the girl said, "It is a rhetorical question, a sort of expression. I knew that you were going to be coming in."

"Ah yes, rhetoric. I read about that. Is it commonly used? Because I may have a problem with that"

"Yes, it is commonly used, but I will try to be as literal with you as possible to avoid any confusion. My name is Rhetta. What's yours?"

"I am Xesca, daughter of Queklian."

"Zestca? How do you spell that?"

"X-E-S-C-A. Xesca." Xesca looked concerned. "Is my name that hard to pronounce?"

"I'll get it. Come on, I'll introduce you to the other roommates." Rhetta led Xesca through the main room. It was decorated in the style of the planet, plainly and with objects that were manually made, not magically made. She would have to get used to these rigid chairs that did not conform themselves to your shape when you sat in them. In the bedroom, the beds were stacked on top of eachother. Xesca was astounded. There were two other girls, both appearing to be around the same age as Rhetta in the room. One sat at a desk, the other on the lower bed of one of the stacks.

"That's Leena at the desk and Casey on the bed," Rhetta said, motioning to the girls. Each girl smiled at Xesca at the mention of her name. "Girls, this is our last roommate, Xesca."

Leena rose and stuck out her hand. "Wow, your green! Are you sick?" She looked down at her hand and Xesca regarded her wonderingly.

"Oh, I'm sorry, you wish to shake my hand," Xesca said, shaking her head. "I read about that. It is a form of greeting in this land." Xesca took Leena's hand and clasped it tightly. She shook Leena's hand so hard that her shoulder cracked. "No, to answer your question, I am not sick. This is my skins natural hue."

"Ugh, that is some grip you've got there," Leena said, shaking her hand as she pulled it back. "What planet are you from?"

"It is called Ohlia." Suddenly, Xesca's face changed to one of joy. "A window! In the sleeping chamber! That means that we will be able to wake up to the sunlight!"

"Of course," Casey said, "don't window's exist on your planet?" she asked, laughing.

"No, unfortunately, they do not. I would love to learn how to make them and pass the knowledge of it on. It would make our structures most extraordinary."

"Wow, no windows?" Rhetta asked. "None at all, not even the little peepholes in doors? How do you see people?"

"I see people with my eyes," Xesca responded, "or was that a rhetorical question?"

"No, that was literal. What about the doors?"

"Oh, we have announce stones. When you step on them, a chime rings inside the house to let someone know that someone is there. When someone inside the house steps on to the other half of the announce stone, they automatically know exactly who is outside there door."

"Incredible!" Rhetta exclaimed. "What form of magic makes those?"

"I'm not sure actually. They are installed in every home. A stoneworker I suppose."

"But," Casey started, "don't stone workers use tools? Do you mean to say all of your stoneworkers have magical abilities?"

"All of our people are very receptive to magic. We use it for everything. In fact, I am as amazed that you do not as you are that the people on my planet do." Xesca looked around the room again. "You read about such things, so you know they must exist, but you never think you will actually see them."

"I suppose so…" Casey trailed off. "Well, I don't know about you girls, but I'm hungry. You think the mess hall is still serving? Or maybe the general stores behind the dormitories are open and we can pick up something to prepare?"

"Hey, before we take off, can we help you unpack your things Xesca?" Leena asked.

"My things?"

"You know, belongings. Didn't you bring anything with you to campus?"

"Actually, just currency. I have read that my clothing would be deemed improper on this planet. In fact, these garments, which are some of my most respectable, have caused nothing but stares from the males on this planet. My superiors instructed me to purchase clothing that would allow me to blend in with the people of this planet as much as possible."

"Hey, that's great!" Casey said. "I love to shop. Leena, can you slide us to your home?" Casey turned to Xesca. "Leena is a native to this planet. She lives on another continent, so we'll have to slide there, but there, it is late morning and we would have plenty of time to spend and everything would be open."

"Well, I'm not a great slider, but I think that I could manage it."

"Actually Leena, I am what you would consider an above average slider." Xesca said. "If you will just set the coordinates in your mind, I can make sure we all get in the hallway."

"Hey great! So, maybe we will have some of the same classes, all of us are training to be Malada."

"Actually, I am training to be Himanoco."

All three of the girls spoke at the same time "Himanoco!"

"But, that is forsaken!" Rhetta said.

"Do they even still train for that?" Casey asked.

"What are you, crazy?" Leena exclaimed. "No one trains Himanoco!"

"I'm sorry," Xesca bowed her head, "I did not mean to cause conflict. I shall find another room to stay in."

"No, No," Rhetta said, standing in front of Xesca, "you didn't cause conflict and we are the ones who are sorry. We shouldn't have started in on you like that. It's just," Rhetta paused, trying to find the most delicate phrasing. "It's just that Himanoco's are so feared, so ruthless. There are so few of them left in the universe, yet the name still makes folks shudder with fear and contempt. Why then, in Jehan's name, would you want to become a part of that?"

"It is a very long story. I would love to relay it to you all, but perhaps we should postpone that for a later time? Or are we no longer going shopping?"

"Oh no, I'm still hungry," Casey piped up, trying to ease the tension. "You ready Leena?"

"Let's go"

Leena opencd the slide corridor and Xesca focused her energy. The corridor tripled in size, allowing all four of them to use it. Leena gasped with amazement. "You are going to have to show me that one!" she said.

Xesca smiled. She was concerned that her stay here would be lonely, but these girls had accepted her already. She was excited to see more of this wonderful planet and find out more about her newfound friends. For the first time that day, duty and obligation were the furthest things from her mind.

Chapter 5

Defalorn

Night had descended on Alden hall and Pagen Defalorn was tired. He sighed and turned toward the door to the room off of his office. *Marshall your wits old man,* Defalorn thought to himself. *Ye be facing down the devil himself.*

He opened the door to a meeting room with a large round table in the center of it circled by ten chairs. Seated at the chair opposite of the door was a man in his early thirties, his black hair was slicked back away from his face and his eyes were a piercing blue. He made no move to rise as Defalorn entered, as would normally have been the custom.

"Ah, Master Defalorn," the man said, smiling, "it is a pleasure to see you again."

"I wish that I could say the same thing to you Kenor. But then," Defalorn chuckled as he sat down, "I dunna really suppose that you

ever liked to see me as it usually meant more work and less fun for ye."
Defalorn realized that his accents from his youth had returned. Kenor's
smile grew and he realized that Kenor had noticed it too.

"Joke all you want old man," Kenor said, the grin looking more
wolfish than before, "I have come because I want to know why is it that
you haven't agreed to join my legion?"

"I have a good job here, why would I want to leave it?"

"Because your master commands you."

"And here I thought that I was the master, ya little plig!" Defalorn
said with some heat rising into his voice.

"It matters not, in any event old man." Kenor said with a dismissive
wave of his hand. "But your support would be helpful to me to sway
some non believers to the idea that I am the Blackwolf." Kenor paused
for a minute. "It also would be good to have your support because it
used to come so freely back when I was you student. I sometimes miss
that."

"Oh, don't ye be feedin' me that plig." Defalorn said as he stood
to rise. "I know that all you want is to get your hands on the power of
Blackwolf. It would be a crime against everything good and natural to
bring back the Blackwolf. He was a traitor and..."

"No more lectures old man." Kenor said and rose to his feet as well.
"Support me or no, I don't need it. I am the Blackwolf. Do not doubt it
and stop trying to find someone to stand in my way. If you haven't got

the strength to do it on your own old man, don't send any more lambs to the slaughter." Kenor winked at Defalorn and then "vanished" from the room.

With a heavy sigh, Defalorn slumped back into his chair. His hands were trembling and beads of sweat broke out on his brow. He knew Kenor would have an idea that he had been trying to turn people against Kenor becoming Blackwolf, but he did not expect that he would throw that at him. It didn't matter anyway. *Marshall your wits around you old man,* Defalorn thought to himself glumly.

He returned to his office and piled up the folders on his desk. Twenty students had passed through his door today. He always laughed at the number. Academy dictate was that, to hold a class on the grounds, you had to have at least twenty students registered. Since only around ten thousand Himanoco warriors existed in the whole universe, with only one hundred produced annually, twenty students at one academy was a ridiculously high number. But, he would keep his class here. For Jehan's sake, Himanoco had founded this academy.

Twenty students, five foursomes. A foursome of Himanoco was considered a unit, what was known as a cordon. It was rare that the cordon one was assigned to train with actually made it through the training together. Usually, a Himanoco warrior just joined a cordon after he finished training. Most of them would wash out in a month, maximum. Maybe all of them. *By Jehan's ears, I pray its not so.* There was potential here. Especially the foursome that he had saved until the last possible week. They would make an unbeatable team, if they all held together and made it through

Gregor Holden was a cocky plig to be sure. But he was a prince, so some of that was upbringing and forgivable. Some of it was not, and Pagen was going to enjoy watching the tower beat that out of him. Gregor brought a strong sense of leadership, but he had to learn to accept the opinions of others as opinions and not assaults. He also had to come to grips with his own fate.

Candace Orthon was a legacy. Steeped in tradition, she longed for training because to her, Himanoco was regal. It was everything she had ever known and she had none of the usual apprehension that was found even in those who claimed they wanted to embrace the ways of the Blackwolf. She would bring strength and unity to the group, if she could conquer her shyness.

Ran Grastle was everything this group needed to fail. More powerful than the other three put together, he is more than twice their age, *Well, not Xesca technically, but twice her equivalent age.* His motivation is revenge, plain and simple, and his heart will be cold for everything else. He must learn to care for someone other than that girl, to transfer her unto the helpless all around the universe. If he could do that, he could be a stronger warrior than Defalorn himself.

Finally, there was Xesca. Sweet and innocent Xesca. She will try everyone's patience with her naiveté. But she will also provide them with a fresh and unspoiled perspective on things.

These four, if no one else, Jehan above let these four make it through!

Chapter 6

Day's Go By

Five weeks can move quite slowly when you are waiting for something to happen. In the weeks to come, Candace found it most disconcerting.

She spent a lot of her time just wandering around the grounds. Most classes started a week after she arrived, so her days were open to herself while her roommates attended class. More often than not, she found herself at the Gingee training fields, watching the sword arms practice their skills.

Alden Hall academy is for advance training. You come to this school with the basic training in the clan that you wish to follow, with the exception of Himanoco. Most of the Gingee trainees were, in Candace's estimation, absolutely phenomenal.

One particular day, while watching the young men and woman move about their forms, the instructor caught her eye. He made his way over to the arch and asked, "You any good with a sword little lady, or are you looking to snag a husband?"

Her eyes narrowed and this would have been stand-offish if she hadn't blushed at the last comment. "I can handle myself."

"Are you here to train, or just watch?"

"My classes haven't started yet."

"Oh, Himanoco," the instructor said, mockingly. "Mayhap you will condescend to show us wee Gingee what you can do?"

"I am not Himanoco yet."

"Still, close enough little lady, close enough." The instructor clapped his hands and everyone stopped. "We have been graced to have a Himanoco trainee watching over our practice sessions. Is anyone here willing to test her abilities?"

"I did not consent to a test." Candace said, more shrilly than she would have liked.

"I would try, Master Grant." A man who looked like he had ten years and fifty pounds on her came forward.

"Please, young Himanoco, show us what you can do." Master Grant was not to be put off.

Candace sighed and leaped the short fence into the training field. "I'll need a sword."

"You don't have your own?" Grant made the question a snicker.

"No, I do not. I could always head back to my dormitory."

Grant snapped and a girl who didn't look much older than Candace herself and about the same size threw her sword. Candace caught it deftly, spinning it softly and testing it's balance. It seemed a superior weapon, quite light and to her liking. "This will do." Candace said simply.

Another clap and the fifty or so troops formed a very large circle. "Now, no magic, young Himanoco. This is a test of our skill, not yours."

"Then perhaps you would like to try me yourself, Master?" Candace asked, finding confidence with a sword in hand.

"Perhaps. First, lets see how you handle Baldwin." A final clap and Baldwin approached.

Casgill would be impressed. Baldwin had all of his fluidness, and the look that he wore was flat. Not determined, not anxious, just confidence. It portrayed a sort of indifference, seeming to say, fight or run, I will win either way.

With no magic at her disposal, Candace was not about to wait for her attacker. Moving just as gracefully, she flowed to close the distance with Baldwin, sword at the ready. She carried it tip up, a broad stance.

The air was loud with the clanging of sword on sword. Candace was fighting with all of her skills, feinting and turning blows she barely saw. The look on Baldwin's face changed only from flatness to disappointment when his attack failed to strike home. Candace recognized most of the techniques that Baldwin employed and still it did her little good.

Something that Anskin had told her when she was younger. "If it looks like a battle that you can't win fair, either fight dirty or don't play at all."

Candace backed away from Baldwin and threw her sword, point down into the dirt. The hilt waved slightly from the force. "I would not beat you with a sword."

"Giving up already, young Himanoco?" Grant called out disappointedly.

"Hardly," Candace used her powers of illusion to make it appear that four of her had formed a ring around Baldwin.

"I said no magic girl!" Grant called, angrily.

"I never agreed," the four Candace's called back, simultaneously. "Besides, if Gingee could best Himanoco with a sword, what chance does and acolyte have against a full fledged Wolfwarrior? I admit that I can't win with a sword. It doesn't mean that I can't win."

Grant tapped three shoulders and now three more students rushed in to occupy the illusionary Candace's. Each one was laughing together.

"I am so formidable that you surround me with four warriors? Will all of you be next?"

"Take her!" Grant called

When Candace picked up the sword, all of the illusionary ones followed the motion and all of them had swords to match. Her illusion prowess was strong and she managed to meet all four blows, the steel clanging through the practice yard.

"Hold!" Grant called. "How did you do that?"

"Do what?" the Candace's replied.

"Illusions are pierced by touching them. How did you meet four blows?"

"I will be Himanoco," Candace said simply.

"Can you finish your duel without magic?"

"The duel was finished. Baldwin would have worn me out. I may have held up another few moments, but he was beginning to get closer. It was just a matter of time."

"Baldwin?"

"Perhaps," he said simply. "She was far better than I would have ever anticipated."

"Finish," the first civil tone Grant had used. He hesitated as though searching for words. "Please."

Candace dropped the illusion. The real Candace was actually standing with her back to Grant, having defended herself against a blow from one of the new students. "Clear out then and let's finish this up."

So, Anskin's advice wasn't going to help her. It was time to go with Casgill's training. She switched hands, spinning the sword in her left hand grip. Scanning the circle of gathered trainees, she found another female her size and saw that she had a sword that looked about right for Candace.

Dancing toward the edge of the circle, fending blows and feinting strikes, Candace finally reached her target. She spu, following a blow, turning her back to Baldwin and making as if to elbow him in the chest. He dodged expectantly but instead of the elbow, Candace reached forward with her right hand and snatched the sword from the startled girl's grip.

Candace could swear that she heard Casgill call out "Now!" as she rushed Baldwin with renewed fury. Slashing, spearing, swords searching desperately for flesh, Baldwin was doing all he could do to keep Candace away from him. She practically snarled as she pressed ever closer. Finally, one of her blades struck home, catching Baldwin high on the shoulder with a downward slash and drawing blood.

"Hold!" Grant called and Candace had to force herself to regain her calm and not press on. "How did she win?" he asked of the gathering.

"She still cheated," the girl whose sword Candace had stolen called. "She used another weapon."

"I said she couldn't use magic," Grant said, just loudly enough to be heard, "I said nothing about the number of weapons. Baldwin, why didn't you draw your swordbreaker at your hip?"

"I thought it was one sword against another. I did not feel it would have been fair."

"If I wanted it to be a fair fight, I would have left her keep her magic. She all but admitted that she couldn't win with just a sword, but chose to fight on. Why did you not expect treachery from a Himanoco?"

"Hey!" Candace exclaimed. "I did nothing treacherous this time!"

"You were pushing the bounds of the exercise and you knew it."

"I wanted to win!" Candace roared back. "I will always win and you will lie bleeding if the only you'll ever fight is fair!"

"See what you are up against, my wolves?" Grant said, as if she had just confirmed the secret of the universe. "Do you understand now what purity and honor can earn you?"

"But," Baldwin said, "better to die pure than to win at any cost."

Now Grant turned to her as if this explained the other great mystery of the universe. Candace shook her head and found the owners of the swords she held. "Sorry, better to go home in one piece. I'll trade honor any day."

Ran stretched languidly, like a happy cat. His life the past few weeks, waiting for the training to begin, had been quite enjoyable. Especially considering what he had left behind. Vos had a penchant for older men so Ran hadn't even had to hide behind illusion. Vos and her servants had also taken excellent care of Ran.

He got up and began packing his room to head back toward Alden Hall, finding himself feeling almost wistful. *Getting soft as you get on old man,* he chided himself. He finished the wine that he had been drinking and tied his bag together.

"Where are you going Lambkin?"

That helped break him out of longing in a hurry. Of all the pet names in all the years, he has both used and had used on him, 'Lambkin' was far and away the most awful thing that he had ever heard.

"It is time I was on, my fetching young Princess," Ran said, wearing his most charming grin. "I have to be at Alden Hall in two days to begin training."

"I thought, after experiencing my…charms," she grinned deviously and Ran fought back a laugh, "you would have consented to be my King."

Ran couldn't help himself this time. He laughed right out loud. "Oh, my dear, that is absolutely the funniest thing that I may have ever heard."

Vos stood aghast. "How dare you!"

"I dare easy as I please, Princess," Ran said with a bow. "I told you that I was here for a few weeks, I stayed on that time, and now it is time for me to go."

"You cannot leave! I won't allow it!"

"What?"

Vos' royal guard came bounding in, swords at the ready. "You are the first man I have ever been with and I will not take another. You are mine, Ran Grastle!"

Laughing still, Ran threw his arms out and wind swept past Vos and blew the three guardsmen off their feet. "You couldn't hold me if you wanted to Princess."

"Oh?" she asked, rage turning to smugness.

Ran licked his lips. Vos was too young to bluff. Her eyes betrayed her though, as they flicked to the empty wine glass. He reached onto his belt and pulled out a small vial that he had in a protected pouch. Drinking the contents down, he returned her smug look with one of cold anger. "Whatever you put in my wine little lady, that antidote will protect me from it."

A look of shock passed across Vos' face. "You cannot leave me! I forbid it!"

"Vos, my patience is reaching its end. This tryst has been fun, to say the least, but I cannot stay. What would you want with an old man like me anyway?"

"So powerful, so wise, so energetic, what would I not want with you?"

Ran's anger broke. He chuckled again. "I am sure that you will meet someone just as charming and powerful over time. If not, who knows? But I can't stay now."

Vos, who could never remember being denied anything in her life, finally resorted to breaking down. Tears flowing unbidden down her cheek, she finally begged, "Please stay!" but Ran was set.

As Halith once again came into sight, his backside once again in pain from being in the saddle all day, Ran wondered if the young bar maid that had been more than happy to help him to his room the last time he was in town was working tonight.

₪

"So, you are all packed?" Marion asked.

"I am all packed."

"You have made all of your goodbyes?"

"I have."

"I will miss you."

"Mom, it isn't like I joined the Marines or something," Gregor said teasingly. "I'm just going to get in some training."

"I know, I know. But I am your mother and I will miss you just the same." Marion breezed about Gregor's room, making sure that he indeed had everything. She placed a kiss on his cheek before heading back down the stairs.

Haley bounded into his room to replace Marion. "You're nervous."

"Mom tell you that or did you work it out on your own?"

"Don't get snippy with me."

"Sorry." Gregor shrugged. He hugged his sister. "I'll see you in a little while. You have a good year at Horton Bay."

Haley hugged back. "You come back in one piece big brother. You are not free of me yet."

"Never dream of it little sister."

It was Alexander next. "You start academy in the fall don't you?" Gregor asked. "Have you chosen one yet?"

"Sulf-du-lak."

"What are you going to study to be little brother?"

"I don't know. Gingee probably."

"No magic."

"Oh, I'll study magic too. But I don't know that I want to follow you. Himanoco isn't really my deal."

"Good luck with that. I hear that some of the professors at Sulf-du-lak are quite hard. It should be good for you."

"I'll see you when you get back." Alex turned to leave.

"Alexander..." Gregor called. He grabbed his younger brother and pulled him into a fierce hug. "I am counting on you little brother." Alex just looked up at him. "You and I might be Holden children, we have a king and a queen as our parents, but we serve our sister. Always remember that. If you ever decide to leave, and I won't blame you, then you'll be free. Until then, I am counting on you to keep Haley safe until I finish with this." Gregor's eyes were beginning to mist.

"She's tough. She'll take care of herself."

"No," Gregor said, more firmly than he meant. "You'll take care of her. I trust you like no other. Promise me that you will do this for me."

"I will." Alexander looked up at Gregor and matched the fierceness. "Nothing will happen to her while you are gone. I promise."

Alexander left and Gregor opened a slide portal. Arthur did not come to his son's room. He had come the night before. He told Gregor just what he had needed to tell and left with no real discussion. "Be well, be safe, and be strong. You are everything that I was and so much more. I am proud of you my son, whether you pass or fail, I am proud."

₪

Xesca had had the time of her life at the academy dormitories. She and her roommates had gone out carousing every night since she had been there. With no classes for her yet, her days were open and Xesca took full advantage of the campus library.

Every afternoon, you could find her at one of the many tables, several different history books laid out for her, studying the ways and means of as many peoples as she could. Sometimes, one of her roommates would stop and they would have lunch together, but more often than not, she was left to her own devices. It was exhilarating to learn so much and have no particular discipline to have to follow.

Other patrons of the library also took note at how much she copied down. Most people were astounded to see the tomes of notation that Xesca appeared to take and many were dismayed to think that there could be a course that would require so much effort.

And the evening fare was enticing. It still amazed Xesca the looks that she got from all of the different students, male and female. Even though her clothes were considered to be far more respectable than the ones that she had arrived with, men still looked at her with barely veiled lust and women with a mixture of resentment and desire to be like her. The fact that she was green did not seem to enter into the equation at all.

All of Xesca's roommates were youngish by comparison, even though she and they were approximately the same age in relationship to the other's life span. Xesca enjoyed watching the way that they would intermingle with the young men that they encountered at the local pubs, the potables that were offered and how many were consumed, as well as the things that they would discuss the next morning. To her, it seemed that emphasis was less on what they were at the academy to accomplish and more on who they could meet while they were there.

And as the date of the training loomed, Xesca found herself concerned with more things than she would have thought possible before she had arrived at Alden Hall. What if she did not get along with her classmates? What if the trials were more difficult than she was prepared for? What if she failed?

She pushed these thoughts out of her mind and went back to the book that she had been reading. What would come, would come.

Chapter 7

The Tower

The northern sun shone brightly as it broke the horizon to start the day's ascent. The Himanoco Tower stood dark and stoic, as it had for over twenty thousand years.

Outside the tower, Gregor, Candace, Ran and Xesca all sized each other up as they awaited entrance. The morning was warm, yet all but Ran trembled slightly with anticipation.

The guards beckoned and the four entered into Himanoco Tower. Inside, the main level was surprisingly bare. There were four benches along each wall, and on each was a black cloak and sword. There were no murals as in Alden Hall but at the other end of the foyer there was a decorative archway.

Pagen Defalorn stood in the center of the foyer and waited patiently for them to come in. As they entered, he spoke loudly "Please, go to any of the benches, put the cloak on, and heft the sword to test the feel of it." They proceeded to the four benches on the left side of the wall, Ran taking the one closest to the archway, with Candace, Xesca, and Gregor following in that order. Each of the cloaks was ill fitting and hung loosely around the wearer.

"Good," Defalorn said. "Now I begin the explanation. This training facility was founded for the specific purpose of producing warriors. It has no other cause. As I am sure you have noticed by now, every other wolf clan has some form of training facility other than the tower except Himanoco. That is simply because by the time you come to train Himanoco, you should have certain abilities and little need for excessive individual training.

"Now, the cloaks are yours only if you decide now to continue. You can leave this tower if you do not feel ready to attempt its challenges. You are entitled to leave four times with no repercussions, but if you choose to leave a fifth time you will not be invited back. Be forewarned, the challenges that you will face in this tower have been faced and failed by many a man and woman, and failure is final. If you fail in the tower, you will not be invited back and will never be Himanoco. I will ask you individually now if you still feel yourself ready and a simple yes or no will suffice." Defalorn turned to Ran. "Ran Grastle, will you continue with the training?"

"Yes."

"Candace Orthon, will you continue with the training?"

"Yes"

"Xesca, daughter of Queklian, will you continue with the training?"

"Yes"

"Gregor Holden, will you continue the training?"

"Yes."

"Good. I am glad." Defalorn waved his hands and the cloaks shrunk up so that the fit more like a waistcoat. Each hung just below the wearer's knees. "Now the swords. Do any of you have any difficulty with their sword? Speak now or be saddled with the hindrance for the rest of your life."

"Mine is a little heave for my tastes," Candace said. "I'm used to a lighter and smaller sword."

Defalorn walked over to her and clasped the blade end of the sword. The sword's blade shrunk two inches and got ounces lighter. "Better?" he asked.

"Yes," Candace sputtered. "Thank you."

"Anyone else?" No one spoke. "Good. Now, if you will all clasp your swords tightly in your sword hand and repeat after me," Defalorn chanted words none of them ever heard. Each followed suit and their swords vanished.

"The sword has now become a part of you. Reach out with your minds and you will find it. If at anytime you want your sword, simply wish it to appear and it will streak out from your sword hand. You will never have need for another sword and that sword will neither break nor is possible to destroy. To send it away, simply swirl your cloak around it and will it gone.

"Next, the cloak's themselves. They are equipped with small bursts of power that will fade quickly but never completely run out. Right now, I'd like you all to concentrate on light illuminating from your cloak." The group did as they were told. Each cloak in turn exuded a bright flash of light that lasted about thirty seconds then faded out. "In time of need, will your cloak and you will have different strengths for about the same period as that light lasted. The cloak can help you do magnificent things; all you have to do is explore its boundaries. This is the extent of the training that I have to give you. I will now tell you about the rest of the tower.

"The tower has four levels and each is the same as this level with the difference that the walls are painted a different color. This is level one, the black level. Level two is gray, level three is silver and level four is white. That archway at the far end was built by Himanoco himself. It is of a design and magic no one has been able to duplicate except Malada, and none of her clan since her. When one passes through the archway when it is inactive they will go up the stairs to the next level. But when it is active, you will be transported to a place and time completely different from the one you left.

"That place and time is where you will meet the challenges that will make you Himanoco. As you travel along, time and space here will be slowed. The journey will take four of our months and your physical age will be the same as when you went in. Only your physical age. If you are injured while in the arch, you will emerge with those injuries. If you are killed while you are in the arch, you will emerge on level one and will have washed out of the training. Inside the arch, time and space will move seemingly normal to you, not slowing at all. Your training could take a day, a week, a year; it is different for everyone. When you see a doorway with an arch similar to the one that you see now, go through it. The training for that level will be over and you will advance to the next level.

"Please remember that once you start, you cannot stop. If you are injured, you must persevere, therefore it is recommend that you either be careful and don't get injured in the first place or remain in the arch long enough that your injuries heal. You must pass at least the first three levels to be considered Himanoco. After the third level, you can decide to conclude your training or continue on through the last archway. If you complete the last archway, you will be considered a Himanoco Master. If you attempt the fourth arch and fail, you do not wash out, however the decision must be made at the time of reaching the arch.

You do not get the option to attempt at a later date as you did when you first came into the tower." At this last, Defalorn paused. "If any of you have any questions, ask them now and I will attempt to answer them, although be warned that there is not much that I can tell you."

Gregor was first. "What was the longest anyone ever spent in the arch?"

"That is unknown. We as the masters do not ask and you as the trainee are not forced to tell. Once and only once in history, we broke that rule. Always four go in and once, three came out on level two and one came out on level one. The man who came out on level one immediately slumped to the floor, dead. When asked about their companion, the other three said that he had met someone on the other side and decided to make a life with her. It was believed that the man died in the archway of old age and when the arch washed him out, he simply stayed dead."

"There are people on the other side?" Gregor asked.

"That too is unknown. As I said, it is different for everyone and we do not ask what one endures inside the arch. In the case of the man who emerged and died, yes."

Next was Ran, "Can we bring items out from the arch?"

"No. You will not emerge from the arch on horseback, even though you may have ridden through the archway on your side. You also cannot bring through some sort of pet or companion. Anyone you meet in the archway, if in fact you do meet anyone at all, belong to the place and time that you meet them. You are just visitors and cannot alter anything. Once your mission is complete, the place will be as though you were never there, and any object that you may have taken will be replaced."

"What if we take in something, will we emerge with that?" Xesca asked.

"Everything you have on your person, you will emerge with."

"Can we run to our quarters and grab some items?" Candace asked.

"No. You should have come to face the trials with everything that you required and ready. If you did not, you should decline to attempt at this time. You still can, if you would like to give up the cloak and sword. The next opportunity to test will be in eleven months."

Xesca seemed to roll that over in her mind, before shaking her head. She really wished that she had brought paper and something to write with along. It would be wonderful to document her journey.

Seeming to read her mind, Defalorn smiled. He held out four journals and a series of charcoal writing utensils. "These are the gift of the master. It is said that the first to present such items to students was Master Havil Gilamesh." Xesca nearly cried out with joy. "Many students have emerged from the archway with new and dazzling magical abilities. It would be a shame if the spell was forgotten due to lack of practice." Each took a journal and writing utensils. "Be careful with what you document. I am allowed to give you one journal per level, but once it is full, it is full. You cannot add pages and bring them through as that would be considered a part of the arch. Are there any other questions that you can pose of me?"

"What about sliding in the archway?" Gregor asked.

"You will find that your slider ability is different. You will only be allowed access to places that you see inside the arch. The 'hallway' won't even show you any other doors."

"Why four people?" Ran asked. "Why not one at a time, or several at once?"

"Four is a cordon in Himanoco. We seldom assemble in any larger group. If a situation dictated that more than a cordon be assembled, the longest running master would assume control. We do not have a ranking system like you will find in other clans.

"As far as training goes, each master sends four in to try to form a solid cordon with trainees who have experienced the same things. If one or more of you wash out, the rest continue on. If only one or two of you make it through, you will be drafted by a cordon that needs a member due to one dying. If three make it through, you will be given the option of staying together as a cordon and recruiting someone to take the place of the fourth, or dissolving the cordon and joining already established ones."

"If all four of us make it through but do not wish to stay together, is that an option?" Candace asked. She had always dreamed of fighting alongside her father and it did not sound as though she would be able to.

"It is permissible, but frowned upon. Questions would arise as to why the group was dissolved. It would be assumed that members did not get along, but which members? Your credibility as a Himanoco would be damaged before you ever really started."

"We were led to believe that the training would take three years. Is this not true?"

"It's a deterrent Gregor. You are invited to stay at the compound for the entire three years and assist the Malada instructors. You are also permitted to drop into any Malada magic classes. You will have to pretend to be studying Malada as a chosen path. Or, you may choose to sharpen other skills, with other clans. In each case, you must make believe, at least for the time of training, that you washed out of Himanoco. Other than that, your training will take four months."

No one else spoke. Finally Defalorn asked, "Are there any more questions?" Everyone shook his or her head no. "All right then, if you are all ready to proceed?" Defalorn went to the archway and made another strange invocation. Suddenly, there was a blinding burst of light then a small humming sound was emanating from the arch. "If you will proceed through, and good luck to you. I will see you when you emerge."

Each stepped through, and this time, even Ran was shaking.

Chapter 8

Level 1 begins.

The foursome emerged onto a plain gravel road. It was the type of road that could be found anywhere. The road was lined with deciduous trees; oak, maple, and birch. Nothing unusual there. The road had no beginning or ending in sight. The sun was overhead, but there was no way to determine its course yet, so they could only make rough estimations as to the time of day.

"Well, now what?" Gregor asked.

"Introductions?" Ran suggested.

"Sure, my name's Gregor. I'm an *ahin dak* and an accomplished slider. I've also studied some geomagic, but am not very good at it yet. I trained under Alexander Blade at the Horton Bay academy to learn battle strategy" Gregor finished.

"My name is Candace and I am a legacy from Baktarus. I am also an *ahin dak*, a conjurer and illusionist."

"Is your illusion any good?" Ran asked.

"I'm licensed. I'm not really sure of your definition of 'good'"

"We can test it out later. What about you, miss lovely green skinned lady?"

"My name is Xesca, not 'lovely green skinned lady'. I am *ahin dak* as well as the others. I am an accomplished slider, as Gregor, and also a battle mage. I have been to the academies at both Horton Bay and Sluf-du-lak to train with some of the universes top strategists. Alexander Blade was also one of my teachers." Xesca smiled at Gregor.

"Well, it would seem that I am a little of all of you plus some. My name is Ran and I do not slide, unfortunately, but that is about all you can do that I can't. I am *sul ahin dak* as well as *sul calen dak*. Illusion, conjuring and battle magic are my specialties. I am also a trained geomage and apothecary.

"Well, now that the niceties are finished, let's get down to business. Does anyone have any ideas as to where we are and what we need to do to advance on to the next level?"

Before anyone could answer, two men atop hovering, metal steeds appeared behind the group. They were dressed in strange armor and a visor covered their eyes. One called out "Halt! Who goes there!"

"Look at that one, she's green!" the other called out.

"Must be carrying some new plague! Do not move!"

"This can't be good," Ran said.

"I am no plague carrier. This is my natural skin tone!" Xesca protested. She started to come toward the two men.

Before anyone could react, one of the men drew a gun-style weapon from his waist holster and fired. A streak of blue light grazed Xesca's shoulder and she cried out. "Do not move!" the man called again to the group.

Snarling in anger, Ran waved his arms. Before the eyes of the two men, the entire group vanished. He held his hand to his mouth to signal everyone to be quiet and rushed to Xesca's side to examine her wound.

"They're magicians!" one of the men called. "Quick, switch your visor to scan for heat signature. It will see through their little ruse!"

"Damn!" Ran muttered. In a flash, his sword appeared in his hand and he leaped at one of the mounted men. He ran him through, carrying both Ran and the rider off of the mount to the ground.

In almost as swift a fashion, Gregor made his sword appear and leaped at the other rider. He severed the rider's hand that was holding the gun like weapon. The two tumbled to the ground and Gregor got back to his feet quickly.

Screaming in pain, the rider called out to his companion. "Hasbit! Help me! The bastard cut off my hand!"

"Hasbit is dead." Ran said simply. "And you're next."

"Hold it," Gregor came between Ran and the fallen soldier. "We can ask him questions, find out where we are and what we are up against."

"I'll not tell you anything!" the soldier spat. "You might as well kill me and be done with it!"

"No, Gregor is right," Xesca said. Candace was holding the taller woman up. "It is just a flesh wound, a warning shot. I should have known better than to startle them." She turned to the soldier on the ground. "Is there anyplace that we can take you to heal you? None of us can do it."

"Speak for yourself darlin'" Ran drawled. "The saddlebags on these mounts have field materials like food and bandages. I can dress that wound." He looked down at the man with a grimace on his face. "I don't really want to, but I can help him. If that is what you want Xesca."

"Yes, and we also need to get off of this road, before someone else passes by and we are accosted again."

"Let's just cut into the woods." Candace suggested.

"We'll be slow moving and we don't have a compass to see our way back out." Gregor reminded her.

"Sure we do. There's one of them in these saddle bags too." He tossed the compass over to Gregor than began wrapping the soldiers wound. "There's also a binding device, so we should be able to subdue this guy"

"Leave me to die, you miserable magicians! You already killed my partner, a Grand Guardsman! You will be flogged and hung!"

"What can we say. We make a hell of a first impression" Ran chuckled.

"Hey, I could fly one of these things," the group turned to see Gregor on top of one of the mounts. "It's really easy, the pedal here on the left is movement, the right one is brake. The left lever for the hand turns left and the right one turns right. Just like driving a car!"

"A what?" Candace asked.

"No worries, I know what the boy means," Ran said. "What about the body? Should we leave it or hide it?"

"Hide it." Xesca said simply. "No use in raising alarms until absolutely necessary and hiding it might buy us some time to escape."

"Fools!" the soldier laughed "Our armor is heart monitored! The minute you killed poor Hasbit it set off an alarm at the castle! Already a unit of Guardsman is on the way to this site and will be here within seconds. They will mow you down!"

"You're bluffing." Ran said, holding a gun underneath the man's chin.

"Stay here and find out fool!" the soldier said, smiling.

"C'mon, leave him too." Gregor called, "Xesca, can you hold on?"

"Yes, I will be fine."

"All right then, Candace, hop on." Gregor helped Candace up onto the back of his mount. "Hey Ran, can you do something with your illusion to make Xesca not green?"

"As long as she is touching me, yes." Ran smiled. "Can I kill him now?"

"Do it and let's go!"

"No," Candace cried out. "I thought you said we needed him."

"If he isn't bluffing, we don't have time." Gregor shook his head sadly. "We can't have him giving our descriptions to his buddies. Do it fast, mount up, and let's see if there is some sort of town down this road. Candace, can you make the two of us look like him?" He pointed to the soldier.

Candace closed her eyes tightly and their appearance changed so that they wore similar armor and visors as the soldier. "This work?"

Ran sliced with his sword and severed the soldier's head. He mounted the other steed and pulled Xesca up. Concentrating, their appearance changed as well.

"It's perfect," Gregor said. "C'mon, let's go."

The four continued down the path. They only traveled about an hour before the lights of a town shone in the distance. They stopped well away from the city.

"Now what?" Gregor asked. "Do we want to go into the town looking like Guardsmen or do we want to go in another way?"

"A better question is do we really want to go into the town at all," Xesca said. "We have enough food to wait and my wound has been dressed nicely. Do we want to raise suspicion at all by entering the city? If that soldier hadn't been bluffing, there is a good chance that more of them will be on our trail and if they question the townspeople, it is likely one of them will say they saw four strange travelers come into town together."

"So we change our appearance to blend in," Candace said.

"But what do the townspeople look like?" Gregor asked. "The only people we have run into so far is the soldiers. We don't know how a traveler would dress. We would be spotted in a minute."

"Well, we better decide quickly," Ran said. "We are all working under the assumption that the soldier was telling the truth about a search party. My guess is that they won't stay long on the scene once they find out that their men are dead. And I would also wager my gold tooth that one of them will realize that we took the mounts and they will start streaking after us to catch up."

A little further down the road, a man appeared in front of the group. He noticed them and when he realized what they were, he lowered his head and sank to the ground. "Hail Guardsman!" he said loudly. Then he got up and continued to walk.

Gregor hopped off of the mount. Immediately, his appearance changed from that of a guardsman to that of a man wearing a black cloak. "Oh shit, I forgot that the illusion wouldn't hold!"

"Magicians!" the man gasped. His eyes rolled back up into his head and Gregor caught him as he fainted dead away.

"Excellent work plig!" Ran chuckled. "Now what?"

"Damnit! Is there a way that we can hold an illusion without touching one of you?"

"Here, give me a couple of those rocks, the smoothest that you can find," Ran said, hopping down. Gregor threw two rocks and Ran caught one with each hand. He closed his eyes and held each tightly, muttering some sort of chant. When he opened his eyes, he looked up at Candace. "Can you hold an illusion on yourself girl, or do I need another rock?"

"As long as I don't get injured, I can keep an illusion on myself indefinitely. Why?"

"You'll need to make yourself look like a man and in clothes similar to what the fainted guy is wearing." Ran said. "Try to change your jaw set a little. He didn't see your eyes, but he did see your mouth." Ran threw a rock to both Gregor and Xesca. Their features changed again. Now Xesca looked like a man a head shorter than she really was. Both she and Gregor were dressed similarly as the man on the ground. "As long as that rock is touching some part of your skin, the illusion will hold." Ran waved his arms slightly and his appearance changed as well.

"You made illusion stones that quickly?" Candace said in amazement. "You really are good. Better than me I am afraid."

"No worries lass, I'll teach you at a later junction. Right now, let's just get into town."

"What about him now?" Candace asked, helping Xesca off of her mount. "Are you going to kill him now too?"

"No need." Gregor said. "He saw four Guardsmen, two male and two female. Then he thought that he saw one of the males change from a guardsman to a man who was dressed in a most unusual way. On the other hand, here are two mounts that belong to the fallen Guardsmen. He'll think that he hallucinated that I changed appearance. Meanwhile, four men with no women will come into town and say that they saw the man be accosted by Guardsmen who, when they saw the four men coming down the path, decided to ditch their mounts and head to the wood. Simple."

"Brilliant plan Gregor" Xesca beamed. "Let us get into town quickly."

"But won't people realize that we do not live here and wonder how we managed to get through the whole town unnoticed?" Ran asked. "We obviously did that if we are coming out the other end. We can't have been coming from the way that the four guardsmen traveled or else they would have spotted us."

"Why not?" Gregor questioned. "Who's to say that the first time the Guardsmen passed us, they even paid us any noticed? If they were on the run, what would they have to fear of four men? They just rode on by and we barely noticed them. It was only after they had stopped and were accosting this poor soul that they became concerned about us."

"Wow," Candace said, scratching her head, "you're really good at this. I'm glad to have met you."

"Yes, he is," Xesca concurred. "It would seem that you learned quite a lot from your training with Alexander Blade."

"Should we take the guy?" Ran asked.

"He was reverent to the Guardsmen, but didn't seem really scared," Gregor mused. "I don't think that four travelers would be too afraid of repercussion if they helped a man into town."

"All right, enough talk," Ran hoisted up the man that they had encountered. "Give me a hand with this sack and let's go before the posse catches up with us."

And so, into town they went.

Chapter 9

Toren

A signpost on the side of the road announced the village name as Toren, population thirteen hundred seventy two. The four saw the sign and heard the music of a tavern and carried their new found travel companion inside.

"Hello, does anyone recognize this man?" Gregor called out.

"Why, that's Patel!" someone called out. "Hey, what happened to Patel?"

Gregor told the story just as they had rehearsed. He told about four guardsmen who had passed them on the road and then of those same guardsmen accosting Patel.

"Ungh," Patel moaned. "What happened to me? How did I end up at the Winespring?"

"These four travelers found you being attacked by the Guard," Someone in the tavern said.

Patel's eyes got wide. "They weren't Guard! They were magicians!"

An older man at the bar laughed and soon the entire tavern was roaring. "Right Patel! Magicians! Way out here in Toren?"

"They were, I swear it. Oh they looked like Guard all right. Two men and two women. But then one of them got off of his Galt and poof, he didn't look like a Guard anymore."

Another roar of laughter. "And I suppose next you'll be telling us that these four are magicians."

Patel took a step away from the group as though he were bitten. "They could have changed their appearance! How do we know that these aren't magicians!"

The tavern nearly shook with laughter. The first man, who had recognized Patel, came up and clapped his friend on the back. "You're crazy Patel. These men saw you and say the Guardsmen ran when there were so many witnesses. Besides, I don't see any women with them, do any of you?"

"No, and a damn shame too, a woman or two would be nice about now," the man at the bar bellowed and the rest of the tavern laughed their assent.

Gregor grinned at his companions. Everything was working out as planned. Suddenly, three Guardsmen burst into the Winespring Tavern.

"Did anyone see the riders on those Galt on the south end of town?" one of them called out.

Most everyone in the tavern turned back to what they were doing. Patel came forward. "There were four of them, Sir Guardsman. Two of them were women and two were men. But I swear sir, they were magicians and not Guards!"

"Heresy to even think such a thing!" one of the other guardsmen called.

The one who spoke originally raised a hand to silence the other. "Did anyone else see them?"

"My self and my travel companions did sir Guardsman," Gregor said, emulating Patel. "They passed us once on the path and we saw them again when we came upon them and this gentleman. They ran into the woods when they noticed us. I did not see any signs of magicians sir Guardsman."

"Let us move quickly then," the guard who had done most of the talking said. "They most likely weren't magicians, but renegades who had stolen the uniforms of Guards. Hear me now good people," the guard held his arms out and addressed the entire tavern, "these four renegades slew two Guardsmen. We will find them and kill them for all to see to avenge our fallen comrades. If any one else can help us as these good men have, we will reward you." The guard reached into a waist pocket and pulled out two small pouches. He handed one to Patel and one to Gregor, "As we have rewarded these two men." No one else in the tavern spoke. "Good evening to you and praise Halen-toc!"

"Praise Halen-toc!" was the shout that the tavern returned and so did Gregor and his companions, if a little late.

The Guardsmen ran from the tavern, hopped onto mounts that they had left outside, and sped off back the way that they had come. None spoke as they left and only started to speak again once the trio was well out of earshot.

"Well," the loudmouth man at the bar said, "it looks like drinks are on Patel and the stranger."

Patel glared at Gregor. "They were magicians I tell you!"

"I did not say that the weren't. I simply said that I saw no evidence that they were." Gregor shrugged indifferently.

"Oh, let it go Patel" was the call from the man at the bar.

Patel pushed past Gregor and stalked his way out of the tavern. Gregor shrugged again and he and the others took a table near the door. Pretty soon the man that had recognized Patel came over and sat with them.

"Sorry about Patel. He thinks that ever since it was found that someone could control the force other than Halen-toc, everyone can and the world is coming to an end. Names Hamel."

"No worries, I was not offended. I am called Gregor." Gregor nodded. "These are my friends, Ran, Candal, and Lester," Gregor motioned to each in turn and he altered the girls names. Their eyebrows shot up at the names that he had come up with for them.

"I don't think that I have ever seen you around before." Hamel examined the group. "You new to town?"

"Actually, we are traveling on. WSe were hopping to find a guide as Lester lost our map and we remembered just enough to get to here." Gregor said, smiling. "We're from a far off land."

"Well, I don't really know of any guides, but you could bed down for the night at my farm. It will have to be in the stable, but it is the least I could do for people who helped my friend. Besides," Hamel eyed the door suspiciously, "if there are people out there who would kill guards, it isn't very safe to be out on the road."

"We appreciate the offer," Gregor said smiling. "Please, I have the reward money here, let me pay you for this evenings lodging."

"Normally I'd turn you down friend, but times have been hard around these parts and the last thing I don't need is more coin." Hamel smiled back. "You folks hungry? I know the place doesn't look like much, but they make a great beef stew."

"Thanks, I think we will take some." Gregor opened the pouch of coins. Inside were ten gold coins and it looked to be twenty silver. "How hard have times been Hamel?"

Hamel was confused for a moment, then grinned. "The stew will set you back two silver for the four of you. Another silver if you order a round of ale and that includes me. As far as the barn goes, will a gold be too much for you?"

"Not at all," Gregor flipped one of the gold coins to Hamel and pulled out another gold. "How many rounds will this buy?"

"Four for us. You know, just because Devlin said that you and Patel were up for a house round doesn't mean you really have to."

Gregor did the math in his head. Around here, four silver were equal to one gold, which meant he had the equivalent of twenty gold in his pouch. A fair amount of money in this area if one gold could feed four. Gregor smiled again. "My father used to say, 'money made easily is money easily lost'. Let's see if we can prove him right." Gregor stood up and shouted, "I think that, Devlin I believe it is, had the right idea. We appreciate the hospitality that we have received so far in Toren and want to return the favor, so a round on the four travelers."

The tavern erupted into cheers. Glasses were raised in the general direction of the foursome and a couple of people actually applauded. Each of them returned the smiles that they received then gave eachother questioning looks. No one was really sure what Gregor had planned.

When a serving girl passed, Gregor ordered stew for each of them and offered to order one for Hamel but he refused. He flipped a gold coin and three silvers onto the tray and told the girl to keep them open and if she needed more, to just ask. "So Hamel, tell me, what has the Winespring full of people this evening?"

"You really aren't from around here are you?" Hamel said, lightly chiding Gregor. "It's almost festival time here. It is spring carnival and a time of celebration, though we have precious little to celebrate. This heat, it is far too early and has stunted the crop. Followers of Halentoc say that the renegade magicians are to blame. Who knows? All we know is that we may be poor but we aren't going to let that stop the celebration."

"A noble line of thinking," Xesca said. "Good for you."

Hamel smiled, "Oh, don't get us wrong. We'd be drinking and carrying on anyway, but at least this way we can say it's for celebration and not because we want to drown all of our troubles in ale. That will be next weeks excuse!"

The table chuckled. Suddenly, Gregor heard Ran's thoughts in his mind. *What do you plan to do here boy? Seems to me, when those guard find no trace of anyone up the road they will be coming back for the men who gave them false information. That may be a day or two or it may be an hour or two. Shouldn't we be keeping a low profile?*

Gregor tried to mask his surprise and continued eating his stew. He focused and thought to himself, *He can project, but can he read thoughts too?*

Aye, I can, Ran thought back, *and it's easier for me than normal because you are holding onto a magical object of my creation.*

Dude, why didn't you say something earlier? We could have been reading people and gotten all kinds of information instead of getting this guy drunk and pumping him dry.

I'm not sure what you just called me, but don't do it again. And as far as why I didn't say anything, it's because I'm a much better thought projector than a thought-reader. The only reason that it is so easy for us is because, like I said, you are holding a magical item of my creation. I have a bond to it and that helps me to communicate with you.

Hey, I have a radical idea Gregor thought, almost blowing his cover and blurting it out. He returned to his stew and tried to remain inconspicuous. He noticed that Xesca was talking to Hamel now, asking him what sort of festivities would be happening in the next couple of days. He also noticed that the only ones really drinking the ale were Ran and Hamel. Gregor didn't want any because it was beer where he was from, and this stuff could only be considered stout. Not what he was used to. *You said that you are a good thought projector? Could you toss out a thought that only a person capable of some sort of magic would 'hear'? And if so, how far could you project?*

Ran waved for another mug of ale. *I could blanket this town, for sure. But who do you think I'm going to pick up?*

Hopefully someone we can speak freely with. We won't be able to open ourselves up too much to Hamel, he doesn't seem to think too well of magicians and I sure think that we would fit his bill. Unless you've come up with something I haven't, I've still got no idea what we are even supposed to accomplish here.

If you think it will work, what the hell. You've been doing good so far. Ran turned to Hamel. "I could use some relief. Is there a place in this tavern?"

"Just to the right of the bar, you'll find the restroom."

"Thank you." Ran left the table and went where he was directed. Inside was exactly what he was looking for, a stall. He went in and sat on the commode. Focusing his thoughts, he remembered what Defalorn had said about his cloak and he hoped he could use his cloak like an antenna. He reached out with his mind and projected the thought, *I and companions are travelers though time and space. We have stumbled upon your planet by accident and are now trapped. We could use information, as it appears that our kind is feared on your planet. We are currently in the town of Toren. If you can help, come to the Winespring inn and ask if anyone has seen a man named Gregor. Claim that he is a relative from a far off land.* Ran felt his cloak amplify his thoughts and smiled. This Himanoco thing might turn out to be handy after all.

Almost immediately, he heard in his mind, *I will be there shortly. I am on the other side of town. Can you describe what this Gregor looks like and brief him on the situation. My name is Cadal.*

Red hair, seated at a table of five. Thank you Cadal. My trust is with you. Ran didn't like it. The men in the bar had said that magicians would not be out this far. Then what was one doing living in the town? How had he gone unnoticed? And what would he want in return for his service to them? Such thoughts played in Ran's mind as he reached out for Gregor. *A man should be coming in to the tavern shortly. His name is Cadal and he answered my call. He will pretend to recognize you, a cousin that he has not seen in some time.*

Do you think we can trust him? came Gregor's thought.

What choice do we have? The dice is thrown and our lot is cast with the man who can reach out with his mind.

Ran got up and headed back to the table. Xesca had left the table and was over talking to the man at the bar named Devlin. He didn't see Candace anywhere. Gregor and Hamel were still seated at the original table, talking to one another and laughing. He noticed that Hamel had a half empty mug of ale in front of him, the same status of his drink as when Ran got up to use the facilities. That would put him up to four, not counting however many he had drunk before the foursome arrived.

Candace appeared at Ran's side and moved him to a corner away from the table, glancing quickly to make sure that Hamel hadn't noticed the duo's segregation from the rest of the group. "I could hear the conversation that you and Gregor were having and the thought that you had sent out. Maybe one of us should stay away from the table so that the man doesn't know our number. You only told him that you and companions had come to this planet."

"But I also told him to look for a table of five. Not to mention, we may still be boarding in Hamel's stable tonight. Don't you think he will wonder where you are when it is time to go? Besides, where would you go? Where would you hide? It seems to me, one person hiding in this town might catch the eye of a Guard, and we already know that they are the types to shoot first and ask questions later. No, we stick together, good or ill."

"All right," Candace conceded. "But this seems awful risky."

"Candace, we are fugitives from the local justice and on the run. We've already killed two men. How can anything we do from here on out not be considered risky?" Ran said, smiling.

"That's a good point." Candace said, not returning any of the mirth. "Let's get back to the table before Cadal arrives."

"Oh and by the way sweetheart, you might want to use some of that illusion ability on your voice. You may look like a man, but you still sound like a girl."

"Oops, I always forget that part."

"Just remember to laugh high pitched, since you've already done that." They got back to the table as Xesca returned from her conversation at the bar with two fresh glasses of ale, one for herself and one for Hamel. Ran noticed that both Xesca's and Hamel's eyes seemed to be closed slightly more than usual, and Xesca's voice seemed a little louder. *Getting drunk. And who can blame them? This stuff that Hamel called ale is pretty strong.*

About the time that everyone was back at the table, a man came up to them. He stood tall, just inches shorter than Xesca and his wide-eyed expression seemed comical on his somewhat scrunched face. His clothes were similar to everyone else's, but Ran did notice a small tattoo on his right had between his thumb and index finger. It was of a circle, with an 'X' in the center and a line through the 'X', the universal mark for a magical fencer.

"Gregor? Cousin Gregor, is that you?"

"Cadal? Why, it's been so long!"

Gregor got up and Cadal came over and wrapped his arms around Gregor. "Why didn't you tell me you were going to be in Toren? Didn't mother tell your father that I moved here a couple of cycles back?"

"Not that I recall. But you know my father, sometimes he tells me things and sometimes he doesn't. Am I glad to see you!"

"Cadal, if I would have known that this was a relation, I would have taken him right over instead of only offering him my stable," Hamel said, slightly slurred.

"Not at all Hamel," Gregor was quick to respond. "I am more than happy at the offer of hospitality. I was about to suggest that we depart anyway, and now that my cousin is here, I hope you don't mind if we go with him? I insist that you keep the gold piece though, as a gift from us for keeping us company and offering to shelter weary travelers for the night."

"Aww, I couldn't do that," Hamel protested.

"No really, I insist that you keep it." Gregor motioned for the others and everyone got up. "But if you don't mind, it really is late and I think we could all use some rest, don't you agree friends." Ran, Candace and Xesca all nodded. Gregor stopped the serving girl as she came by and dug out another four silver coins to settle up their bill. "It has been a pleasure and if we are still in town for the festival, I hope we can spend more time together."

"Hey, you bet!" Hamel swayed as he stood up. "You're all a great bunch of guys and I mean that. You can come and celebrate with us any time."

"Well cousin, shall we be going?" Cadal asked. Everyone else was already by the door.

"Let's cousin."

Once outside, the four fell in behind Cadal. He led them over to a hovering vehicle that, to Gregor, resembled a convertible automobile. As they headed further into town, each was scanning the buildings, now dark at this late hour. They saw two other taverns, a clothing shop, a general store and some small houses. There were a few side streets, but it looked like they mostly had homes on them and that the street that they were on was the main one thoroughfare in town. On the outskirts of the town were a couple of farm houses and Cadal pulled into the last one. The ride was a short one and no one spoke.

"Come on in," Cadal said as the others got out of the car. "And maybe someone can tell me what the devil is going on here and why there is a whole group of Guardsmen outside our nice little town?"

"Happily," Gregor said. "And we hope to get just as much information from you."

Chapter 10

Cadal and friends

The house was large and the main entrance opened to a living room style room. There were several chairs and a hearth in the corner opposite the door. A hallway connected the room to what appeared to be a dining room and kitchen combination. There was a staircase in the middle of the hallway heading up to the next level. Gregor, Ran, Candace and Xesca all sat in a row of chairs while Cadal sat in a chair opposite them.

From the hallway, two more men in similar clothes to everyone else in the town came in. The only difference was that each had a belt knife cinched to his side. One had dark hair and a mustache; the other was shorter and had sandy hair. Both were slight of build and both seemed to have eyes that missed nothing. The shorter ones eyebrows shot up as he looked at Candace and Xesca.

"But they're women," he said.

"Oh sorry, we were disguised," Candace apologized. She made a slashing with her hands and returned to her normal appearance, Xesca removed the illusion stone from where it was tied to her wrist. Meanwhile, Gregor took off his stone while Ran made a similar motion to Candace and returned to his original appearance. Ran had made the stone so well that no one even saw them.

" A handy trick," moustache said. "Much the same as that thought projection. You four are a formidable group, I'm sure. And I'm guessing that that is why there are six Guardsmen combing the wood on the south end of town?"

"In a manner of speaking," Ran said. "We have several questions."

"But first," Gregor broke in, "an exchanging of trust? My name is Gregor Holden. These are my friends, Ran Grastle, Candace Orthon, and Xesca. We are the ones that the guardsmen are looking for and they are looking for us because we killed two of their kind." Ran winced and Candace went wide-eyed at the last. Only Xesca maintained her calm, but it might have been the ale. "If you do not want to associate with us, that is fine and we understand. I warn you though, we are not to be taken lightly and I would not recommend you attempt to turn us over to the Guard. Just say the word and we will be on our way."

"Killed them? With what?' Cadal asked. "You are unarmed."

"Don't count on it Cadal," moustache said. He looked at the shorter man but he only shook his head. "In any event, we may be able to associate with you a little longer at least. My name is Favel and this is Destin. Along with Cadal, we own and operate this farm. Since you have been so forthcoming, even if you do underestimate us, allow me to give you some base information. A man named Halen-toc rules this entire continent that you are on. He is an incredibly powerful magician. His castle is about five hundred spans from here, a minimum six-day ride in any hovercraft. Halen-toc has issued a decree in the past four cycles claiming that anyone else who can do any sort of magic is 'unholy' and must be killed. Your turn for more information."

"We aren't exactly sure how or why we arrived on your planet," Gregor continued. "We are on a quest. We meant no trouble with the guards that we encountered, but they did not believe us. They thought that our friend," he motioned to Xesca, "was carrying some sort of new plague. She is not, just to assure you. Green is her natural skin tone. She frightened them and they fired a shot, grazing her arm. Reacting quickly, Ran used his illusion powers to cover us in an invisible cloak. This enraged the guards and they took aim to kill us on site. We killed the guard in self-defense."

Favel nodded. "Halen-toc has killed an estimated thirty thousand peaceful magic users. Recently, a rebel band has formed. We call ourselves *Cultat Ne Zau,* which, in our ancient language means…"

125

"Oppressed ones." Xesca said softly.

"Yes," Favel said, surprised. "We have outposts, hiding places like this farm, in almost every town in the land. The method of finding these places is thought projection, like you used. Cadal is our receiver and he said he had never heard anything as powerful as your call. Destin and I are skilled at hand to hand fighting and we help to defend this place. Destin also can see through illusion. Myself, I am a telekinetic. We fear death, but will not run from it if it is our time to die."

"Well, we are not about to die, any of us," Ran piped up. "Why don't the people rise up and overthrow this Halen-toc?"

"Only, on average I'd say, ten percent of our population can do magic. Halen-toc actually has the people believing that magic is evil and so they help him hunt the magic users down. Few side with us."

"How organized is your resistance?" Xesca said. "Do you have a leader? Do you have a plan other than hide?"

"You seem to ask a lot of questions about the others," Cadal said suspiciously. "I think that this has gone on long enough. They are professed Guard killers. Let us hand them over to the Guard and collect the reward."

"Patience Cadal, patience," Favel said soothingly. "I don't think that would be a good idea. I think these people can see injustice when it stares them in the face and won't stand for it. You will help us, yes?" Favel asked them.

"Help you what?" Candace asked.

Favel looked at his companions, then leaned in toward the foursome, "Help us kill Halen-toc!"

"*You* plan on killing him?" Ran said, smiling.

"Not us in particular, but our group, the *Cultat Ne Zau*!"

"Perhaps we will, but not tonight." Gregor said, standing and yawning. "Either throw us out or let us rest. It has been a taxing day."

"Yes, enough talk for tonight," Favel said. "Cadal, would you kindly get the Guard out in the stable and let them know that we have killers in our house." He and Destin stood up and faced the group.

"What!" Candace said, leaping to her feet.

"Damn!" Ran said. "I knew it!" In a flash his sword was at his side.

"Wait a minute for Crissakes!" Gregor shouted. "Don't be foolish! We'll never fight our way out of town!" He opened a slide passage.

"Is that a good idea," Xesca asked. "Defalorn warned us about attempting to slide when you asked him back in the tower. My coordination may be disrupted due to that drink called ale, but I do not think that I would be a hindrance in a fight. Perhaps we should attempt to battle our way out."

"The house is surrounded." A voice boomed from outside. "Throw down any weapons and come out slowly. There is no escape."

Gregor let the slide portal close. "Are you certain you want to do this." He directed his question toward his companions, but looked at Favel when he asked it.

"Absolutely" everyone responded.

"Do not attempt to resist," the voice outside seemed to finish their thoughts. "I repeat, you are surrounded. Come out!"

"Cadal had the mark of a magical fencer. I saw it on his hand," Ran said. "You know that we can do magic. Why do you wish to turn us in?"

"We serve Halen-toc," Destin said simply "That is what happens when you get branded, either serve him or be killed. We find rogue magicians like you and put them down."

"How many outside Candace?" Gregor asked.

"I'm guessing that the house is ringed by about ten guards. Cadal is out there too, and he has one of those strange weapons. All of them have weapons trained on the house. Lights too."

"You can't be seriously considering escape?" Favel asked. "You did not tell us of any other of your kind and you did not actually agree to kill our ruler. I believe you when you say that you are not even from this planet. The guards may go easy on you, a simple flogging. Then, either you leave the planet in peace or stay as the branded ones."

"She recognized the name of the group!" Destin said, pointing at Xesca. "She knows our ancient language. How can you believe that story that they are from another planet?"

"She's also green!" Favel shouted back. "How many green people have you seen in your lifetime?"

"Gregor," Ran broke in. "Those weapons may be powerful and may have range, but if we strike hard and fast I think the cloaks will protect us."

"I forgot about the cloaks," Gregor said, slapping his forehead. "Ran, you said you were a good geomage? Can you raise up a mist that will help disguise our escape?"

"Enough of this," Destin said. He drew his knife and started toward Gregor. Gregor shot his sword out and, before Destin had a chance to react, he sliced across the man's thigh. Destin slumped into a chair and Gregor leveled his sword at the man's neck. He motioned for Favel to move next to his companion.

"You just sit tight boys, you've done enough damage tonight and I don't want to kill any more people than I have to." Gregor turned back to Ran. "Well?"

"Easy there boy, it's coming, it's coming"

"Candace, how many vehicles are out there?" Gregor asked.

"Well, Cadal's is out there. Plus it looks like five or six of those horse type things we rode in on. What were they called, Galts?"

"Which can go faster, the Galt or Cadal's vehicle?" Gregor asked, holding his sword to Destin's chest. "And don't lie to me, there is a chance that you can come out of this alive and I don't think that you want to do anything to change that."

"The cruiser," Favel said. "The Galts are more for show than high speed travel."

"Be careful," Destin scowled at Favel. "I don't want to have to tell them that four traitors escaped but one stayed behind."

"I'll take that as confirmation that you told the truth Favel," Gregor said smiling. "I wonder how many others had this hard of a first day?"

"Well, the fog is up, and is it thick," Candace said. "Good job Ran!"

"This is your last warning," the outside voice boomed. "If you do not come out, we will come in after you."

"All right, Ran put your sword away," Gregor said. "You and Xesca are going to lay us down as many strong and wide blasts of battle magic that you can. Candace, can you make an illusion behind them, some sort of monster?"

"Sure, not a problem."

"I'll make a bee line for the cruiser. Once I've got it, I'll pull it out onto the road. Everyone hops in and we are out of here."

"Sounds fine Gregor," Xesca said. "I'm ready."

"Me too," Candace said.

"Just say the word boy," Ran said.

Gregor turned to Favel. "You could come with us. You are already branded an outlaw. You can live a miserable life helping a ruler that you hate or you can live on the run with us. It's up to you."

Favel thought on it for a moment. "My powers aren't as strong as yours, but I might be able to throw one or two of them aside to give you a clear lane to the cruiser."

"You fool!" Destin said. "The guard will hunt you down and kill you. All of you!"

"I meant what I said when I told them that I am not afraid of death. I am not!" Favel leaned in until his face was just inches from Destin's. "I will not toil any longer under the heel of a tyrant! I won't!"

"Fine, Favel, you made your point," Gregor said, pulling the man away. "Time to go to work."

"Can we trust him?" Ran said, eyeing Favel up.

"We still need a guide." Gregor said simply. "On three. One... Two...Three!"

Gregor kicked the door open and ran into the night. Shots were fired from the line of guards and he had to move quickly to avoid them. Suddenly, shots were being fired in the other direction, as a creature appeared behind a small cluster of guardsmen.

Gregor kept running. Flashes of yellow light streaked from over his shoulder as Ran and Xesca's magic attacked the guards. Two guards stood between Gregor and the cruiser and he was about to draw his sword when the two went flying backwards, as though struck by some invisible hand. Gregor leaped into the cruiser and fired the engine. He pulled it out onto the street just in time to see his companions and Favel emerge from the fog. They jumped in and he sped them all into the night.

Chapter 11

Plots

Kenor Anor knew that his time was approaching. He could feel things shifting. What he was uncertain of was where things were shifting to.

His tower-like castle loomed high on Mt. Vazramzin, overlooking the little town of the same name. Kenor's home planet of Capval was said to be one of the oldest known planets in the galaxy, stretching back over fifty millennia. It's peoples had always been strong in the ways of magic and little had changed in all of it's time. The planet was also so large that the population never really grew to the astronomical amounts that it sometimes did on other planets.

Sitting at the head of a rectangular table in his battle room, looking down onto the city below, Kenor had his hands folded in a steeple under his chin. The walls were lined in maps, almost to the point that they were papered. At the table with him were seven other black-clad Himanoco warriors, waiting somewhat patiently for the leader to speak.

"Markus, what news do you have for me on the Himanoco who do not follow us?"

The man seated on Kenor's right drew up at the sound of his name. "Of the remaining 40,000 warriors, several have stated that while they do not openly support our movement, they do not seek to hinder it. Nor will they deny that the Blackwolf is risen, at such time as we announce it. Many claim to feel the presence of powers that they cannot explain away."

Another man, this one seated next to Markus, broke in. "Opinions vary on the source of this disturbance as well as the cause." Markus glared but Kenor motioned for the other man to continue, before putting his hands back in the steeple-like position. "Some say that it is emanating from this very planet. Others claim from Ohlia. Still others say it is Alden Hall academy. A dozen of other places, from forbidden planets to uninhabitable ones are all also named. Whatever the case, they all think that it has something to do with the return of the Wolf Warriors."

"Anton," Kenor regarded the man at the foot of the table, "what of our contacts in other clans? Do the Gingee, Malada, Bayer, and Kivkavzed concur with what Haxil says our clan feels?"

"Lord Anor, the Bayer are as impenetrable as ever. All I have been able to learn is that they have gathered a very large number on the plains of Ameradeo, located on the planet Mawrice. The Malada as a clan claim to feel nothing, although the *Raes can Mitlon* say that the time is ripe for the return of their beloved, whatever that means. The Gingee are never in tune with such things and say that the workings of magic as well as that of the Himanoco clan are of no concern of theirs, so long as it does not interfere with them. Kivkavzed have taken to openly opposing the other clans and battling any Wolfwarrior that they come in contact with."

"The Malada Travelers of Knowledge are not as reliable as they make themselves out to be, Lord Anor." The man to the right of Kenor interrupted. "And I have it on good terms that the Bayer are gathering because they do think that the 'Time of the Return' as they put it, is coming."

"Pren forgets himself my lord and speaks when he should listen," Anton retorted. "The Bayer legend of the 'Time of Return' is said to take place on the planet Kosivo and the land of Thom, which is believed by almost all Bayer to be the birthplace of the Brownwolf himself."

Pren glared murderously at Anton but held his tongue. "Have you anything to add Unaag?" Kenor asked the only man to not yet speak.

"Only that the recent expedition that I led has uncovered some very interesting artifacts. I do not believe that any of them actually belonged to Himanoco yet, but it is only a matter of time before one of these scoutings uncovers one of the weapons of the Blackwolf."

"Good. Now," standing, Kenor turned to Haxil and fired a beam of battle magic energy that reduced the man to ash. "That was for interrupting. Pren," He turned to the man on his right, Pren's complexion was sickly pale, "open your mouth." He did as he was told and a much smaller beam of energy shot out from the end of Kenor's finger, severing the man's tongue. Pren would have screamed had he been able to. "You would have shared Haxil's fate but you schooled your tongue when Anton upbraided you. In my mercy, I have helped you to never have to school your tongue again."

Some of the remaining men trembled visibly. Kenor continued. "Markus, you will assist Unaag in his search of artifacts. I want the Sword of Himanoco found and brought to me before the close of the year, understood?" Markus shook his head in assent.

"Anton, you will be sure to bring envoys of representatives from each of the wolf clans to me in the next few months so that I can meet with them and explain exactly what I expect in the way of support. Also, let Pad Bever know that he has been promoted to Council in replacement of Pren and that he is to assist you in communication with the clans. Also, you may want to tell him what type of manners I expect of my Council." Anton saluted.

"Unaag, tell Piotren Valse that she is now the on the Council as well. Her job is to get the number of Himanoco that do not openly support me down from 40,000 to 15,000 in the next three months. Tell her to use whatever means necessary and also that failure will be met in a similar fashion to how I dealt with Haxil." Unaag murmured his assent.

Kenor stood glaring at the men as they awaited further instructions. "You're still here?" Saluting, they turned and opened slide portals and headed through. Left alone in to his thoughts, Kenor mused on something Haxil had said. He claimed people believed that the source of disturbance was emanating from Alden Hall. Kenor had felt something a month ago, when he knew that Defalorn had been interviewing students. Shifting.

He had to find out what was going on. No more mistakes and no more suffering of fools. His time was coming and nothing was going to stop him now.

Chapter 12

On the Run

The lights on the vehicle were starting to dim. The group had been riding now for nearly three hours and fatigue was definitely setting in. It was Favel that spoke first.

"I think you should know that this hovercraft is powered by the sun and is not designed to be run for too long in the dark. It would be advisable to head into the woods for the night and come up with a plan as to where we are going to go next."

"I think he might be right Gregor," Xesca said. "There is still a lot of information that we will need to have if we are going to be successful in this mission."

Ran spoke up next. "I'm still not sure that it was a good idea bringing Favel with us." He shot the man a hard look. "He turned us over to these damnable Guardsmen."

"I'm with Ran," Candace said. "I know that we still need information on this planet and all but," she glanced sidelong at Favel, "it may be that we will just be caught by a larger group where this man takes us."

"I think that I proved myself by helping you escape," Favel said, defensively. "I could have just let the Guard take you."

"On the other hand, the Guard would still be out searching for us if you hadn't told them who we were when I reached out for your help"

"Enough!" Gregor exclaimed. "We need to think logically. Logically speaking, we will be able to blend in better and cover more ground if we split up and I don't see where we have any other choice. The Guard are going to be looking for us, a group of four or five people who will be inquiring about all kinds of information." Gregor paused. "The only thing I am uncertain on is how we will get back together after we have our information."

"Not to mention where will go?" Xesca asked. "We have no maps and no knowledge of the topography. We also don't know where to go or how to get there."

"But I do," Favel said. "We could split up. Some of us could cut through the woods and come out to a different town than the one on the road. Then, we could meet up at the capitol, Langeria. There is a tavern that is popular to people of the resistance called the Raging Warrior. We could meet there in about, oh, a weeks time."

"Does it take a week to get to Langeria?" Gregor asked.

"About that, yes."

"Then why don't we make it ten days to meet up again."

"Who should split with who?" Candace asked.

"Why don't you, Ran and Xesca go along the road to this town up ahead, what was it called Favel?"

"Vavally."

"Vavally." Gregor said. "Favel and I will cut through the woods to another town. You can pick up a map in Vavally and meet us at the tavern in a couple of days."

"Gregor, are you sure that is wise?" Xesca asked. "Splitting us up could be a disastrous move. Besides, you are not an illusionist, you won't be able to hide without either Candace or Ran."

"I don't think it will be a problem. We will stick to the woods and cut through to the next town, you will move as a smaller group than what they are looking for." Gregor pulled the vehicle over. "And I think it best if we move into the woods now and hide. You will want to come out on the road a ways ahead of the vehicle so if asked you can say that you heard it coming but never saw it or any of the people. We will make a camp tonight and talk more about this."

"If you think that is the way that we should do things, you've been doing fine so far" Ran said. "We've got the supplies to stay in the woods tonight, but no sort of shelter. It will be cold and we could light a fire, but it will probably alert the Guardsmen."

"I think that we can cover too much smoke and light with a large illusion," Candace said.

"Favel, do you think that there is a place that we could get something to sleep in fast?" Gregor asked.

"No need, Gregor," Candace piped up. "You've got a conjurer with you. It will be no problem for me to whip up a tent and a couple of bed rolls. It will however, take some time."

"Perfect, let's go."

The group headed into the woods. They went on until they found a fairly large clearing. Ran set to getting some sticks and wood to make a fire and Xesca gathered as many rocks in the dark as she could find so that she could make a ring to contain it. Gregor and Favel found some logs to use as benches to sit on. Candace sat quietly, focusing her energy to form the items that they would need.

Half of the night had passed when they had finally finished. They had a fire, two large canvas tents and five bed rolls. Candace had fallen asleep from the exhaustion of creating all of the different items. Favel had also retired to a tent to get some rest. Ran, Xesca and Gregor sat in the warmth of the fire and Gregor yawned tiredly.

Ran spoke first. "You know Gregor, there was a time not that long ago that I was following men about as young as you and hated it. But, you seem to know what you are doing. Why then would you split our numbers and why would you yourself decide to go it alone with the one person who you can't fully trust?"

"I have to agree with Ran, Gregor," Xesca said. "I have studied with one of the same strategists as you, but have also studied with others. It is wise to ally ourselves with a citizen of this planet. But is it wise to ally ourselves with one who has the potential to betray us again?

"It is also a wise idea to split the group up. But is it wise to have the larger of the two groups go without you, the man who has established himself as leader? I also have to question the decision to make the smaller group just you and the citizen from this planet. Not necessarily a bad decision if the citizen had come willingly or had proven that they would be a good ally. But Favel has had one betrayal and one assistance in his history. He also is a fugitive who, if caught, would most likely trade any information on us to get a more lenient sentence. Not to mention, you give up the advantage of outnumbering him two to one if you don't take one of us along with you.

"Finally, what is it that you hope to accomplish by leaving with Favel? You think that you can trust him? What are you planning?"

"O.K., O.K., first things first," Gregor held up his hand so his companions would stop talking. "Do I think that I can trust Favel, no. But I know that I can watch him. And I know that I could defeat him one on one if he gets out of line. And I know that if I took Ran," he turned to the older man, "you might get angry and kill Favel before I'm ready. If I take Xesca," he eyed up the woman, "I put both strategists in the same group. That would leave Candace, and I thought about it. Has either of you noticed that she hasn't really said or done much so far? She did a great job as a conjurer, and she can follow direction, but I don't know what her potential is and I don't think that I will see it right away. All of you already think of me as a leader, and if that's fine with you, it's fine with me. But you two are the ones who are questioning me and keeping me on my toes. You don't follow blindly. I think that if Candace went with me, should would follow blindly and maybe advance to the next level of training without earning it. I am hoping that you two will push her a little and get her to come out of her shell.

"Now we can all agree that these Guardsmen are looking for us, but I wonder if they are truly our enemy or just an enemy because of extenuating circumstances? If we all stick with Favel, not only would we be easier to spot, but we also would only get his one, colored version of the story. But you three, together, are resourceful and untainted by Favel's opinions. You could learn things. Our survival may depend on that."

Xesca and Ran mulled over Gregor's opinions. It was Ran who spoke first. "You know son, I've followed many men in my time into one battle or another. As I grew older, it got harder and harder to follow anyone with a hint of youth because, in my eyes, they just hadn't lived, hadn't seen enough to be telling me things about the world. But you,

you see not only with an old man's eyes, but with a cunning that would make most of the warlord's I know turn green," he turned to Xesca, "no offense girl."

She smiled. "I thought that expression was a compliment to my people before I looked up the true meaning of it." Turning to Gregor, Xesca held the smile, "You would have made Lord Alex proud. If I may ask, are you just a traveling warrior Gregor? You seem like so much more."

Gregor grinned sheepishly. "Actually, I am a prince on the planet Kanderfain. I am Defender of the Realm of Holden and that is why I train so hard."

"Defender of the Realm?" Xesca asked.

"I've got this one kid," Ran chimed in. "On some planets, the male is seen to be the dominate of the sexes, with his strength. Other planets see the female as the dominate one, with her ability to grow life. Kanderfain is one of the latter types. Gregor is the oldest male heir, but he has a sister. She will ascend to the throne in his land and he is her sworn defender, the war chief of all her armies."

"Is the sister older or younger than you Gregor?" Xesca asked.

"Younger actually, but it wouldn't matter. She is queen and I am her defender. My younger brother Alexander is the only one of us whose future is undecided."

"That is just so much different from my home," Xesca said, shaking her head. "Age is the primary factor in our hierarchy. Bloodline or sex have very little to do with it. We are ruled by a panel of elders, and if one should die the remainder of the elders have to choose someone else to fill the empty space."

"Now my planet is the former I described, one ruled by males. My father was a *culdat*, a landowner. I think you call the title duke on your planet Gregor. It isn't really, because technically speaking, *culdat* are appointed by a governing body called the *magih*. Usually though, as long as there is a male heir, he ascends without resistance. All the *magih* really do is make sure that taxes are paid to the monarch and assign *culdat* to recently conquered lands. I have an older brother and sister, as well as two more younger sisters. They all live on an estate referred to as a *sig-culdat*. The *culdat* and his family live in the main house at the near center point of the lands that the *culdat* ruled at the time of his ascension. Depending on the size of the land and the length of time the *culdat* and his family have ruled in the area, the house can be basic or incredibly elaborate and castle like. All the siblings have the same style house as one another, with the oldest sibling being directly to the west, next in age to the east, next south, and the final is north. This set up is deliberate because the continent that I live is not nearly as long north-south as it is east-west. Also, in relationship to the land of my family, the majority of the continent stretches eastward. For others, the

First House, as it is referred to, is in the in the west. But always south, then north."

"So your house is in the west?" Xesca asked.

"It would be, heart, if I lived with my family. Unfortunately I had a falling out with my brother after my father had died and, well,..." Ran just shrugged.

"What was the 'falling out' about?" Gregor asked.

"Rather not talk about it son, if that's fine."

"That's all right. We should really be getting to sleep anyway, we've all got early days ahead of us tomorrow, and a lot more running. Oh, and just to let you know, I wouldn't recommend using illusion. That is exactly what those Guardsmen will be looking for. Lucky for us, most everyone who has seen what we truly look like is either dead or has only saw us in the dark on the run.

It was on that note that the threesome retired. Each of their hearts weighed heavy with what they had seen and what they knew was lying ahead.

Chapter 13

More of the Strange Planet

The camp broke with the first rays of the dawn and Gregor and Favel set out to reach Bethel on the other side of the wood. They had a long hike and it was very possible that they would not make it to the city walls today, so they made sure to pack up one of the tents and two bed rolls to take along on their journey.

They walked on for what Gregor gauged to be about an hour, well out of range of anything but the birds that were busy flying to and fro. He figured that now would be as good a time as any to start questioning Favel about this planet.

"So Favel, how did Halen-toc come into power?"

"Well, he wasn't always referred to as Halen-toc. About thirty years ago he was know as just plan old Halen Tocartel. He was a magician, and a powerful one at that. But this was back when magic wasn't outlawed. Halen was a recluse, he kept away from cities and sometimes would go without being spotted by anyone for months, even a year at a time.

"Then, he stumbled across a power most mages only dream of. He became immortal, his magic seemingly limitless. It was then that he named himself Halen-toc and began to assert himself as the supreme leader of our continent, Corda. He knew that no one could oppose him, and if they did, he would dispatch them mercilessly.

"You see, at the time that Halen-toc came to be, not only was magic legal, it was encouraged. We used it for many of our daily activities. Also, there were four different controlling factions in Corda. Each had been fighting for some years and many people had felt the despair of war. Halen-toc promised an end to the fighting as long as the people followed him. That was his motto, 'Worship me and live in peace.'"

"So, why didn't you follow him?"

"Oh, we did at first. Then, when he had successfully quelled any uprisings and had the entire continent under his boot heel, I don't know, it just seemed as though he had to have a hobby or something to occupy his time. So, he turned against magic, saying that it was one of the reasons that people had fought in the first place. He said that only he could control the power and anyone else caught using magic for anything would be branded as an infidel and either killed or cast in to slavery."

"That was when you rose up?"

"Aye, what choice did we have? But we didn't know about the damnable Guard. Halen-toc had been amassing those soldiers for years, unbeknownst to everyone I think. I'd wager that the Guardsmen that he had were stronger and better trained than any army that had existed before him. He had spent an incredible amount of money in the development of weapons and war technology as well as building training facilities for soldiers. Our resistance, with no nation or ruler like the three factions once were, was little match for what we faced.

"We became an underground movement. The fly that is always buzzing around Halen-toc's ear, but is never more than an annoyance. Slaves like myself become double agents, learning about the Guard and their weaknesses under the guise of slavery."

"Guise?" Gregor asked. "You're branded."

"Yes, and I had to plead my life to get this brand. Thankfully, Halen-toc and his Guard keep the brand secret. They don't want the people to know who is a slave so as to use the slaves not only to catch magic-users but also to spy on the everyday citizens. Many a young person has been surprised and then tortured into secrecy because they chose to mimic a marking that they saw. In fact, brand's in general, once very prominent, are now frowned upon because no one knows if the brand you wear is one you chose or one that was forced upon you.

"No, my mission was to get caught. To turn myself in and get the brand so that I could become a spy and try to find more people like ourselves. To try to find people like you and your friends; dynamic and powerful. There may have been war under the three factions, but at least the people were free."

"A hard choice that is," Gregor mused quietly. "Do you trade freedom for peace, or live free and in a state of perpetual war?"

The two traveled on the rest of the day in mostly silence. Their pace was strong and it was not long into the night that they saw the lights of Bethel were just visible in the distance. They decided to camp for the evening, as Favel said that most people would become suspicious of two people traveling through the woods at night.

They kept their camp small and the fire low so as not to alert any Guard to where they were hiding. Favel had foraged for some of the local vegetation along their hike. It wasn't very filling, but it had helped to keep their stomachs from rumbling too much. Gregor stilled had a few questions nagging him that finally he felt he had to ask.

"So Favel, I need to know, this Halen-toc, how could we get to him? Wouldn't he have round the clock protection?"

"He has grown soft," Favel spat. "After ten years of complete rule, he is lazy. He doesn't fear the fly anymore. Now is the time to show him that the fly was really a bee and to remind him he can still be stung!"

"But I still don't understand, what will it accomplish? Who will rise up to take his place? You kill him and the continent may very well be plunged into anarchy!"

"No," Favel said, shaking his head. "The *Cultat Ne Zau* has a strong hierarchy. We will be able to either lead or appoint leaders."

"But won't that be the same thing, the magician's ruling the common?"

"But don't you see?" Favel was becoming exasperated. "People will be free! They will be able to live their lives how ever they would like! There will be no total dictator!"

"Like I said, anarchy."

"You will see, you and your friends. It is not just my kind that wants to be rid of Halen-toc. It is everyone!"

Gregor asked no more. He had let Favel retire and sat looking at the fire for a while after the tent flap had closed. Gregor agreed with Favel on most points and he was fairly certain that this Halen-toc should be put down and that his group would be the ones to do it. But he couldn't help but think that he was overlooking something. He couldn't shake the nagging feeling that there was a reason why they shouldn't kill Halen-toc. That maybe rule by a dictator, oppression of a small group of people, maybe that had to be the price of peace.

His own planet had been beleaguered by war for as long as any generation could remember. His people, his country, weren't involved directly with any current wars. At least, he didn't think they were. There was that whole Middle-East crisis, but who knew if they were even still involved in that other than trying to mediate a peace treaty between two counties that had been at war for hundreds of years. There was, however, always a war.

And oppression. Every race on his planet seemed to oppress every other. All over skin tone and religion. Sometimes, it would disgust him so much that he would escape to hiatus on Kanderfain just to be with people who didn't care what you looked like. That would only last until an aristocrat from a visiting nation would either show up with a entourage of slaves or would make some sort of comment on how the common folk of his land seemed to need more "discipline". Gregor was born a prince, by definition he was supposed to be above people, and yet he had never understood what made people think that. If anything, he was a servant to the people, to his followers. He was their slave, not the other way around and he loved it. In turn, his people loved him.

And that was the rub. Was civil unrest enough to kill a man who had calmed the world? Did the people not liking Halen-toc justify upsetting the whole balance of this continent, and of the lives of the quiet individual that was indifferent to the whole "hunt the magicians"?

Gregor just didn't know. And it was these thoughts that held sleep off for quite some time even after he had lain down for the night.

While Gregor and Favel traveled on through the woods, Candace, Ran, and Xesca made it to Vavally easily enough. No one came upon them while they were on the road and no one seemed to notice them when they came into town.

Xesca was the only one of the group to have any illusion on her. It wasn't that they wanted to, but clothes alone would not hide her height or her skin tone. They knew that it might draw the Guard if they were making random searches of people who were traveling, but when one has no choice, they make due with what they can.

Vavally was laid out similar to Toren, a main street where most of the business' were, side streets with modest homes and farms on the outskirts. A tavern called the Hulking Warrior sat near the center of town. It was still somewhat early in the day and so it was fairly empty.

Xesca spoke first. "I think that we will have to divide up even more. Candace, I feel it best if you stay with me. Ran, you are strong and wise, I think that once you find out how far the next town toward Langeria is, you move out of town. That will lessen our numbers and will leave us even more vulnerable, but it will also draw suspicion away if we are broken up even more."

"Are you sure that we can handle things on our own Xesca?" Candace asked.

"The girl has a point m'lady. Three swords are always better than two."

"Please, do not worry about us Ran. I am more than confident in our skills. Also, since this is an illusion stone of your creation, I will be able to contact you mentally if necessary and vice versa. I think I see," Xesca paused and held her hand up to block the sun from her eyes, "yes. It is another caravan. See if you can slip on to the end of it."

"If you insist." Ran grinned and made a mock bow. When he looked back though, his face was stoic, "be careful girls. I wouldn't forgive myself if either of you washed out because I wasn't there to help."

"We will be fine Ran Grastle. You be careful as well and do not worry us with anymore death and destruction."

Ran trotted off quickly and Candace watched him the whole way. Then she turned to Xesca, "Now what are we supposed to do?"

"That was the exact question that I had for you Candace. What do you think should be our next course of action."

"How should I know? I'm not the strategist!"

"One of my professors often said that 'One does not have to be a strategist to come up with a plan. Some of the greatest plans I have ever seen were devised by so-called layman and some of the most disastrous plans were created by those that referred to themselves as strategists.' This by a man who devoted his life and made his livelihood by coming up with the best battle plans. You have been far too quiet and too willing. It is most likely stemming from your youth. Do not fear any sort of repercussion from your decision. We will analyze it together."

"Well...," Candace was still hesitant. *Get a grip on yourself girl. You have earned the right to be here. Show these people!* "Well, I guess that if we are splitting up, we should split up completely. I noticed some male travelers head toward the one inn. One of us could warm up to them, maybe be a little friendly with them and see if we can get any information out of them. The other could apply for that part-time job over at that farm we saw coming into town. It would give them a place to stay and glimpse of family life; I saw the two children running around in the back yard. What do you think?"

Xesca regarded Candace. "I think that you have a far more brilliant mind than anyone was willing to give you credit for Candace. I am thoroughly impressed. I think that it would be best if you took the position with the farm house. Please do not take me the wrong way, but I am still having some difficulty with the amount of manual labor on these planets."

"Not at all," Candace said smiling. "Part of my original training had me doing some farm work to build muscle and teach humility to the daughter of a Lord. I was thinking the same thing." *Besides, flirting with those dirty men would just be more than I could handle.*

"Wonderful. Favel had said that it would take approximately one week to reach Langeria and the Raging Warrior tavern. Do you think that you could help them for three days and then start out for the capitol of this planet on your own?"

"I don't see that as being a problem."

"Then it is settled. Good luck to you Candace and I will see you in nine days time."

"And to you as well Xesca."

Candace watched the other member of her party leave and then turned to head back to the farm that they had all passed. There was a smile on her face. For the first time, she felt that she had made a real contribution. *I made the camping stuff sure, and they group has benefited in other ways from my powers, but that is the first time that I made a decision. And to think, someone as learned as Xesca giving me praise. Why, this is wonderful.*

It was those thoughts that followed her to the farm house as she knocked on the door. A smallish woman in what could only be described as her late-middle years answered the door, drying her hands in the apron that she was wearing. "Yes, what can I do for you young lady?"

"Well, I seem to have run out of money and the group I was traveling with has refused to take me any farther." Candace looked as sheepish as she could, trying to play on the woman's sympathy. "If it is alright, may I work for a few days on your farm to earn enough to travel on. I noticed the sign." The woman regarded her. "Oh, I am a farmers daughter, I will be no trouble at all."

"And what would a farmers daughter need with traveling money?"

Putting on her most pitiful face, Candace took a chance. "I just couldn't marry that man, no matter what my father said." She even managed to make her lip tremble.

The woman's hard look faded quickly. *Boy was that a luck guess!* Candace thought to herself. "I'm sorry for you sweetheart," the woman said softly. "We need someone to watch the children and take care of the chickens. You'll sleep in the loft above the barn. Can you handle that?"

"I hope to move on in three days time. Would that be fine with you?" Candace asked.

"It will work for now. We will just leave the sign up. But if someone comes in for the job while you are still here, I'm going to have to give it to them."

Candace gave the woman the biggest smile she could muster without hurting her face. "It's perfect, thank you so much!"

₪

Ran caught up to the group heading out of town without a problem. He walked up to the lead man and was about to ask him if he could join the group when he noticed the mark of a magical fencer on his hand between his thumb and forefinger. Quickly, Ran used his power of telepathy so that the man could hear his thoughts *Boy, that's a nice brand.* "Excuse me sir, is there room for one more weary traveler? These days, it isn't really safe for a lone man on the road." Using as much energy as he could without making some sort of physical sign, Ran tried to tune in on the man's thoughts.

Blamed fools thoughts are like a beacon. Not really an active magic ability, so I bet that's why he's never been branded. Also, not much use to the resistance, but always good to have another man on board with this group. "You certainly may join us wanderer. What is your name?"

"My name is Ran," *and I am not quite as useless to your resistance as you think.*

The man was startled for a moment, but quickly regained his composure. "Welcome aboard Ran, I'm Casidan." *And if you can read this, then you're a man that would be good to have around.*

"Thanks. I'll try to be a man worth having around." Ran flashed one of his winning smiles and made his way back through the caravan to meet some of the other travelers. *I must warn you Casidan, I am on the run from the Guard of this planet. I am a traveler of time and space and am currently stuck on a planet that I crossed early on by a mistake. I shall try to keep hidden, but I do not want to see any harm come to your group because of me.*

Do not worry, Casidan thought back, *we heard of the problems and the escape of the people from the town over. By the time the Guard catches up to you, you will be well gone. Who aided in your escape?*

A man by the name of Favel. He and a companion of mine have headed in another direction.

As the group cleared town, Ran noticed Casidan was glancing at his companions. That was when he noticed the guns.

"By the beard of Jehan, it is a trap!" Ran leapt to the side of the road and his drew his cloak from his pack. A shot caught him in the left shoulder and his whole arm went numb. He shot his sword out from his right hand. Drawing magic through himself like a tuning fork, he summoned the geomagic spell of steelgrass and held four of the six travelers in place.

"Damnable magicuser!" One of them growled. "Surrender now or die in obscurity."

"You cannot hope to defeat six Guardsmen. Slave," one of them turned to Casidan, "seal his magic!"

Sweet Jehan no! A 'blocker' as they were called on his planet specialized in cutting off magicusers from the source of their power. Ran would be left at their mercy and his arm was starting to throb.

Reacting by more instinct than actual thought, he launched a battle magic blast through his cloak and down the end of his sword directly at Casidan. It cut the man in two, his scream cut short. Rolling to the ground, he focused the energy in his cloak into giving him control again over the left side of his body.

The two Guard who were not locked by the grass flanked around the wagon to get a shot at Ran. Leaping from the ground and snarling furiously, Ran threw another battle magic beam with his left hand that cut right through the wagon and decapitated the Guard behind it. He sliced at the other with his sword, effectively knocking the pistol-like device from the man's hand. Ran scooped it up.

The other four Guard, regaining their senses and realizing that their feet may be bound but their hands are free, resumed firing at Ran. Leaping and twisting, Ran managed to duck behind a boulder along the side of the road as they continued to fire. *Good thing you didn't tell them the entire plans you langin buffoon. And I was worried about one of the girls washing out because we split up. Now, how am I going to get myself out of this mess?*

More shots exploded around him as Ran stayed crouched down behind the boulder. The steelgrass was starting to loosen. Ran knew that it would only be a matter of time before the remaining Guardsmen would flank his boulder and shoot him dead. *Four left. These damnable Guard are well trained. Come on old man, think!*

Suddenly, it hit him. With a gesture, Ran made an image of himself appear behind the Guards. "Here I am, fools!"

All four swung around and fired. As they swung, Ran popped up from behind the boulder. He knew that they wouldn't have the frame of mind to see through that illusion. He fired upon them with the gun he had picked up and fatally shot all four before they swung back around.

Jehan, but I hope that the girls are doing better than I am.

₪

Xesca walked into the Inn just as the last of a group of four rough looking men sat down at the bar. Even though she didn't feel all that attractive with her skin tone changed to match the pink-ish hue of the humans and clothes that covered every inch of her body other than her head, she knew by the looks that she received when she walked in that the men of this Inn felt differently. *The male of this species is just too easy to arouse.*

She walked up to the men at the bar. Xesca had noticed that most everyone she had talked to, including her fellow trainees, had been using a much more casual form of speech than was in her nature to use. But to blend in, she tried her best. "I'm looking to head to Langeria and I really don't want to go it alone. You boys wouldn't be heading that way, would you?" *By the Elders, they are nearly salivating!*

"Sure, we were heading in that general direction anyway." When the man spoke, it looked to Xesca that he only had four teeth left in his mouth. "With all that excitement coming out of Toren, it isn't safe for a flower like you to be alone."

One of the other's reached down to his belt knife. "Besides, with all the Guard running around plus us, you'll be as safe as if you were in your mothers arms."

Ugh, do the females of this race find this to be attractive? Xesca smiled at them. "Wonderful! Than, shall we leave this morning?"

"We shall," another toothless one snickered.

"Meet us at the far end of town in an hour or we will be forced to leave without you sweetcheeks," the first toothless one said, patting Xesca's bottom. She almost smacked him but was unsure if this was an actual custom or just an aroused male trying to arouse the female.

Xesca made her way to one of the tables and a young serving girl came to ask her if she wanted anything. Waving her hand slightly, Xesca felt a sudden pain in her arm. She tried to focus in on why, but could not.

She maintained the focus though, turning her thoughts to the task at hand. She didn't trust anyone outside of their group and she realized that her monetary resources were non-existent. She needed a way to make some currency quickly as the thought of paying for these dirty men to escort her to Langeria with anything other than the local coin made her shudder.

The pain in her arm was starting to ebb as she got up from the table and headed into the town. The streets were narrow here and the buildings built very closely together. There were many small alleyways that served as side streets. She noticed one such alleyway close to a building marked "Bank". She walked down it and found a back door to the bank that was locked.

Xesca took off her illusion stone and set it near the door. She then focused a small beam of battle magic at the lock, causing it to melt away. *Your ancestors will be shocked at the course of action you are about to take Xesca, daughter of Queklain. Pray that they understand.* She kicked the back door open and swung her sword from her cloak with one deft motion. The startled teller yelped as Xesca flowed toward him, bringing her sword up and pointing it at the mans throat. "I need two belt pouches, one with thirty silver coins and one with thirty gold, and I need them now."

The teller only stammered as he wet himself. "You...You...You're green!"

"I realize that. I have been green my entire life. I have grown somewhat accustomed to the hue. Now, if you please, the currency, and do be quick about it."

Stumbling to the vault, the teller put the money in the belt pouches. "Will anyone else be along this morning?" Candace questioned

"S...S...S...Someone will check if the bank doesn't open in an h...h...hour"

"Good. If you would kindly step into the vault." The teller stood, shaking. "By the Suns of Ramdoor!" Xesca cursed and pushed the teller into the vault and closed it behind him. She ran to the back door and returned her illusion stone to her wrist. Stepping out of the alleyway looking like a woman of this planet again, she headed to the other end of town to join up with the men.

Chapter 14

Reconvene

Candace thoroughly enjoyed her time at the small farm in Favally. The children were not difficult at all and the farm work reminded her of a not too distant time when she spent her days doing chores and her nights practicing swords with Casgill. She talked to the farm wife and her husband about the times that they lived in. In Candace's opinion, they were much like most older people she had been around, hard on the youth of today and reminiscent about how much easier times were in their youth.

What she did learn was that all of the commotion that she and her friends had caused had the farmer worried. The common people of the village seemed to be afraid that all of this activity would mean that things would plunge back into war. They weren't all that happy with the rule of Halen-toc, but it also didn't target the common man and it did protect them from the war and hunger, so their was precious little to complain about.

After her three days were up, she found herself traveling with a band of minstrels. Candace could carry a tune and had a good voice, so they took her in. In lieu of payment, Candace dined for free in the inns that the band stopped to play. In years past, even during war times, the people of the smallest village would still have enough money to pay to have the band stop in their town, if just for a night, to perform for the people and lift their spirits. But times were hard financially and the people had nothing to spend. The band was heading toward the capitol hoping that business would be better and a few inns would be willing to pay them to play in their common rooms and restaurants.

Candace didn't recognize all the words, but she did recognize the tunes of a few of the songs. In fact, some of the songs had the same tune and theme with only a few of the words changed. This, among other things, was striking her as very familiar and somewhat unsettling.

She noted in her working journal that the people here were of human descent. Not a particularly advanced peoples, their growth seemed stunted at first by the constant war and then secondly to the total dictatorship. Trade and farming were the main sources of commerce. Arts, science and other creative outlets that typify evolution and social advancement seemed fairly non-existent with the exception of the few traveling shows.

She also noted a fact which she gathered from the farmers about life prior to Halen-toc. It seemed that the warlords of the lands were very powerful magic users in their own rights. Legend held that the wars were initiated by the warlords as though they were large games of skill, only instead of using game pieces, these warlords choose to use live people. Gains in land and power were oft times minimal and if any truces were signed in the mornings they would be dissolved by the sunset. All in all it sounded as though the standards for life had improved, if the standard of life had not.

While traveling with the minstrels, she took in and logged in her journal the topography of the land, the style of buildings, the sizes of most towns, as well as anything else that crossed her mind. She may not learn many new spells or techniques, but at least she would have a record and notes to study of her journey. What Candace was really having difficulty with was what this was supposed to be teaching her. She was a learned woman from a land that was more advanced. What could she possibly learn from these people?

These were the thoughts that plagued her as the towers of Langeria came into view. She finished writing her thoughts, put her journal away, and put on a smile.

₪

Gregor and Favel emerged from the woods as the sun glanced off of the copper towers of Langeria. Gregor marveled at the beauty in the simplicity of the structures. Most of the towers were of traditional circular shape, with the same copper tops like something out of a cartoon "Aladdin" Gregor had seen in his youth. The city itself was surrounded by a moat of water and a great wall like a medieval castle. He could see that Guardsmen patrolled the walls as well as guarded the three gates that Favel had told him about during the journey.

In fact, Favel had told him quite a bit while they were traversing the wood. Mostly, he prattled on about how noble the cause of the resistance, how oppressive the rule of Halen-toc was, and so on and so on. But occasionally, he would let a kernel of information slip about the past, about the townspeople, or about the ruler in general. Gregor was convinced he had deduced what was necessary to complete the training on this planet, but he wanted to discuss it with his companions before making any hasty decisions.

The duo came through the arch with no difficulty at all. Favel had already said that the Guardsmen were mainly just a show of power, not really assigned any sort of checking. Gregor had also deduced that Halen-toc might like to know that the brunt of the resistance members resided in his own walls. Like the old adage said, 'keep your friends close and your enemies closer'.

ℿ

Ran had managed to reach the capitol in an uneventful way. He simply used his survival training to maintain a closeness to the road while keeping out of sight. Normally, he would have used his illusion tactics, but he didn't want to tip off the Guard and he figured that they would be sweeping regularly for any magical disturbances.

He checked on Xesca regularly through the bond with his illusion stone. Other than a brief moment after his battle, when he had regained his senses and realized that she was no longer wearing the stone, she seemed fine. Shortly after, she was back in contact with the stone and maintained a constant motion toward him, and he kept her about a half the day's walk behind him, just to be safe.

Ran's shoulder had burned for two days from the blast he had taken. During his travel, he had found some plants and using his apothecary skills, made a make-shift poultice to help relieve the pain. He noted in his log that the plants of this planet were very similar to Baktarus. He also noted that the dialect, as well as many of the mannerisms reminded him of planets like Baktarus, only in a much earlier stage of their development than what they had currently attained.

There were exceptions though. The gun-like device he had kept from his battle on the outskirts of the last town and studied it at length. It was like nothing Ran had ever seen before and he marveled at both the complexity and simplicity. Outwardly, it was like any other gun-like device he had ever seen, a trigger, sights, different lever switches for varying degrees of potency and burst ratio. Ran did manage to break the gun down, and it's interior workings were like something else entirely.

It seemed powered both by the sun and by the users body heat. It fired both a laser-like beam that the strength-varying lever controlled as well as solid rounds of lead, which was what Ran was more familiar with. Surprisingly, the barrel had very little rifling, meaning that it did not have a very long range, at least when it came to using the solid rounds. In his experience it was rare to find a device like this that was designed for close combat. He was unsure about the range of the laser, but the device itself relied on open sights, so he assumed that maximum range anyone ever used it was about fifty to seventy yards. He took down notes and drew diagrams in his journal.

He noticed an increase in activity by the Guard on this road and he assumed that was largely due to his battle. Ran was surprised again by the skill of the Guard offset by their apparent lack of thoroughness. He recalled his short stint as a soldier and knew that he would never have avoided his battalion this long without someone finding him or his trail. The Guardsmen were ready for a war and seemed ill equipped to handle the single rogue warrior. He made note of this as well.

Ran figured that was going to come in handy if someone was going to have to kill this Halen-toc. He was more than ready to volunteer once the group was back together. Anything to get off of this planet and on to the next challenge.

ℼ

Xesca had had her fill of the men of anywhere but her home planet. Having very limited dealings with women in general, all she had learned was that the male of the species was driven not to knowledge or betterment like her own people, but procreation. Constant procreation. Not even really concerned with procreation so much as the *act* of procreation. It was truly amazing to Xesca.

She had learned early on that the men that she traveled with were a masonry camp for hire. They were out of work builders that had banded together to travel to town to town and earn the equivalent of two years wages in half the time. They had traveled approximately two hundred of their 'miles' and built several structures to arrive at the capitol.

What she also learned though, disturbed her even more. They were banded together as a sort of brigand group of collection agents for the Guardsmen. One of them was a squat man dressed in robes who typically rode in a carriage. He was a tax collector and he had hired these men to work as enforcing agents when the citizens claimed they could not pay their tax.

Xesca tended to ride with the tax collector, whose name was Gavren. He had made several sexual advances toward her throughout the trip, which she had managed to avoid. He did also tell her many useful facts about the area, about the capitol itself, and about Halen-toc himself, with whom he claimed to a be a ready acquaintance. Xesca tended to believe the last was more of a boast, but if even a half of the information he had given were true, this Halen-toc was truly a unique and powerful leader.

Most nights, the traveling group camped right along the side of the road. Many nights found her by the fireside, listening intently to the discussions and the dialect. The men themselves were unscrupulous, the only moral standpoint they had was that while it was perfectly acceptable to make as many lewd and innuendo comments, still they would not force themselves on her against her will. It seemed that even they, who would drive people from their homes, frowned upon that particular action.

She did learn that their interpretation of Halen-toc differed greatly from that of Gavren's. It seemed that they cared little for their leader or even expected him to remain in power. They didn't long for war times again, when the land was split into factions, but they didn't necessarily want what they had either.

It all puzzled Xesca greatly. She had never heard of nor experienced political unrest on her planet, only read of it in the different texts. She found that living it was something else entirely. She had decided on a course of action and looked forward to reconvening with the group.

Finally, the wall and towers of Langeria were coming into view. Xesca could see the windows on the towers and she caught her breath. The moat, the brick and mortar built wall and buildings, the heavy chains that controlled the drawbridge for the main entrance, the hard-packed streets with their wagon wheel ruts, it was all just too much for her at times. *Do the Elder's really believe what they teach when they talk of such wonders? Have they seen them with the same eyes that I have?*

They crossed the bridge into the town proper with no resistance. Xesca was riding in the carriage, and she wanted to get out and explore some of this city before meeting up with her companions. "Can you stop to let me out please, I can find my way from here."

"Nonsense my dear girl," Gavren patted her thigh, a little higher than Xesca would have liked. "We have given you safe passage this far and will continue until you have reached your complete destination. Now, where exactly were you headed to again?"

"Really, I feel as though I have bothered you far too much," Xesca reached for and began to open the door. "I appreciate all of the kindness you have shown me, but I must be off."

"What, and do you mean to leap out of a moving carriage?" Graven was incredulous. "I forbid it! Sit down, dear Sara and relax. Have we not treated you with respect throughout the journey here? Would you disrespect me so now?" He made to close the carriage door.

The commotion and the carriage door opening had gotten the attention of the men walking behind the carriage as well as the driver. He began to slow. "I do apologize, I mean no disrespect..." Xesca trailed off, then dove headlong through the door, ripping it out of Graven's hand. She hit the ground and somersaulted to her feet. "I really do need to be going"

Xesca cut quickly down a few alleyways before slowing, just in case someone was trying to follow her. She suddenly became acutely aware that she was standing in the nation's capitol, the home of the Guardsmen, and she was shrouded completely in illusion.

Taking in things as quickly as possible, she moved through the streets scanning for the Raging Warrior. She needed to get off of the streets and somewhere where there wouldn't be so many eyes on her moves.

₪

Gregor and Favel did not head directly to the inn, much to the dismay of Favel. Gregor wanted to take in some of the city. He questioned Favel at length of museums, galleries, libraries, or music houses. Favel's response was always that time did not allow such diversions, but Gregor persisted. "I have traveled through time and space to help. I want to know more about the people that I am here to help. I want to know their culture, what they value and what they regard as garbage. I want to know what motivates people to get out of their beds, if everything is as horrible as you paint it to be."

"But surely your companions..." Favel protested.

"Surely my companions feel the same way. We are learned individuals and appreciate the aesthetic side of culture. Before the night falls on this day, I want to see some of the beauty that this land has to offer. Is that so much to ask?"

Grumbling under his breath more protests, finally Favel led Gregor to a library near the very center of the city. It was surrounded by street merchants, peddling wears, tools, food, and anything else a shopper may need. The duo was met almost as soon as they came in by a young lady, "What may I get for you gentlemen?"

"I would like to browse, thank you," Gregor replied.

The young lady looked aghast and confused and Favel quickly filled the gap, "History, you would like to browse the Grand History of Halen-toc. Just because you tell me something Gregor, you cannot expect it is common knowledge."

Relief spread across the young lady's face. "And anything for you sir?"

"No thank you, I will just look with my friend. We will sit over there?"

"Wonderful," she replied and spun away.

Gregor and Favel made their way over to a bench and table. As they sat down, Favel whispered, "A person is not allowed to just look at anything they want. In some cases, permission notices are required to even view the work you want. Also, no books are allowed to leave the library, that is why the aide goes and gets the books for you. She will sign it out and be responsible for it's consequent return."

"Intriguing," Gregor mused, "but why? Are there a finite number of copies?"

"Of course," Favel replied, "but here she is."

The lady returned with a large, leather bound book, the words <u>The Glory of Halen-toc, ruler of the known world</u> embossed in gold on the cover. Gregor opened the book to find it hand written in a fine calligraphy. "Thank you very much." Gregor said.

"It is no trouble at all," the lady said, regarding him intently. "Just beckon me over when you are finished and I will come to collect the book. Enjoy gentlemen."

Gregor thumbed the pages. It was fine, papyrus paper. Gregor likened it to the ancient Egyptian style from his planet. *No printing press. I will have to question Favel how news travels and how quickly.* He read as quickly as he could, learning all he could from the legend and exaggeration that the book contained. Favel was astounded.

"How do you read so quickly?"

"It is a talent that can be learned on my planet. Plus, we have a device that produce printed pages at high rates of speed. Many copies of books exist in our libraries." Gregor tried to speed up his reading and focused out Favel as much as possible.

Time still marched and after about three quarters of an hour, Favel was like a child tugging an adults shoulder. "Have you not learned enough?", "Are you not finished yet?", "Should we not head to the inn?", he asked in an almost constant stream.

"Just a few more pages. Is there nothing else, as far as a museum of art, a statue in a town square, anything?"

"I already told you, Halen-toc has no respect for such things. Why do you not believe me?"

"It's not that I don't believe you all that much, it's more that I find it hard to believe in general," Gregor said as he finished his three-hundredth page. He closed the book and motioned to the attendant to pick it up.

"Did you gentlemen care to look over any other works? Perhaps some fiction?"

"No, thank you though." Gregor nodded and the two headed for the door. Gregor allowed himself to be led to the inn, digesting the knowledge he felt they needed.

ℸ

Candace found the city to be charming, in a backward sort of way. It had some unique aspects, but she could tell that a refined element did not really exist. The people seemed haggard and tired, the streets were just hardpack and wagon ruts, and the vendors were all street style. There were few real shops that existed.

She bid the troupe farewell and headed to find the Raging Warrior Inn. She came upon it straight away and headed into the common room. It was bench style seating with a stage at the north end. A handful of people were spread out throughout the room, but no one she recognized.

As she took a seat, Ran came in, looking tired and a little disheveled. He spotted Candace and came over to sit across from her. "What happened to you?" she asked.

"S'long story sweetheart. I'd be happy to tell you over some food?"

"I'm not sure. I only have six silver pieces left from my travel. I'll get for you what I can."

A serving girl came over and they ordered food. It took all of Candace's money, so they drank water. Ran relayed his run in with the Guard, again, as he escaped Favally. When he was finished, Candace regarded him and said, "So far, you've got my vote for earning the next level. This one has been pretty hard on you."

"So tell me, what have you learned?" Ran asked.

"Not much really, except this whole thing seems vaguely familiar. I mean, the topography, the language and dialect, even the music that we played. It all feels like home."

"And that was Baktarus, right?"

"Yes, why?"

"It's not just the topography. The plant life is just like the stuff indigenous to your planet. It is strange we both notice that. What about the people that you have come in contact with? What were they like?"

Candace recounted her experience on the farm, as well as her travels with the traveling minstrels. "It is just a backward planet all the way around."

"Some claim Baktarus still is, but I know what you mean. Even these Guard make foolish mistakes. I saw many from the cover of the road, and since they were scanning for illusion or other magic, they didn't even notice me. They have become too reliant on their tools and have lost their instincts."

"So you think that their time is almost up and that the resistance has a chance?"

"You two will want to keep your voices down and your eyes open, lest next time I am the serving girl over there regarding you to see if you need any more service." Xesca sat next to Ran. "You were injured. I felt it and did not know what it was."

As the girl came over, Xesca ordered a plate of food and a pitcher of ale for the table. She threw two of her eight remaining gold on the tray. Ran whistled, "Where did you come into the money, darlin'?"

"Robbed a bank," Xesca said smiling. "It was really rather invigorating."

Candce's mouth hung open and Ran laughed heartily. "Well, I'm proud of ya girl. That was definitely imaginative."

Xesca recounted her travel here and her harrowing escape from the moving carriage and Ran and Candace brought her up to speed on what they had been discussing.

"I had thought it strange that I should recognize their ancient dialect," Xesca mused. "The ale must have been clouding my mind not to place it before."

"So what do you think our plan of action should be?" Candace asked

"I have an idea about that," Gregor said, taking a seat next to Candace. Favel sat next to him. "And it may come as a shock to you." Gregor motioned for the serving girl to come over and placed an order. "I'm guessing you have realized where we are?"

"So you have confirmation that we are on Baktarus?" Xesca asked.

"Oh, I have a lot more than that, but yes, this is Baktarus. As far as I could gather from the history, it is about six hundred years *after* we went into the arch."

"But how can that be?" Candace asked. "Baktarus is already much more advanced than this. With the exception of the devices to travel and the gun-like things, we are more developed socially and scientifically. What would have caused the planet to regress so badly?"

"We did, apparently." Gregor said.

"Excuse me?" Ran said

"Apparently, four black-clad warriors took this planet and held it in their grasp until this Halen-toc managed to overthrow them. That part was probably more legend than fact, but it was the truth apparently. The warriors, two men and two women, all had the same sigil of a wolf's head, yet they all used different colors. Red to the west, Green to the north, Blue to the east, and Yellow to the south. The women were north and south while the men ruled east and west. I don't know about your individual house colors, Ran and Candace, but mine is blue and green for Xesca was too coincidental for me.

"Also, for a time, there was peace. Great thinkers built the machines that could travel by using the sun. Other great things, legendary in their scope, were created and later lost. No one knows how or why the war started, at least it wasn't in the history. But war waged until just two generations ago." Gregor took a bite of his food.

Favel was astounded. It was not possible. He did not know what to say. Listening on, Gregor continued. "I can only guess one thing, I don't know where we all stand on Kenor Anor, but I would guess that half swore fealty to him and half didn't. That was what started us on war. What I am not sure about is who Halen-toc really is? But if I had to guess, I would have to say..."

"By Jehan above and below, it is Himanoco!" Ran shouted and jumped to his feet.

The table drew up as a handsome, blond haired man came in, surrounded by the Guard. Quickly the Guard raised their weapons and took aim at the group. "Hold," was all the man said. "Let the branded one come forward to confess his sins and be cleansed."

Favel was sweating profusely. He was shaking all over and fell to his knees. "Oh great and powerful Halen-toc," he started, "I was beguiled! I had no control over my actions! I have swore fealty to you and would serve you all of my days!"

"Well, you were one of my guesses," Gregor said and sat back down to finish his meal. The entire room was taken aback, including the members of his group. "Oh, I'm sorry, would you like something to eat?" he asked as he turned back to Himanoco.

Laughing, Himanoco headed toward the table. The Guard opened around him to let him pass, and as he did, he struck Favel in the throat, killing him instantly. "Cocky as I remember Gregor." He waved a hand dismissively and everyone left; the Guard, the lookers-on, everyone. "No food for me, but I will take up a chair. And by the way Mr. Grastle, the name is Halen-toc, not Himanoco. Do you want to blow my cover?"

"Boy am I confused," Candace said.

"Have a seat sweet Orthon, last of your line, and I will explain what happened to you so you can tell me how it is that you survived."

Chapter 15

Explanation and the end of Arch 1

"It would seem that Gregor pieced most of it together already. Candace, you and Xesca stood against Anor as Blackwolf.

"Gregor, you stood with Anor. Your sister had been killed, your brother ascended because you refused. With no female heir, you had no bond to hold you to Alexander and you left to pursue what you had always dreamed, adventure.

"Ran, you disavowed the wolf but kept the sigil anyway. You were never much of a joiner, as memory serves. You took up against your old cordon due to some sort of conflict that you had had. I don't know all the details."

"But that doesn't tell us what you are doing here!" Candace exclaimed.

"Oh, that is easy. I had always guessed that summoning you, claiming to be you, might just be enough to bring you back." Xesca stammered. "You were always the crafty one Blackwolf. With enough power, channeled through something of your own creation, perhaps the Himanoco Armor, the Mace of Chaos, or maybe even the sought after Sword of the Blackwolf, you would be released. I always had my doubts that Malada had vanquished you completely."

"Very good Xesca. Although, you already know that. Or at least, you knew it when I killed you.

"Kenor had finally found my long hidden sword. I had stored my psyche in it's jeweled hilt, waiting. Malada, that bitch, murdered an empty shell."

"You speak of murder?" Ran shouted. "You, who killed your own brethren for no reason. You who then killed your own disciples, us?"

"Oh, he had reason. Just as the other four wolves had coveted power in the past, so had we." Gregor scraped his plate clean. "That was the secret that your history held that no one bothered to let us know. You did not murder your brethren, you liberated the galaxy. I'm guessing that the originals of us that you killed failed to believe that point, just like most of the other Blackwolves."

"Always a sharp one as well," Himanoco said, smiling. "I was proud that you four were part of my newest breed, right up until the time that I killed you.

"The wolves of my era had been the greatest warlords of the time. Universally known, we conquered for knowledge, for power, for the glory of battle. We would hold wars just to see who could win a battle here and there. We played games with real people, just because we had the power to." Himanoco shook his head. "I was tired of it. I wanted out. But it is hard to let go of someone who is powerful. The rest of the wolves didn't trust me on my own. Maybe just as well, I may have built an army to challenge them, who is to say?

"In any event, I killed them. An ambush that they never suspected. I got all but Malada. When she chose to mourn as opposed to coming right after me, I figured that maybe the two of us could live in peace. I figured wrong. I never imagined to revive so many generations later and not find her ruling the entire galaxy in her iron fist. She always was a strange girl." Himanoco almost seemed wistful.

"So, why us?" Candace asked. "What was the point? I still don't understand what it is that we should learn?"

"Silly girl," Himanoco actually reached out and tussled her hair. She recoiled in fear and disgust. "Always the last to know, you have given me the answer that I sought, so I suppose that I should give you yours so you can be on your way?

"You four had been the strongest cordon in memory. You were chosen to be the deciding factor, set to bring unity to the clan and to be sure that no one claimed the full power of Blackwolf. You were good too, as I heard it. But, and as I said I never really bothered to find out the exact circumstance, something split your loyalties. The cordon dissolved and you four scattered. You came together on this planet and took the same type of roles as the wolves of my era, warlords. More powerful than most Himanoco, you were dangerous. I went with you first to get rid of the danger."

"And why'd you chose to hide your true identity?" Ran asked.

"No one will believe that I have completely submerged Kenor. They will just think that he has become delusional. Even his faithful will begin to wonder. I set it up so that you killed him, figuratively speaking of course, and an unknown killed you. I got my invitation to train today. I figured once inside, I can rise through the ranks and decide what I will do next from there.

"And there is your archway," Himanoco motioned toward the doorway that they had passed through to get into the common room from outside. Its appearance had changed to resemble that of the archway in Himanoco Tower. "I have to guess that all things have come to light and that everyone now truly understands, as do I. My curiosity now is wondering what will happen when I pass through my own arch? Will I end up battling with myself? It's kind of interesting."

"So," Xesca started, "It would seem that what we learned is that the scope of our own powers is not yet known, even to us."

"And that together, we could be strong enough to rule the entire galaxy," Ran continued.

"But we are destined to battling each other for supremacy, leaving us wide open to be destroyed by someone like you," Candace chimed in.

"So our only choice is to try to hold together, as best we can, and hope that we all still graduate as this little glimpse into the future has taught us." Gregor finished. "Oh, one more thing before we all go home," he shot his sword from his cloak and the others did the same. "Did you ever wonder there what it would have been like to go up against the four of us together, as opposed to picking us off one at a time? Even if it is the four of us before we have realized the, how did you put it Xesca, 'full scope of our power'?"

Himanoco's grin faded slightly. It returned quickly though. "You won't do it. Why risk failing in the arch for something that you cannot change in this particular here and now? Stay together, continue on, and live to fight another day and who knows, maybe none or only a part of this will actually happen."

"S'worth the risk to me," Ran said, circling around the bench and flanking Himanoco to the right.

"Don't be foolish. You are the disciples, I am the master." Himanoco seemed actually concerned. He drew his sword from his cloak in his right hand and whirled a dagger from thin air for his left.

"I think that I might like to try you," Candace said, taking the left flank. "Not many that I know of can say that they went up against the Blackwolf and survived."

"You have no plan of attack," Himanoco was backing toward the wall so that no one could get behind him. "Do you think that those Guard went far? Just because they are not inside does not mean they won't come charging in as soon as a battle starts. I will be away and they will mow you down. You can still be killed and this will wash you out of the training. Just take the archway and go!"

"No," Xesca said firmly. "This day, a Ohlian with a sword will defend the honor of her people and fight the way we should have when first we met you."

"What do you hope to accomplish?" Himanoco croaked. His back was firmly against the wall and he was twirling the dagger quickly, getting ready to throw it. "Nothing can come of this. You stand to lose everything. What could possibly motivate you to continue?"

"For the sake of unity," Gregor said summarily. "Because normally, better judgement would have come over me and I would have agreed with you. Just take the arch and live to fight another day. Maybe that is what went wrong with the me who you killed. Maybe that was part of the rift between us. Who knows?" Rocking back on his heels, Gregor licked his lips nervously. "What I do know is this, the group has spoken. Here we go!"

Quickly, Himanoco waved his arms and a shield formed in front of him, protecting his entire person. Ran drew the Guardsman's weapon he was still carrying and fired. It's laser sliced right through the shield and struck Himanoco in the arm.

Outside, the Guard were rushing the door, but, due to its change into the Himanoco Tower archway, some invisible force was blocking them. They fired their weapons over and over, yet nothing could get through. Confused, they scrambled to try to find an alternate entrance.

Himanoco was stunned from the beam, but his shield was more than it appeared. The minute it had been pierced, it split apart and had become shrapnel-like. Pieces caught Ran and Candace in the arms and legs, knocking them down. He let his dagger go and it caught Xesca in her already wounded shoulder. She cried out in pain and surprise as the dagger lifted and carried her the length of the room to pin her to the far wall.

Leaping forward, Gregor slashed only to hear the clang of metal on metal as Himanoco swung his sword up to block. They matched swords, clanging in the common room. Neither breaking their barrage long enough to use some sort of magic.

Ran struggled to his feet as Candace made it to Xesca and worked on pulling out the dagger. Gregor and Himanoco were battling furiously and Himanoco was having a tough time keeping up. "I must say, Gingee would have never had a chance against you," he said

"Where do you think I learned these moves from?" Gregor huffed. "Himanoco was not always my chosen path."

Seeing that Ran had made it to his feet and that Candace had Xesca down, Himanoco growled deep in his throat. "Give over," he exhaled. "This is pointless and you will still have an injured cordon to take through the arch to the next level."

With one deft motion, Gregor knocked Himanoco's sword out of his hand and into the air. Ran leapt and caught it as Candace and Xesca made their way to the archway. The Guardsmen outside were using their guns to cut a hole in the wall and were starting to break through. Himanoco stumbled backward and tripped, sitting hard on the floor.

Gregor leveled his sword to Himanoco's chest. "You were just playing with me?" Himanoco stuttered. "How? You were not nearly this good when I met you the first time!"

"I figured as much." Gregor breathed heavily. "My guess is that our battle that you won was more a test of magic?"

"Yes."

"That is what draws me to follow in your path. It is not that strong now, but if you met me later in life, I'm sure that I grew much more powerful in many different magical arts, at the expense of my sword skill. But now," he grinned boyishly, "now I'm one major badass with a blade!"

"Gregor, c'mon son," Ran called from the archway. He threw Himanoco's sword in the wall that Xesca had been stuck to. She and Candace were already through the arch. "It's over. You won."

Gregor helped Himanoco up. "Lesson learned for me master. The sad thing is, I will remember this, you will not. Good luck."

"You too, young Holden." Himanoco clasped his hand tightly. "I must say, this was more interesting than I could have ever imagined. I see now why you and yours were so formidable. I hope the course of history that found me putting you down does not repeat."

"As do I. And I may be foolish to say this, but I look forward to meeting again, if we ever get to."

"I would trade this entire lifetime for that opportunity," Himanoco said, sincerely. "So this is not a goodbye. Merely until we meet again?"

Ran passed through the archway. "Until we met again," Gregor smiled. He ran to the archway and vanished.

Chapter 16

Interlude: Back in the tower 1

The light seemed blinding as the group rubbed their collective eyes. "Congratulations, all of you have managed to complete level one," Defalorn's voice said. "I see that you have suffered some injuries that you did not wait to heal though."

"Master, might we have a collective moment to gather our thoughts before we continue?" Xesca asked. "We are all a little jostled."

"You'll never believe what happened to us!" Candace exclaimed.

Defalorn's eyebrows went up. "You do not have to tell me," he said.

"No, we want to," Gregor said. "I didn't write anything down in my journal, so go ahead and I will be the secretary of our final moments in the arch before we get our new journals and head on."

"We went to the future!" Candace shouted. "It was Baktarus."

"Has anyone ever reported going into the future," Xesca asked.

"Not to the best of my knowledge," Defalorn said. "But not everyone has reported their exploits in the archways. It is possible that others have."

"Anyway," Candace continued, "we met Himanoco. The real Himanoco!"

"How could you have possibly met him in the future?" Defalorn asked.

"He reincarnated through Kenor Anor," Ran said. "Kenor had found the Sword of Himanoco and somehow released his psyche. Himanoco then submerged Kenor and took over his body."

Gregor was not only writing their story. He grabbed his illusion stone and shot a thought through to Ran; *Can you heal yourself and the girls a little before we head through the next archway without Defalorn getting to upset?*

I'm an apothecary, not a healer. I need supplies of some sort. Herbs, flowers, roots, blessed water, something.

Candace continued, "The four of us had been at war over Baktarus. It all sounded crazy but Gregor found it out. Anyway, we sat down with *the* Himanoco! Gregor even mocked him!" Candace beamed in Gregor's direction. *I heard that. I have been training to heal. But, I was so excited I've made myself the center of attention and can't really heal anyone behind the scenes.* "We battled with him. Himanoco! He knocked the three of us around. But Gregor, he beat Himanoco one on one in a sword fight!"

Xesca chimed in now, "I watched the whole thing. Gregor was hiding his true abilities. He, what is the expression that your people use? He 'played possum'"

Gregor smiled at her. "Yeah, I guess I did. I took a chance, knowing myself and the path that I intend, or intended to take. If the future hadn't held true for me, I would have been beaten handedly."

Candace rattled on about the guns, the shield that Himanoco had used, how his dagger had flown, and on and on. Gregor finished his notes. Finally, Defalorn cut Candace off, "its very fascinating Candace, but it is past time to continue. Are you all ready to go on?"

The foursome nodded their assent. Defalorn handed them the new journals to take with, then went to the archway at the far end of the room, and again came the blinding burst of light then the small humming sound. "If you will proceed through, and good luck to you. I will see you when you emerge."

In turn, they all went through, and once again vanished.

₪

After they were through, Defalorn slumped onto one of the benches on the side of the room. He was shocked. They had met and battled *the* Himanoco. Gregor had overcome him, single-handedly. Defalorn had never heard anything like that before. He looked in his lap and saw their four journals. Protocol dictated he store them until they emerged to claim the journals at the end of their training. It said nothing about reading them. *Doesn't say anywheres that I can't either!*

He began with Xesca's. Ordered and clerical, it was mainly full of thoughts, which he did find interesting. Next, to Ran's, where he stumbled upon the notes and schematic of the gun-like device of the Guardsmen. He spent some time studying this and was curious if the technology of the day could reproduce such a weapon. He decided against finding out as he felt that would be too invasive.

Next, to Candace's, where he learned more of what they saw. Candace took in many things and wrote to herself as though the journal was more of a personal log. Finally, Gregor and his notes about Himanoco. Defalorn was struck by the fact that most of what Gregor noted was not the tactics he used in the fight, nor how Himanoco fought back. What Gregor noted was the quotes and conversations, the history he had learned, and his feelings toward Himanoco in general. Defalorn would later log this in his own journal as a quote:

It seemed that, above all else, Himanoco missed the Wolves not because he wanted to be part of them again, but because he missed equals with whom he could converse. Surrounded by servants, what Favel had said about him attacking magic-user's because he needed a hobby may well have been true.

I meant what I said when I told him I hope that we meet again. I relish another opportunity to have conversations with him, realizations about why he did what he did, and when he did it. Learning what he is all about has made me that much prouder that I have chosen to follow in his teachings and that much more the glad for having believed and defended him all the while that I have. He truly was the greatest of them all and it is sad that I could not meet the others, as a barometer for what the times were like. Perhaps another arch or two?

Defalorn hoped. He truly hoped.

Chapter 17

Level 2 begins

The foursome emerged and it was Gregor who spoke first. "I'm home?"

"What do you mean?" Candace asked.

They stood in the front yard of a three story house, the lake in the background. "This is my family's home on Earth. It is where I live my life when I am not the Prince of Kanderfain. Like I said, I'm home."

"What are we doing here?" Ran asked.

"Are you sure? Does it not just resemble your living quarters?" Xesca asked.

"Only one way to find out." Gregor headed up to the front door and tried it to find it unlocked. Nothing unusual there. The interior was his home, no mistaking it. He motioned for the others and headed inside. "Hello," he called out. "Anybody home?"

"Greg, that you?" Haley called back. She was upstairs. "What are you doing home?"

Gregor searched the bond he shared with her and found that, at least here, he felt her. He knew it was her before she answered. Haley bounded down the stairs. "What are you doing home? I thought that you were on a mission?" she asked.

"Mission? You mean training don't you?"

"No," she hesitated, "mission. You were supposed to be battling Lord Drahmak's minions near the Mexican border."

Gregor stood agape. "Who? What? In Mexico? What are you talking about?"

Haley regarded him suspiciously. "What's wrong with you? Did they do something to you while you were down there? I don't feel any difference in the bond, but..."she trailed off, looking at his neck and the back of his head, "No sign of entry."

"Uh...Gregor, I'm sorry to interrupt but," Ran broke in, "I can't kindle a flame."

Gregor was still looking incredulously at his sister. Finally, he shook his head, "You can't what Ran?"

"I can't kindle a flame. I can't cast any magic. Nothing. I don't feel the usual panic that follows with this type of complete cut-of, but I can't do any sort of magic, can any of you?"

"Of course you can't," Haley chimed up. "None of you can unless you are wearing these," she held out her arm and showed off a multicolored bracelet. "Gregor, you're worrying me."

"Haley honey, let me talk to you just for a second, and believe every word I say. You'd feel it if I lied. I went to a planet a month ago to study in the ways of an intergalactic warrior sect known as the Himanoco. This planet," he pointed to the ground, "Earth, had held forbidden status by all intergalactic councils and there were nothing but humanoid and animal life on it when I left.

"We are an aristocratic family on another planet, where you are heir-apparent to the throne and I am your sworn defender. Hence the bond between us. How much of this is true and how much is different?"

Haley mused it over in her head. Finally, "You didn't lie. It really doesn't make a whole lot of sense, but you didn't lie. Well, I guess then I should start from the beginning. Mom and Dad have got to hear this!"

She turned and headed toward the living room. "You and your friends head into the dining room and I'll bring them. This is so weird!"

Gregor, Ran, Candace and Xesca took chairs at the end of the Holden family's large dining room table. The table sits eight normally, so there was plenty of room. Gregor sat himself at the foot of the table, Candace and Xesca in the two chairs to the left, Ran on his right. Although Xesca had proven to be his best council, he sat her farthest because he had felt a closer bond with Ran and because he wanted to spark interest in Candace. He regarded Xesca and she did not seem to mind.

Arthur, Marion, and Haley Holden came into the dining room for the other entrance. Arthur sat at the head of the table, his wife on his right and his daughter on his left. "Son, what has you home so early from your quest and has my daughter so confused her mother felt a problem the minute she entered the room?"

"Father, I am sorry to disturb the home, but I am not sure of my surroundings or my life. These three people will verify for you and your wife and daughter will be able to sense the truth of the matter. I am not the Gregor Holden that you know. I appear to be him. I have the same talents and abilities as he. But my parents are the king and queen of a land God knows how far from Earth. They were placed here for their own protection when they were newlyweds, and have portaled back and forth since. All three of their children have been born on this planet and trained in the ways of the other.

"I am Prince Gregor Holden, Defender of the Realm of Kanderfain, sworn to protect the princess and heir-apparent to the throne. I am studying with an intergalactic sect of warriors known as the Himanoco and am currently in the process of that study. Everything I see and hear is an illusion. It is not real and eventually, I will move on to the next level of training."

Arthur sat, stunned. Marion and Haley's mouths were agape and they regarded each other, hoping that one had felt something different than the other. Finally, it was Arthur who broke the silence, "This is all a rather fantastic scenario you have painted for us my son." He stood up and drew his sword, "Now, if you do not give me some answers that make sense, I will have to assume that you are some spawn of Drahmak's and I will slay you where you sit."

"Arthur, wait, please," Marion jumped up and put a hand on her husbands shoulder. "Gregor, come here for a moment."

"Marion, no!" Arthur exclaimed. "It may be a trap!"

"I will never know what happened to my son if we do not do this!" Marion replied, a composed and resolute look on her face. "Place your head in my hands my son, let me see all that you know."

Gregor had heard that his mother had this power, but he had never seen it in action. It was rumored that she once, when very young, was going to work as a Inquisitor on Kanderfain, but that the empathetic side of her power had made it impossible.

Gregor moved to his mother slowly, so as not to provoke his father. He kneeled down at her feet and she put her hands on his head. Suddenly, they took on a bluish glow.

Marion caught her breath. Her eyes rolled back into her head and she moaned softly. Arthur had completely disregarded everyone else in the room and was looking on his wife with total concern. Haley moved around the table and behind her mother, focusing her own energies to try to glimpse what her mother was seeing in Gregor's minds eye. The others leaned in over the table so that they could whisper to each other.

"I have never seen a power like that before," Xesca said. "What is she doing?"

"She's an empath," Candace explained. "She can sense emotion, feelings. She can also tell if you are lying."

"More than that darlin'," Ran drawled. "She's powerful enough to draw the thoughts right out of your head if she is touching you. It's not like reading a mind. You see, feel, experience everything that the person you are reading has ever seen, felt, and experienced. It's a rare power and I have known people who have studied years to learn it."

Marion cried out and slumped back into her chair, cutting their conversation short. Arthur and Haley rushed to either side of her while Gregor crumpled to the floor. "It was amazing husband," she whispered. "Everything he said. I saw it all. Never touched by Drahmak. Never even seen him."

"Hush, we can talk more when you are ready."

"No, Arthur, he has to be helped somehow. He may not be the Gregor we know, but he is our son." She turned to him, sitting up. Tears began to well in her eyes. "He is our son!"

Gregor began to rise up, and Ran went over to help him. He got Gregor into his chair. Candace and Xesca came over and looked at him closely. Gregor's eyes were blank and he stared into space. His mouth hung open and a small amount of drool was beginning to form in the corners.

"Is he going to be all right?" Candace asked.

Haley snapped out of her amazement. "Geez, I forgot." She dashed into the kitchen and came out with two glasses of water. One she threw in Gregor's face and the other she sat down in on the table.

Gregor jumped with surprise and looked around, confused. He took the water and drank it down. "Wow," finally said, "was that ever weird!" He looked at his companions. "You ever hear how they say that your whole life flashes before your eyes right as you are about to die? Well, that was my life. Every second of it, right before my eyes in high speed." Gregor shook his head, trying to regain full consciousness.

"So you are who you said you are?" Haley asked him. "Then what of the brother that I know? Where is he?"

"Haley, is this the only Gregor that you can feel?" Marion asked. "Search the bond, reach for it. Is this the only brother that you can feel?"

Haley closed her eyes tightly and struggled. "It may be because he is so close, but he is all that I can sense."

Marion hung her head sadly. Arthur straightened himself and put his hand on his wife's shoulder. "Gregor, let me tell you the reality that we know. Then maybe we will all be able to find out what exactly you were sent here to accomplish?"

Chapter 18

Home

The group moved from the dining room into the living room for the comfort. Everyone sat on either of the two leather sofa's or in the overstuffed armchairs with the exception of Arthur, who paced the room. Haley turned off the television as Ran, Candace, and Xesca were all marveling at the images. Gregor had recovered from his ordeal with his mother, his mind racing to try to piece together everything that was happening.

"Well," Arthur started, "I am your father, and we are aristocrats, but I am no king. I was not born on some other planet and have never possessed the power to slide, as you and your brother have. Holden's have been named Lords and Ladies of Michigan for seven generations counting you. We have fought the darkspawn of evil lords for as long as we have been aristocracy, and our line has produced many strong and just warriors."

"You and your sister are two of the greatest hopes for this planet," Marion continued. "The current sovereign of the Great Eastern States, Annabella Johnson, is the last of her line and has no successor. Your sister has been named heir-apparent and you are her guardian. That happened three years ago."

"You were down in Texas, trying to push back the denizens and gain more land as the, how did you put it, 'Holden legacy'," Haley spoke. "My ascension to the throne was to happen in three weeks and you were going to attend with the new maps showing the further territories of the Great Eastern States. You left a month ago."

"Bizarre," Gregor said. His family looked at him. "The symmetry I mean. The me from this planet took on a quest a month ago, I started my training a month ago. Just a little odd is all."

"If we may continue," Arthur asked. "Your brother Alexander is currently abroad undergoing the same training that you had in weapons and tactics at Oxford Academy in England. He has a leave coming tomorrow and should be home soon. He was going to join you on the battlefield, to see if he could be any help.

"You are already a legend in your time. A Hunter of the highest caliber, you have battled with some of the greatest dark fiends of all time and either held your own or defeated them totally. It is said that you are the main reason that the Holden line is ascending the throne.

"My brothers Nelson and Troy both have lost children to these battles. Currently, Nelson's son Benjamin is with you, a trusted friend and consort. He is the only child left of three, both of his brothers dying in the War of Dallas seven years ago. Troy's son Jeremy was killed in the Battle of Waco, just two years ago, but James is still abroad. He is currently hunting deep in South America. Now, with this ascension, it is their right to recall their boys home and move up from the level of Lord and Lady to that of Duke and Duchess. I doubt that they will, but it is their right."

"Annabella had no siblings, and never married. She is a good and just queen who has done well with her thirty years on the throne." Marion shook her head sadly as she spoke. "She and I had grown up together. I was touched that she chose our line."

"Mom, what's your background?" Gregor asked.

"I was born the youngest of three girls, to the Lord and Lady Bornhold of Florida. One of the southernmost states in the union, my family is a legacy similar to the Holden's. My father was disappointed that he had no sons, but when my powers began to show themselves, his outlook changed. Then, when I married your father, a respected lord from a similar family, he was pleased. My cousins, as well as nieces and nephews, will also travel on to Washington D.C. when Haley ascends the throne. My sister Janell's son Jared has fought along side you before. He and Danielle's son Marcus."

"Go back further if you can," Gregor asked. "The layout of planet is still somewhat familiar, but I did not leave a Great Eastern States union. This family tree is enlightening, but I need more history, more depth."

"All right," Arthur said, composing his thoughts. "Seventeen eighty five, only a handful of years after the Americans had established their freedom from England, strange and inexplicable creatures had begun to appear on the frontier of the known land. At first believed to be some form of wildlife, little attention was given to these creatures, just a general avoidance as they were fierce and deadly beings.

"Then, the creatures masters began appearing. Dark skinned, brooding men the likes of which no one had seen before. They claimed the land theirs and opposed the new, pale inhabitants as trespassers. They demanded that we sail back to the place of our ancestors and leave their land or they would destroy us.

"Well, having stood down the greatest army in the known world, our ancestors were a little cocky and told their new neighbors that they could, well, 'shove it' would be the best way of putting it. The battle lines were drawn and war raged. The new weapons that had been so productive, cannons, muskets and the like, had little effect on the new enemies. Shoot them and you would slow them down, only to see them rise back up and battle on.

"It was then that the 'old world' methods of battling evil were re-instituted. Silver and swords, garlic and herbs, might and magic. The hordes only attacked at night, so counterstrikes were launched in the daylight to learn that the sun was a weakness. Vampire Hunters were born."

"Vampires?" Gregor asked.

"We have studied such a culture," Xesca offered. "Anyone who claims to be immortal is intriguing to a group of people with our longevity. It seems that there are several different strains of these creatures, all blood drinkers. Immortality does seem to be their gift, along with others, but their weaknesses were not deemed worth the risk to pursue the means. It also seemed that in all the different strains, becoming such a creature brought out an innate evil. It is all very interesting."

"No one is sure where they came from," Haley said. "It is widely believed that they have lied about how long they have existed on the planet, but no one is sure. They lie about everything."

"They have brought with them creatures," Marion shook slightly, as if chilled. "Hounds of enormous size, goblin creatures, large sea hydras. They can control the carrion eaters on this planet, crows, rats and buzzards being their favorites. They have been known to have incredible powers, mind reading, shape shifting, and flight, just to name a few."

"What about those bracelets and our inability to use magic?" Gregor asked.

Arthur sighed. "In the year Eighteen eighty three, a powerful magician named Herman Blain managed to cast a spell so powerful that it blocked all forms of magic that weren't inborn. He created these bracelets so that he could still cast. He taught many, and for many years it was a crippling blow to the Dark Lords. Eventually though, they got their hands on one of the bracelets and learned how to duplicate them. A way to modify the spell is currently being researched.

"For over two hundred twenty five years, wars have waged and battles have been fought all through the America's. South America and its countries are nearly entirely wiped clean of human inhabitants. North America, stretching its entire length from the Mississippi River to the Pacific Ocean is also inhabited by the Dark Lords and their minions. Mexico is entirely, with the exception of what you went to retrieve, submerged."

"Man," Gregor said, slumping back into the sofa, "you thought my story was fantastic. This is incredible!"

"Gregor," Candace started, "do you know what it is that we are here to do?"

"I haven't the foggiest," Gregor confessed. "I'm still trying to process all of this. It is all just too odd." He turned back to his family. "How do I travel?"

"Either by vehicle or portal. You have the ability to slide," Haley answered.

"And the eastern continents? Africa, Europe, Asia, Australia?"

"Europe and Asia are still entirely human. They have known of our plight low these many years and have profited from it. With a few exceptions, Africa is of no interest to anyone, it's peoples too powerful in mystic ways for the vampires to care and too backward in a civilized way for the humans to care. We were on the most minimal of terms with most of the European nations until probably the last fifty or so years, while our affinity with the Asian countries has been strong for decades."

"That would explain the appliances," Gregor said to himself. "Monetarily speaking, how has this nation survived?"

"The vampires have no use for currency," Arthur stated simply. "Precious metals seem to hurt them, so we have taken much off of their hands."

"Why did the U.S. revert back to a monarchy after it had established its freedom?"

"Control mainly. The democratic process, while being wonderfully idealistic, would and did take too much time to make hard decisions. The monarchy now is still very representative and there is an 'oversight' council, the elected House of Representatives. While their overall power would be considered as weak, they are the only people who can and have called sovereigns to account for their actions. In Nineteen fifteen they actually beheaded Cathleen Ferrand, great grandmother of Annabella Johnson, for the crime of collusion with the enemy."

"So then the standard of living?" Gregor asked.

"Good, actually," Marion answered. "Most citizens are so used to war that they don't pay much attention. Only those with children who are hunters. There hasn't been an invasion of our territory for over one hundred fifty years now, so we have built a high standard of living."

"Music, art, culture," Xesca asked. "All of this during such a long era of war for your people. That must have been very difficult to manage?"

"Yes and no," Arthur replied. "Our culture has thrived mainly because after the invasion had ceased, we choose to stop spending so much time and energy on war. Oh, people do still research weaponry, tactics and the like, but it does not consume all of our resources, leaving us time to explore all avenues."

"The decadent West will never change," Gregor laughed to himself.

"Asian Prime Ministers have referred to us in that manner, yes. But they use it as a scare technique."

"Well, I don't know about you all but I am starting to get hungry," Ran said, trying to break the mood.

Gregor laughed again. "Thanks, I think we may have needed that. Mom, Dad, do you know what fast food is?"

Marion smiled, "Yes dear. There is a McDonald's just down the street in the same place that you left it. It should be an interesting treat for them," she motioned toward Gregor's companions.

"What about livestock and farms? They were mostly in the West in my reality."

"Import mainly," Arthur answered.

"From who?"

"Oh, all over I suppose."

"Weird." Gregor went to the garage to find his green convertible where he left it, top down and keys in the driver's side visor. "Hop in everybody."

"Another cruiser type vehicle?" Xesca questioned.

"Sort of. Hang on just a sec," Gregor ran back into the house. "Hey Mom, is Xesca going to be all right in public or do we need one of those bracelets? She's the green one."

"Oh my, let me get you all bracelets. We have several extra on hand, just in case of emergency." She went up to her room and hurriedly returned with four bracelets that looked large enough to be worn as necklaces. "They will size themselves. And here," she handed her son two fifty dollar bills and two twenty dollar bills. They had names and faces that Gregor didn't recognize. "For food and whatever else might pop up," his mother said.

"Thanks Mom," Gregor kissed his mothers cheek. "I am sorry for all the trouble."

"You didn't do it my son. None of this is your fault."

"Ran, grab a rock and make Xesca pale," Gregor yelled as he threw each one a bracelet. "Sorry."

"It's all right. It is to be expected when one of my race has to travel amongst your kind. I am not offended."

Once the illusion was in place, Gregor drove them to McDonalds and took them inside. "Unusual inn," Candace remarked.

"Go ahead and sit at any unoccupied table. I'll bring the food."

Gregor went up to the counter to order. "Samantha?" he exclaimed.

"Well, hello Master Holden. What can I get for you and your friends?"

"Master Holden? Are we not on less formal terms than 'Master Holden'?"

The girl behind the counter seemed confused. "Not really Master Holden. You eat here a lot but have never said to call you anything else."

"Well, call me Gregor from now on, okay?"

"O.K.," Samantha said, still confused. "What'll it be?"

Gregor ordered and brought the meal back to the table. He handed everyone a sandwich and fries, with some ketchup in the little paper cups for dipping. Each regarded their food suspiciously as Gregor stared at Samantha.

"You eat this stuff?" Candace asked.

"Does not look very appetizing." Xesca said.

"What the heck is this?" Ran exclaimed.

"How could she not even know who I am?" Gregor asked.

"Who?" asked Ran

"The girl behind the counter there. Where I am from, she and I are what you'd call "an item". We have been together for a couple of years and I am working up the nerve to tell her all about my other life. I may even marry that girl. In this reality though, it doesn't appear that she knows me more than because I am a regular."

"You're a regular here?" Candace asked. "Why, this food is terrible."

"It isn't so bad I guess," Ran said. "Not overly flavorful, but not too bad."

"I am sorry that she does not know you Gregor, but should we not concentrate more on the task at hand?" Xesca asked.

"Yes, and I am the one who's sorry Xesca," Gregor said. "I'm just still baffled. What lessons are we to learn? What is it that we are supposed to accomplish? Why Earth, a month after I started training but a completely different reality? It doesn't seem to have any logic to it."

"Well, these, what did you call them, 'fries', are great!" Candace said.

"Darlin', I think that we've moved on from the food issue," Ran said, smiling. "The question is, what do we do now?"

"Oh, well, I don't have the slightest idea. Gregor, what do we do now?"

"Maybe we should head toward Mexico and see if I am still alive? I mean the me that is normally on this planet."

"Normally, I would think that that would be cosmically disastrous," Xesca said. "But, since we are in the Himanoco Tower in one of the training arches and we know that whatever happens, nothing will be affected once we have vacated the arch, I can see no reason not to follow that line of thinking."

"Well, we can drive and it will take us a couple of days, or we can wait for my little brother and he can slide us down. Personally, I would just as soon wait as I don't even know in Mexico where the heck I am supposed to be"

"Seems logical to me. So," Ran started, "what'll we do till your brother gets home? Hit the sights? Tear up the town?"

Xesca frowned. "What does 'tear up the town' mean? I may not condone such action."

Ran's smile broadened and even Candace grinned, showing her youth. "No worries Xesca, we won't do anything that you'd regret."

"We can try. I'm not even sure of the hang-outs." Gregor got up from the table. "And if she doesn't know me now, I'll make sure she knows me before the night is over." He headed toward the counter.

"She?"

"That girl he mentioned when we came in Candace," Ran said. "Must mean quite a bit to him."

Back at the counter, Gregor waived Samantha over. "So, if I may be so bold, when do you get out of here?"

"Master Holden," Samantha started.

"Gregor"

She sighed. "Gregor, I don't think it appropriate for us to see each other socially. You are to be the Defender of the Realm. A hunter and aristocrat. I am just a citizen. It would not be proper."

"To hell with proper, I find you incredibly attractive and I would like to get to know you socially. Now, I ask again, when do you get out of here?"

This time, Samantha managed to blush. "I'm finished in about an hour or so."

As Gregor turned back to the table, he paused. "What did you call me?"

"Gregor?"

"No, you said 'Defender of the Realm'. What does that mean?"

"Oh, I know it isn't official yet, but everyone around here knows that your sister Haley will be queen and you will be her Defender of the Realm."

"Sweet Jesus, it seems that is my fate no matter what reality I am in."

Gregor left Samantha with a confused look on her face and gathered up his companions. As they left the restaurant, Gregor promised Samantha that they would return to pick her up in an hour.

Back at the car, Gregor drove down US 31 to a scenic turnoff. He pulled the car in and everyone climbed out. "I'm really at a loss guys."

"This is the land that you hail from?" Candace said in awe of the bay. "It is just incredible!"

"Thanks." Gregor looked out over the water. The sun had completed half of it's descent and sunset was only two hours or so away. "You wake up to this view every day and you begin to take it for granted."

"Gregor, I beg you please to not be offended, but I recommend that I take the lead in this mission," Xesca said. "It would appear by your actions and comments that your emotions are in turmoil and you may make some unnecessarily rash decisions."

"By all means Xesca." Gregor shrugged. "I'm confused, concerned, and down right pissed off to be honest. What are these monsters doing on my planet? How did my family even come about? I was the first native. And why is it that every where I go I'm the damn Defender of the Realm? Why can't I just once be a normal, everyday guy?"

"D'yea really think that would be better lad?" Ran asked. "Sounds to me ya got yourself thinking life would be easier if you lived obliviously. Don't you think life is better when you have a hand in it? Oh sure, ignorance can be blissful, but if you're informed you can decide. Plus, if you find out that you lived in ignorance longer than necessary, wouldn't that really piss ya off?"

"Your strong, smart, and a warrior," Candace continued. "Wouldn't the average person love to be you?"

"Do not worry about the future Gregor," Xesca chimed in. "If my species has learned anything, it is that nothing can be done that time cannot undo."

"O.K., O.K, no more self-pity session, I got it." Gregor looked back out over the bay. "Alex is home."

"How can you tell?" Candace asked.

"I can feel it through the bond that I have with my sister. She is projecting thoughts of him. To be so strong that I can feel it, he has to be in her eye line."

"Should we head back to the house?" Ran asked.

"No way," Gregor turned back to the group, a smile on his face. "I told a pretty young lady that I would meet her and be damned if I'm going to let duty come in the way of her again."

"Do you have ale?"

"Better"

Chapter 19

Prepare for battle

After a night of pub crawling, dancing, and entertainment, the foursome awoke the next morning hung over and exhausted. Gregor slept on one of the couches in the family room, Ran on the other. Candace and Xesca had shared Gregor's king size bed. Haley had bounded down and was now harassing the men.

"Boy, Dad is gonna kill you two if you don't snap out of it. I can't believe you just went out bar hopping! What were you thinking!"

"Haley, If you don't leave us alone for at least another hour, I will personally..."

"Gregor!" Arthur Holden boomed. "Where is your head boy!"

Gregor sat up on the couch, then slid back down as his head spun. "Sorry dad, we just wanted to slip out and have some fun."

"Drunk and passed out is fun!" Arthur raged. "This is no way for a Holden to act! I can't believe you could have been so thoughtless!"

"Ahh, ease up old man," Ran said, groggily, "I was hoping for a little more sleep."

"You're old enough to be this boy's father!" Arthur harumphed. "I would have expected more sense out of a man of your age."

"More sense usually isn't nearly as much fun" Ran said, hoarsely. Haley chuckled and Gregor winced.

Arthur apparently gave up on Ran and turned his attention once more on Gregor. "I will tell you this only once boy, if you are or aren't the son I know, you are still my son. Do not embarrass this family again!"

"For the millionth time, we are not really even here!" Ran yelled now. "As soon as we leave this arch, no one will have any memory of our even existing!"

"Enough, please," Marion spoke as she came into the room. "Arthur, let them have their fun. Leave it be."

Arthur did not look pleased at his wife's stand on the subject, but he conceded and followed her out of the room without another word. Ran lay back down. Gregor got up and went over to his sister. "C'mon, let him get some more sleep. Is Alex up yet?"

"Yeah, he is."

"We'll go into the dining room. Have you got the maps and info that we need?"

"Alex is already setting everything up in there. Do you really think that you should all go down to Texas? I mean, seriously, you don't know what the hell is down there."

"Hey," Gregor shot his sister one of his winning smiles, "is 'what the hell' proper queen speak?"

"You know what I mean you jerk," Haley replied as she playfully punched her brother in the shoulder. "I just want you to be careful."

"Did you want to come?"

"What?!"

"Why not?" Gregor asked. "Like we keep telling you, once we leave, everything goes back like we were never here. Our understanding of it is it goes all the way back to the time when we landed on the planet. So, if you went down, even in the event that something were to happen to you, everything would be undone."

"Cool!" Haley exclaimed. "I've always wanted to see it for myself!"

"Now, you won't remember anything..." Gregor started.

"So what!" Haley said, cutting him off. "I will see it now. Just the opportunity, even if I won't remember anything, is awesome!"

"The opportunity for what?" Alexander asked.

"I'm going to Mexico!"

"Get out!" Alex said. "Mom and Dad will let you?"

"Oh probably not, so let's just keep this to ourselves!" Gregor winked. "Now," he said, turning toward the maps laid out on the table, "let's get serious, shall we?"

"Well, from what I understand, Mom and Dad have already given you a lot of background information. Let me bring you up on your current mission." Alex pointed to a dot on one of the maps. "This is the last known coordinates of you and your infantry."

"Infantry?"

"A hand-picked team of crack soldiers. Twenty-five to be exact, not counting you of course. Cousin Benji and I think Marcus are with you."

"Yeah, Mom and Dad mentioned Ben fights with me. They said Marcus and Jared have as well. Tell me about them."

"Well, Benji is tough. He is a great swordsman, maybe the best in the country. Marcus and Jared are more the healing types, they come along to help the injured."

"Aren't they warriors in your reality?" Haley asked.

"Sort of. Ben is. But none of Mom's family came to this planet, and Marcus and Jared are both dukes. They would never think of getting anywhere close to a battle."

"Discussing strategy?" Candace asked from the doorway.

"Hey Candace, good morning. Did you sleep all right?"

"Fine Gregor," Candace said, making a face at the brightness of the light. "Should we wait for the others?"

"I'm just looking right now. Getting a feel for what it must be like to live on this planet. I'll leave the major planning up to Xesca. It was what we agreed to after all."

"So, about last night then, what was that you called our drinks?"

"Whiskey. We were drinking a drink named a 7 and 7. Then we switched you girls over to Rum and Coke."

"They were really good." The other two Holden children snickered at this remark. "And that music was great. It was like nothing I had ever heard before."

"I'm glad you enjoyed it sweetheart. It's good that you are getting to see some of this culture. I would love to have you come and visit me and my family when all of our training is through."

"That would be great! My father doesn't let me hardly ever leave the castle without at least one escort, much less to go to different inns and enjoy myself like last night."

"It sounds like you and I would have a lot in common Candace," Haley said.

"We need to focus a little don't we?" Alexander asked. "I thought that you wanted to be south by noon."

"Sorry little brother, please, continue."

"Well, if all reports are correct, two days ago you and your team stopped reporting in. No word, no contact. We expect you may have been ambushed and even scattered. Our new mission will be that of retrieval, not expansion."

"Then we will need a guide to help us try to find out exactly what happened to the original Gregor." Xesca said, emerging into the dining room. Ran was following her, grumbling about how he had just about fallen back to sleep. "And more data on our enemy. These maps will do us little good, we do not have time to study. Alexander was it? My name is Xesca. We will need weaponry. What is the standard weaponry used in battles like this?"

"Typically, you'll have a couple of riflemen for distance and perimeter protection. We outfit them will silver bullets, and from what I've read, it hurts the vamps pretty bad. Next, ya need a good set of crossbow or longbow troops. Somewhere in the neighborhood of eight to ten. Wooden stakes, through the heart, and a vamp is dust in a hurry. One or two magic users, one or two healers, finish with eight to ten swordsmen and you've got yourself a crack infantry."

"Gregor, can you handle this rifle device Alexander mentioned?" Xesca asked. Gregor nodded. "Good. I will take the bow. Candace and Ran, you will comprise our main swords. Ran, we will use your battle magic more than my own so as to allow me to direct the battle. Not to offend Gregor, but the 'let's go' approach we employed against

225

Himanoco is not the style of attack that I would like to use in this situation."

"Sounds fine to me," Ran said, stifling a yawn. "When do we leave?"

"After you have had time to eat and freshen up," Marion said, breezing into the dining room with stack of dishes and a heaping plate of pancakes. "Alex, move those maps and Haley, run into the kitchen and grab knives and forks for everyone. Greg, where are your manners? Get the milk and juice and bring some glasses." She turned to the room, "I've got more cooking, and I'll send the kids in with hashbrowns. Eat, you'll need your strength." The group eyed the food wearily. "Hey, I could have made you eggs. Now eat!"

After breakfast was finished and the dishes cleared, the elder Holden's left the room so that the plans could be continued. "Alexander," Xesca started, "you said silver bullets and stakes through the heart. With this particular strain of vampires, am I correct in assuming that decapitation and sunlight are also viable means of destroying them?"

"Oh cutting off their heads will do just fine, sure, but they can move about in the daylight fine. Their powers are diminished, but it doesn't dust 'em".

"All right, what of garlic and other herbs?"

"Make 'em sick. Vamps puke blood, how gross is that?" Candace's stomach gave a lurch and her face looked a little paler. "I have heard that they dust out when mass quantities are injected," Alexander continued, "but that was during an experiment and I don't know how we could use it in battle."

"Holy symbols?"

"Nah, they just laugh at that stuff."

"Well, this has been very educational," Xesca said, pleased. "I suggest that today we go down and see if we can find the team. If it is nearly sunset and nothing has been turned up, we portal out. Haley, you can portal in and out with us, but we will need you and Alexander to be somewhat close but in safe territory."

"Aww, why?" Haley whined.

"I believe that you will be the only thing that will be able to determine where we are. You will be able to guide Alexander to us and get us out of harms way." Xesca regarded the rest of the group, "Any ideas yet as to why we are here and what we are supposed to be learning?" Everyone shook their heads. "Then we will take no undue risks. I am not certain what advantages we will have with our powers and abilities. I estimate that being wolf trained will be to our benefit, but do not know for certain, so until we face the enemy, no heroics from anyone!"

The group nodded their consent. They left the dining room and went upstairs to freshen up and to get into their gear. Alex and Haley went out to the garage to get the weapons that they would be taking.

Gregor and Ran were in his room, getting changed, when Ran asked "You think that Candace might have a bit of a crush on ya?"

"I never really thought about it, why?"

"She was watching you and that girl Samantha pretty close last night. Just wondering."

"Wondering?"

"Will it affect the two of ya?"

"I don't know why it should? She's proven herself worthy of being here. I had my doubts in the beginning but she has been much more active in this venture and concluded well in the last arch. If she does have feelings for me, I don't feel the same way about her and last night should have shown her that. I don't really know what it should matter whether she thinks of me in that way or not."

"Just wondering, that's all. She's seems a sweet girl. They both do really. I'm glad that we were put together." Ran stuck out his hand.

Gregor took it. "I am too. It occurs to me that we would be a textbook example of a good battle team. The young aristocrat with a chip on his shoulder, the seasoned veteran with the mysterious past and youthful demeanor, the analyst, and the wide-eyed rookie who will do anything to succeed. We're perfect."

"And if this hadn't brought us together, we would have never met and would definitely not have ever sought each other types out."

"Ran, why are you here? You never did answer that question in Corda."

Ran sighed heavily. "Not now Gregor. I promise later. But please, let me keep my wits for the tasks at hand. More probing questions at a later date?"

Gregor smiled. "I will hold you to that you know." Ran opened his mouth to protest. "But I will concede for now and let you keep your secrets. C'mon, are you ready to go?"

"Let's"

₪

In the spare bedroom, Candace and Xesca were putting on some clothes that Marion had provided them. Loose and ill-fitting, they regarded each other. "These are the ugliest things I have ever seen," Candace spat.

"I am glad that I am not the only one who thinks so. But then, I have not felt that I have had anything nice to wear since I began this training. I will never understand the homosapien desire to cover as much of the body as possible."

"I was more referring to the color than the style." Candace said, looking at herself in the mirror. "So, what did you think of last night?"

"What do you mean?"

"Well, the drinks, the music, the people. Those boys dancing with you were kind of cute."

"I suppose. Potables so far have been very interesting. I have never tasted anything like these before. The music was loud, but the rhythms were incredible and very enjoyable. I am not attracted to pale skin, so I did not really notice if the men I was dancing with last night were 'cute'".

"It's just so unique. The experiences so far. Going to the future and seeing my home planet. Meeting Himanoco head on and coming away in good condition. Now, all of the experiences here, where Gregor should have the advantage and doesn't because it is nothing like he is used to. It's all so," Candace struggled for the words, "special."

"That is one outlook I suppose. Why do you bring it up?"

"Well, I just am so impressed is all." Candace shrugged. "I guess I never imagined that the testing would be like this. I am used to much more structure in my training."

"I am also more disciplined than this in usual circumstances. But, the circumstances that we have faced are highly unusual. Also, as Gregor has established himself as the leader of this group, we tend to follow his example." Now Xesca was regarding her clothing and the pale skin that the illusion stone gave her. "Unorthodox as it may be."

"But you are more in control this mission. Maybe that will be a precedent and we will each get a chance to lead a mission."

"Do you feel that your opinions are being overlooked?" Xesca asked. "Is there anything about the plans that we discussed or the mission in general that you are unsure or uncomfortable with?"

"No, it's not that. It's just that I feel so much younger and inexperienced. You all have done and experienced so many different things, trained with so many different people, been to different planets..." Candace trailed off.

"Candace, you are a valid member of our team, therefore your views, opinions, and characteristics are just as important as anyone else. Do not measure yourself against us if it is your intention of finding yourself lacking. We may be more trained in different areas, obviously less trained in conjuring, but we are all of the same level while we are training Himanoco. Do you understand?"

"Yes, I do. I'm sorry if I appear sheepish."

"Do not apologize. If it makes you feel any better, I am probably learning more from you than you are of me."

"Do you think so?"

"Definitely. I told my roommates this back at the Alden Hall dormitories, you can read all you want about things, but until you actually witness them, you just do not believe."

"I suppose that's true." Candace took one last look at herself in the mirror. "Well, let's go see if the boy's are ready."

The group reconvened in the living room. To their surprise, the weaponry that they were going to use was somewhat primitive.

"I guess I expected something more like those gun devices that we used in the last arch," Ran said.

"I'm used to seeing more devastating weaponry on this planet," Gregor started, "but I guess if this is the stuff that works, and works well, I can see why only small modifications were made throughout the years."

"We have to consider the time-line that you are used to as well Gregor," Xesca said. "Without the intervention of these creatures, humans were allowed to thrive."

Candace was hefting a sword. "It's one of the best in the land," Alexander said. She shot her arm out and the Himanoco sword was in her hand, "Thanks, I've already got a sword," she said, smiling.

The rifle that Gregor had was a lever action, "It holds six shots," Haley said. "Do you know how to use it?" Gregor spun the gun like something out of a movie, "Yeah, I'll manage."

"We have binoculars as well," Alex handed a pair to Gregor. "Very powerful, these can see in any light up to seven hundred yards."

The crossbow Xesca was looking at had an automatic bolt loader with five on each side. "Just cock the string and pull the trigger, very nice." She turned to the rest of the group, "Ready?"

"Heart, I was born ready," Ran grinned.

Chapter 20

Plots Continue

To Kenor, it seemed he lived in his battle room these days. Studying the reports on the table in front of him, his scowl was so hard he had to focus to keep his teeth from grinding.

"Master Anor," a liveried young woman entered cautiously, "your guard-captain sent me in to tell you that the envoy from..." she hesitated on the names, trying to make syllables and sounds not native to her tongue, "Gialmesh of Malada and Rodain of Bayer have arrived."

"They arrived together?"

"Captain Edwart did not tell such as me sire."

Kenor sighed and the liveried young woman flinched badly. "Violetta, if you see the good Captain, tell him that next time he sends the likes of you instead of coming to me himself, he will be able to watch his own heart beating when I rip it from his chest."

The serving woman fainted dead away and Kenor sighed again. He never understood why people were afraid of dying. If they didn't want to die, why didn't they seek out the power to live, as he had? If anything, in Kenor's estimation, if a person was contented to live a bland and everyday life, they should be content to die at any given moment.

Stepping over the girl, he headed to the back entrance of his throne room that was right down the hall. His guard-captain would not be so foolish as to take any envoy anywhere other than the throne room, even if he did think so highly of himself that he thought he did not have to deliver messages anymore. That would change.

As he entered, Kenor immediately noticed the lack of people. He was the first to arrive. *Edwart had better be bringing them and just given me time to be here, looking overpowering. If he took them directly to the battle room, I think I may not even bother with his heart and instead pull his brain out through his nose.* He had an ornately worked golden dais on a platform three foot off the floor. Leaping, he flew up to the platform and sat on the throne.

A slide portal opened and two men and a woman stepped out. They were all black-clad and all menacing looking until they saw that Kenor was in the room. Softening their features quickly, the two men took positions on either side of the platform on the floor level, the woman leapt up and flew in the same manner as Kenor to stand next to the dais.

"My Lord," the woman started, "we attempted to have these two envoys meet with you separately but they had spoken with eachother and wanted both to be present. It appears that the Malada are afraid of our power and want the Bayer backing, while the Bayer are afraid of our magic and wanted the Malada to bring blockers with to cut us off if necessary."

"Piotren, relax. You are part of my council. School your emotions or have them schooled for you."

Piotren's jaw snapped shut. Pad's voice rang out as the main doors to the throne room opened. "Councilman Verstach, representing Lord Gialmesh of the Malada and his entourage. Councilwoman Wav representing Lord Rodain of the Bayer and her entourage. You are in the presence of Lord Kenor Anor, the Blackwolf incarnate and leader of the clan of Himanoco." The speech sounded by rote a little more than Kenor had wanted, but at least the fool had gotten it right.

Each speaker had three other clan members with them. The only way to tell which were the council and which were honor guard were bright sigils of wolves on their cloak backs as well as the shoulders. Verstach was the first to enter and the first to speak. He did not even suffer a salute, much less a bow for the man who should have him prostrating himself on the floor. "Lord Anor, my Lord Gialmesh has sent me to inform you that your claim of leadership of your clan has not been substantiated and that he can not support you at this time.

Perhaps if more of the Himanoco clan can agree on you as their leader, he will join you."

Wav not only saluted, she also bowed deeply for Kenor, yet her message was mostly the same. "With regret Lord Anor, my liege Rodain can also not join you in fulfillment of the prophecies at this time. His own friend, Mitris Orthon has advised him patience and suggested that the Time of Return might be yet in our futures. He begs understanding and is quick to add that no disrespect is meant to the mighty Lord Anor, nor does he not honor your claim as leader of the Himanoco." Wav shot a withering glance at Verstach, clearly indicating that this was more the way to address a person of power and that he should have waited for her to speak so that she could have educated him.

Kenor had already cast a geomancer trick of the wind to make his voice sound like it was coming from all directions. "Is that all?"

"My Lord Gialmesh," Verstach spoke up, trying to make his voice boom as Kenor's had, "has also instructed me to tell you that the presence of your Himanoco warriors on sacred Frotnefalt is a travesty and demands that they are removed at once."

This time Wav gaped at her counterpart, but she also spoke loudly and perhaps harsher than before. "My lord has also asked me to relay the message that claiming the forsaken is quite dangerous and may invoke contempt from the other clans. Certainly, he did not mean to imply that he held any contempt of you, quite the opposite. Lord

Rodain simply wanted me to caution someone whom he would like to consider friend."

When Kenor sighed again, it sounded as if the room itself had released it's breath in a huff. He rose and spoke "Each of you will return to your lord's with this message. If you will not openly support me and lay your claims to be the Wolf warrior incarnate as I know each of you to be, the forsaken son will have no choice but to follow in his fathers footsteps. I will not tolerate weakness in my presence, so I suggest you remove yourselves before I lose my temper."

As quickly as possible, one of Verstach's honor guard opened a slide portal and all eight representatives vanished. Kenor turned to look down at Anton and Pad. "Anton, if you will kindly make sure that the message I just gave gets delivered in the intention that I meant it?" Anton saluted and left by slide portal.

"Pad, tell Tartusk to double the number of Himanoco warriors in Frotnefalt and make sure Unaag knows that we are uninvited. I think that the Malada may be hiding something and I want to find out what." Pad mirrored Anton's salute and left in similar fashion.

"Piotren, I have not seen any new Himanoco faces in over a week. Do not disappoint me." She bowed, saluted, and left quickly.

Kenor sat back down and pondered before returning to his battle room. It did not make sense for two envoys of different clans to come at the same time and not provide a unified front. Mitris' hand was in this, and that meant that Defalorn was most likely involved as well. He was going to make those two old fools squeal before he killed them. He promised himself that.

Chapter 21

Into the Heart of Battle

A slice of pure, white light opened somewhere in south Texas and six figures emerged. Immediately, Candace and Ran took the flanks while Gregor moved toward higher ground to scope the perimeter. Xesca stuffed her illusion stone into a pocket and turned to Alexander and Haley. "Move out of harmful territory and maintain a lock on your brothers location. If he does not signal within three hours, slide to our location. Do you understand?" They nodded. "Good."

Ran came back up to Xesca, "Nothing on the right."

"Nothing to the left," Candace said.

"There is a keep about four, wait, it's five hundred yards." Gregor called down from a bluff. "Well guarded. Looks like some sort of troglodyte."

"Troglodyte?" Candace asked.

"Half lizard, half man" Ran answered. "They are legendary creatures. Fierce and strong, they are believed to be formidable fighters."

"Great," Candace said sarcastically.

"Ran, you'll take the lead. Scout no more than fifty yards ahead so that we may close the gap if necessary. This terrain is not very concealing but you can use your illusion powers to protect yourself.

"Candace, stay fifteen yards in front of me and to my right. If Ran gets attacked, I will throw you the crossbow and use my battle magic. If the attack comes on your side, draw your sword and stand fast, Gregor and I will provide cover fire.

"Gregor, keep at least twenty-five yards behind me, making sure that nothing comes up from behind. We need to be looking for signs that a group of people traveled through here."

The group quickly took their positions and headed toward the keep that loomed on the horizon. After forty or fifty yards, Ran called out, "It looks as though we have signs of a battle."

Everyone quickly converged on the spot. "See here," Ran crouched and pointed at the ground, "powder burns and chipped rocks. Your gun devices firing into the ground."

"Can't be that old if it is still here," Gregor mused. "Seems like the wind would have shifted that stuff."

"Aye, but maybe not if they were close enough to the ground to leave powder burns like that," Ran corrected him. He rubbed with his foot and there were still some black powder remnants. "Would take a whole lot of wind to do what my foot just did."

"We at least know that they came this way," Candace asked.

"Yes, and they ran into what ever is now attacking us!" Xesca called out.

In the sky were three large, bird-like lizards that reminded Gregor of Pterodactyls he had seen in school science books. Gregor quickly took aim and fired a shot into the lead bird's head. It came crashing to the ground. The other two birds began to circle, not sure if they should move in to attack.

"Here comes the cavalry!" Ran pointed.

Roaring down on the foursome was the sound of hooves as nearly thirty of the troglodytes rode toward where the pterodactyls were circling. Each of their faces bore a nasty snarl and they had a myriad of swords, lances, maces, and clubs brandished and ready to strike. They were about one hundred and fifty yards away and closing quickly.

"Ran, we will need whatever geomagic spell you can come up with to slow them down," Xesca yelled out her instructions. "Candace," she threw the crossbow, "take aim at the troglodytes and make sure every shot counts. Gregor, you take out those birds and then provide us with cover fire." She stepped forward slightly and her green skin took on a glow. Channeling fiercely, Xesca fired beams of pure, yellow energy from fists that she pointed toward the riders.

Ran closed his eyes and started a chant under his breath. Dust began to swirl at his feet and when he threw his arms out, the swirl became a wave of dust and wind that he launched toward the riders, knocking about a dozen off of their horses. Gregor quickly downed the other two birds and turned his attention on the riders. Firing quickly, he managed to take out three riders and began to reload. Meanwhile Candace waited until the riders were within fifty yards, then began firing furiously, taking six more riders off of their horses.

Finally, as the remaining riders closed in the foursome, they all drew their swords and stood their ground for battle. "This is going to be tough!" Gregor shouted

"Make all of your blows lethal," Xesca called. "Save any fleeing for questioning."

Leaping, Ran took one rider off in a deft motion, ran him through, and swung up to mount the horse. Gregor and Candace flanked the horse on either side and Xesca stayed behind it. Swords clanged against the weapons and the armor as they sought to kill. Clouds of dust stung their eyes and made breathing hard as the horses pounded and circled. Shouts and roars filled the air, and in the end, Xesca and Gregor had both taken substantial wounds to the shoulders and arms. Twenty two dead troglodytes lay at their feet and Candace had one snarling on the ground, her sword pointed at it's throat.

Ran climbed off of the horse and chanted again. The ground formed in manacles that bound their captive's feet and wrists. "Think they understand what we say?"

"I undersstand," he hissed. "you will all die at the handsss of my masster!"

"Strong words considering we just mowed ya down." Ran growled.

"We have killed many of your kind in the passst pale-skin. I am proud to die!"

Gregor moved in front of Ran, who looked ready to kill the beast himself. When the troglodyte saw him, he began to lose he confident sneer. "I make you uneasy?" Gregor asked.

"I know your face hunter! But it cannot be you!"

"Why?"

"Only the massters come back from death and I ssaw you killed by Drahmak's own hand!"

"When was this?"

"Jusst the lasst time that the curssed ssun made it'ss asscent."

"And the people that were with me?"

"We dined on their flessh!"

"Well, that solves that mystery." Gregor turned to the rest of his companions. "Now what? What on God's green Earth can I hope to accomplish now? No one to rescue."

"Are we sure this thing is telling the truth?" Ran snarled.

"He is truthful. He has no reason to lie." Xesca stated simply. She was rubbing her chin. "Ran, finish him off. Gregor, call to your sister and have them take us out of here. My shoulder pains me very much."

Ran shoved his sword through the beasts head as the slice of light from a slide appeared to the right of them. Haley and Alexander came out. "I see you didn't have to go far." Alexander commented.

"Wow" was all Haley could say, as they both surveyed the area.

"Alexander, take us to where you just were so that we can get some medical attention and decide what it is we should do next, if you would please." Xesca asked.

Alexander made the slide reappear and all six passed through. They came out at a large, plantation style house. "Louisiana, and some friends of ours."

"Ran, please catch me as I am going to..." Xesca didn't finish her sentence as she slumped from the shock of her wounds.

"We have got to take care of these two," he could see Gregor getting paler as he hoisted Xesca up over his shoulder. "Can we do it in there?" Ran asked as he motioned toward the house.

"Yeah, sure."

"All right then," Ran bounded up the steps. He lay Xesca down on a couch in the living room and Candace helped Gregor to a chair. "Fetch me lots of water and something to dress these wounds. It would be nice if you had some sort of herbs or other medicine with which to clean 'em to."

Alexander ran to the kitchen and got the water while Haley went upstairs to get dressings for the wounds from a bathroom on the second floor. Chanting to herself, Candace produced some healing herbs native to her home planet for Ran to use.

"Thanks darlin'. Sure is handy to have a conjurer around."

"I do what I can."

Gregor's head started to bob as he fought to maintain consciousness. "I just don't understand. What are we doing here?"

"Hush now, Gregor," Candace said, soothingly, "we'll figure it all out. Don't worry."

"It just seems a little too familiar to me..." Ran mused.

"To you?" Candace asked.

"Yeah, the troglodytes, the fassels, which is the name of those flying things, vampires..." Ran trailed off. "Something about this is striking a chord with me and I can't place where."

Xesca moaned softly as Ran attended her wound. The herbs that Candace had conjured stopped the bleeding and helped to close the wound. He used the bandages Haley brought down and then turned his attention to Gregor. His wounds were not as severe, and Candace's herbs were enough to take care of him.

"Alex, can you take me back to the scene of the attack?" Ran asked.

"Sure, why?"

"Actually, I want you to slide me right up to that keep."

"Ran are you insane?" Candace cried. "It will nearly be sundown! How do you expect to go unnoticed?"

"I need to see something." He turned to Xesca. "I may need to take rubbings or pictures of things. I expect that there is some hieroglyphics on the walls of the keep and my ancient language translations are a little weak. Xesca could probably decipher them though."

"How do you know this?" Candace asked.

"I told you honey, this is very familiar to me. Maybe I read it somewhere before, I can't remember. I can't put my finger on it, but I know what this is about."

"Then you'll wait until we can go together," Gregor whispered from his chair. All eyes in the room turned to him. "If you can go, you figure out why we are here, what is going on, and we have to go through the arch wounded. With two tests to go, we can't risk that."

"Good point," Ran said, almost glumly. "Then we wait. It will be a couple of days 'fore Xesca is up and moving around."

"That's fine," Gregor said. "Alexander, I need you to tell me more about Drahmak."

"Well, Lord Drahmak is a vampire king of this region. Many of the other vampire lords fear him."

"What about the creatures?"

"Most vampire lords have an army of troglodytes, as well as dire hounds, goblins, and flyers at their disposal. No one knows for sure where they all come from, and most think that they import them from other planets. Some people contest that that all of those creatures are created from the vampire itself, in some sort of torture lab."

"We defeated them easily, how?" Candace asked. "It seems that if four can stand down thirty, this planet should have been taken back by the humans years ago."

"You four are better trained that anyone we have ever seen," Haley said. "You seem almost as omnipotent as the vampires themselves. Weapons out of thin air, spells and chants, it's all amazing!"

"Four legendary heroes from time and space sent to battle an impossible evil force." Ran said. "One more and you could accuse us of being the wolf warriors."

"I want to go to another area little brother," Gregor said. "Boarder lands always have the best defenses. I want to go to the heart of another overrun area."

"What about the missing people, your troops? The you that we are familiar with?" Haley asked.

"I'm sorry." Gregor shook his head. "One of the troglodytes we captured said that the me that you know and everyone that I was with was killed."

"No," Alexander shook his head. "It can't be! There's no way that my brother was killed! I don't believe any stinking trog!"

Candace took Alexander's hand, "What would he have to gain by lying to us? He knew that he was going to die."

Alexadner jerked his hand away. "It's not possible."

"Lad, I wish that it weren't, but it's true." Ran held Haley in his arms as she began to cry into his chest. "We saw evidence of a struggle. They were wiped out."

"What are we going to do?" Haley sobbed. "What am I going to do without my defender? As soon as you leave, I will feel my brother die through the bond that we share and you won't arrive at that same instant to take his place."

"I wish that there was more that we could do little sister, but there isn't" Gregor said sadly. "You're right. And from what I gather, without me, you will be in big trouble."

"Than maybe that is it?" Candace asked. "Maybe we are supposed to leave, just so we can come back from outside the arch to help these people?"

"Nope," Gregor said. "This is only an arch reality. I couldn't take you to the planet that I know and have it be like this."

"This is so unfair," Alexander said. "Somehow, we should be able to keep the knowledge that we can get from you. You should stay for a few years and train people how to fight like you."

"It doesn't work that way," Gregor said. "No amount of time will change the fact that when we leave, no knowledge of us ever being here will remain."

"Why do you want to see another area Gregor?" Candace asked.

"I tend to agree with Alexander and I want to get an estimate if my death on this planet will set them back or not. There may yet be something we can do to help these people."

"You know that there isn't lad," Ran said. "I'm sorry. I want to do things for them too. But the longer we stay and the more involved we get, the more likely we will be here for a long time, get hurt, or wash out." He placed his hand on Gregor's shoulder. "I know how you feel. But you have to remember that these are only mirror images of the people that you love. When all of the training is over, you will head back to your home planet and meet back up with all of your relatives who have absolutely no clue about this reality. Until then, you have to keep the focus. We need you." He looked almost pleadingly at Gregor. "Please."

"Your right," Gregor said, sighing heavily. "Fine. Let's go home."

"Home?" Haley asked.

"I am going to spend the next few days with my family. I may not be the exact brother that you two knew, or the son that mom and dad raised but," Gregor looked up at them with the tears welling up in his eyes, "I will just have to do. I want you to have the opportunity to say goodbye to your brother. Even if you won't remember it, I'm here now and you deserve the opportunity."

Haley collapsed onto him and he winced from the pain in his shoulder. Alexander was crying now as well as he fell into the heap. It was all Candace and Ran could do not to join in.

"Can she be moved?" Gregor asked, motioning toward Xesca.

"Yes, she can be moved," Xesca said quietly. "She is hurt, but not dead."

"We move dead people around here too." Gregor said smiling.

"I may never learn these customs," Xesca said, smiling back. "I heard what you said. It seems that you are back in charge?"

"Not at all m'lady. If you have another idea, we go with it. I will simply ask for the leave to spend with my family."

"No, you are right. We cannot press on." Xesca started to sit up and slumped back down. "If we were to go through the arch now, we would be at a great disadvantage for the third level."

"Alex, you want to slide us home?"

"Hang on, we need to check out with the people here. I'll be right back." Alexander headed into the other room.

"Boy, this has sure been odd," Haley said. "I can't believe that there are other realities out there."

Alexander came back in, his face ashen. "They are attacking! The vampires have launched an initiative into our territory!"

"Where?" Gregor asked.

"All the way along the Mississippi, north and south," Alexander stammered. "Most of that area hasn't been an active border in over a hundred years!"

"Why now?" Ran asked.

"They say that Drahmak is looking for you," Alexander motioned to his brother. "People claim he is calling out the new vampire Gregor Holden. His minions saw you alive and he knows your dead because he killed you himself. He thinks then that you must be a vamp."

"What are we going to do?" Candace asked. "This is all our fault!"

"You don't think he is headed to Michigan do you?" Haley asked.

"He might be. Who knows if he knows where we come from." Alexander said, his voice cracking.

"Ran, can you heal us faster?" Xesca asked.

"No honey, I'm an apothecary, not a healing magic user. I mix medicinal potions and dress wounds. No magic involved."

"I know a magical healer," Alexander said. "He lived in my dorm at Oxford. I'll see if I can summon him to us."

"Summon him to the border where they are attacking," Xesca said. "Then get us there. The people will be mowed down and we need to help them."

"But we can't risk it," Ran said. "There isn't anything that we can do."

"I want to meet this Drahmak. I think he may hold some of the answers as to what we are supposed to be learning from all of this." This time, Xesca actually did sit up. "And the only way that we will be able to meet him is if we are on the border where they are attacking. Besides," she grinned at Ran, "when has there ever been a time that you did not want to get involved in a fight since we have known eachother?"

Ran grinned back. "We need to rearm these weapons and get ourselves ready. If you guys have anything else stronger," he turned Haley, "we would love to use it too."

"Haley, I want you to get our entire family to the boarder," Gregor said. "The Holden's, the Bornhold's, everyone. Drahmak wants a run, we give it to him. When Alex gets back, have him slide you."

"Greg, we aren't as strong as you and your friends," Haley said, quietly. "We will be killed."

"Not on my watch," Ran said before Gregor could respond. "Nothing will harm any of you, I promise that."

"Ran, why didn't I think of this earlier!" Candace exclaimed.

"What is it?"

"You asked about weaponry. I can conjure any weapon that we need!"

Ran's face brightened. "Candace honey, remind me when this is all over to give you a very large kiss." Candace blushed. "Do you think that you had enough experience with those laser gun devices from the past arch to create a working one?"

"That was just what I was thinking," Candace said. She closed her eyes and began to chant. She waved her arms and four of the weapons appeared on the closest table. She chanted again and pointed at the ground, creating six strange looking swords. Ran regarded her. "Plasma blades," she said. "Almost pure energy in a sword. They are very coveted on Baktarus and I though that whoever we have fighting with us could use them. We won't need them with our swords."

"This may be worth more than one kiss," Gregor said, regarding the weaponry. Sitting down from the exertion, Candace blushed harder. He picked up the laser and fired a perfect beam that cut right through the wall of the house. "You're great Candace!"

Alexander returned in a slide of light. "Christopher is on his way to the boarder. He is the healer and he will be waiting for us to arrive."

"Fine. Alex, after you drop us off at the boarder, slide sis to where she can get our family together. We are going to make a stand against Drahmak."

"Alright! I've been waiting my whole life to fight that bastard!"

"Here," Candace handed them the blades. "When you go to use this sword, make sure you keep them away from each other."

When Alex grabbed the hilt of one, a beam of light formed the blade. "Cool! It's like something out of a sci-fi movie!"

"C'mon little brother, let's get back to the fight!"

Chapter 22

Meeting the enemy face to face...Again

After the healing, Xesca, Gregor, Ran and Candace stood on a wall of a fort looking out at an army of hundreds of goblins and troglodytes. Large, worm-like beasts were being ridden around the perimeter of the army by what appeared to be men in dark hoods and the men were shouting orders. The army occasionally attempted to take the fort with a barrage of arrows, but a few magic users inside of the wall would deflect the arrows with a spell.

Gregor's family were all inside the fort, waiting for some sign that it was time to die. There were other families here as well, some warriors, some not. They weren't positive who the four were that were standing on the wall, but they knew that they were important and in charge.

"So, now what?" Ran asked. "I can see us beating thirty, but there must be three thousand out there!"

"We wait," Xesca said. "They have seen us standing on this wall. They have seen Gregor. We wait until Drahmak comes, then we get some of our answers."

"Boy, I hope that you're right," Candace said. "Otherwise, I don't know how we're getting out of this one."

"Why don't we stir 'em up a little bit?" Ran asked, patting his laser gun. "We could knock out a few of 'em from here without a problem."

"Might hurry Drahmak along," Gregor added.

"Very well," Xesca said. "Everyone target one of those worm riders." She set her sights on one. "On three. One...Two...Three"

The four shot together and each took out one of the riders. This incensed the group of beasts and they began to shout curses and prepared to charge. Ran set his gun down, threw his arms wide and three twisters shot from the wall and threw bodies in every direction as they cut paths through the army outside.

Xesca turned to Ran, scowling. "What?" He said, grinning boyishly. "Can I help it if they were going to charge? I was just trying to stop them."

"That you did," Candace said. "They look pretty confused."

"I don't think it's confusion Candace," Gregor said. "They are parting to let someone through."

The worms without riders were moving forward toward the fort. "Something," Xesca said, correcting him. "It appears that without their riders, these creatures charge the nearest thing to them." She shook her head. "I am guessing that this will not be the best idea we ever had."

Ran swung the gun back up and began to fire at the nearest worm. The laser beams bounced off of the hide. Cursing under his breath, he focused his energy and channeled a beam of battle magic, only to watch it have the same effect as the laser gun.

"Our swords," Xesca said. "They will penetrate the worms skin. Defalorn said that nothing could ever break them." Xesca waited patiently as finally one of the worms reached the wall and began to inch it's way up. She drew her sword and threw it down at the worm. It pierced the skin and drove into the worms head. Howling in pain, it fell off the wall and lay, writhing. Xesca waived her hand and her sword was there. "We will see if hurting one of them will cause the others to reconsider attacking this fort." It did just that. Seeing one of their kind hurt, the other worms stopped their charge and began to retreat. This caused the army to wait. "I would suggest that we do not stir them up anymore Ran."

"Yes m'lady," Ran said, the boyish grin still on his face. "You have to admit, that was a bit more fun than just staring at each other over the wall."

"We will delve into your definition of 'fun' at a later juncture," Xesca said, not quite as sternly as she had anticipated. "Perhaps Drahmak does not realize that you are here?"

Gregor shrugged. "How do I know? He knew that we were in the South even though we left nothing alive. I have to assume that if any of his minions see me, that he knows."

"So, when do we get to charge down the army?" Alexander asked. "We are all prepared to die since we know that this won't last past when you all leave, we aren't afraid of anything."

"Be patient please," Xesca cautioned. "Who knows how long it will take us to discern the lesson we are to be learning and find the arch to pass through."

"But you will pass through, right?"

"Either that, or we will be killed, effectively ending our time in this and any other arches."

"So you see, we realize now that we have nothing to lose. Let us charge down the guns so to speak."

"As I asked, please be patient." Xesca turned her attention back over the wall. "Candace, what is going on over in that group over there?" She asked, pointing.

Candace peered through her binoculars. "Someone is standing in the middle of a large group of trogs and goblins. He is talking to them."

"Do you think it's him?" Gregor asked.

"We shall see," was all Xesca replied.

"How's the wound honey?" Ran asked.

"The healer did an excellent job. I will be fine."

"He's coming this way!" Candace shouted. "What are we going to do?"

"We are going to let him in," Xesca said simply.

"What!" Alexander exclaimed.

She turned to him and smiled softly. Taking off the illusion stone, Xesca stood in her green hue, looking lovely. "Alexander, you have done everything we asked and we have shared all we can. You say you are prepared to die because you face no reprisal, so it is mostly the same with us. In the last arch, we met our enemy and defeated him handedly." She turned her gaze to Gregor. "Actually, your brother handled him." Xesca sighed deeply, " We will meet our fate head on and unafraid. Few can brag the same."

Alexander had no reply. He just watched as the figure came closer and closer. "It is him you know. I've seen pictures."

"The sun still shines and he will be weak," Xesca said. "You and Haley should ride out and meet him. Invite him in and we can discuss things. Just him."

"I'll go with you," Gregor said.

"No, you will not." Xesca turned to him. "You will remain inside this fort and will talk to Drahmak only if he agrees to come inside."

"They'll be mowed down if one of us doesn't go with them," Ran said. "I promised."

"I am sorry, but you will also remain inside. We remain together and safe for now. I am in charge and I am not loosing any member of this cordon unnecessarily."

Ran shuffled his feet. "Liked it better when Gregor was in charge," he mumbled.

"Are you sure Xesca?" Alexander asked timidly. "I think that Ran is right and they will just kill us."

"Warn him that we are still on the wall watching. Remind him that he saw what our weapons can do and the sun does still shine. Invite him to come inside the fort and meet with us personally, or else he can stay outside and relay any terms he may have to you."

"O.K." Alexander went down and got his sister. As they headed to the gate, an uproar from the Holden's began.

"Please, please," Gregor said, trying to quiet them, "trust us. We know what we're doing." The din began to subside, but faces were still grim. They watched in a mixture of horror and awe as the two Holden youths rode out of the gate. "Do we know what we're doing?" Gregor whispered to Xesca.

"I hope so." They met up not fifty yards from the wall. "Ran, Candace, train your guns on him. Fire if he makes a threatening move."

"Yes ma'am"

The trio talked for awhile, then they all began to ride toward the wall. "They are coming in!" Candace yelled.

A sigh of relief passed over the Holden family. "Prepare us a place to meet please." Xesca called down. "Gregor, come with me. Ran, Candace, keep your weapons on him, even as he passes through the gate. Then, you two follow the escort to wherever we are meeting."

"Got it." Candace said. She was smiling a smile similar to Ran's.

"I am serious you two, a discussion about what you find amusing will be following this tenure in the arch." Xesca said, smiling back.

Gregor and Xesca hurried to a small building near the center of the compound. It was basically a room with a table and three chairs. Maps lined the walls. Xesca took the chair that faced the door, Gregor stood beside her on her right.

When the door opened, it was the first time that they saw Drahmak. Both were immediately struck by his size, standing well over seven and a half feet tall. Dark skin and black eyes, he stooped to come into the building and took the chair in the middle of the table. Candace, Ran, Haley and Alex followed. Haley took the last chair and Alex took up a position on her left after he closed the door.

"So," Drahmak said in a silky, deep voice, regarding Gregor, "you do not like my attack on your territory and wish to discuss things with me? Hardly the vampiric thing to do."

"What makes you think that I am a vampire?"

"Resurrection is beyond the reach of this people and I killed you and drained you of all of your blood personally. I still have some of it chilling, which I plan to enjoy on a special occasion. So vampire you must be."

"Sorry to disappoint but vampire I am not." Gregor said, mockingly.

"Enough," Xesca said, with a dismissing wave of her hand. "I tire of this banter already. We have done it before with people more important than this." She nodded toward Drahmak and now her face was contorted with contempt. "I am green. Do green people exist on this planet?"

"Not that I am aware of," Drahmak said calmly. "How do I know it is not a trick?"

"To do what?" Xesca asked. "What could possibly be gained by appearing to be green?"

Drahmak shrugged. "Then what is the point of your hue in general?"

"To prove this story…" Xesca told Drahmak all about the Himanoco tower, the training, and the arches themselves that brought the foursome to this reality. "So you see, this is not the Gregor Holden that you have chilling, waiting for a special occasion. This is a completely alternate Gregor Holden who will soon be out of your way. If you could refrain then from this initiative and allow us to continue in peace, we would all appreciate it."

"Fairy tales and bedtime stories will not stop me from routing your pathetic people," Drahmak grinned wolfishly. "It is long overdue you understand. We have enjoyed toying with the people of this planet over the centuries because we knew that at any given time, we could crush you. Your puny attacks over the years have cost us so very little and you so very much.

"But now," he pointed at Gregor, "you embrace one of us as your own. I care not what you say about him, vampire he must be and must then be stopped at all costs!"

"This is ridiculous!" Candace shouted. "You don't believe a thing we said!"

"Can I kill him now?" Ran asked.

Shouting, Drahmak leapt to his feet and lunged toward Gregor. Immediately, Gregor's sword shot out of his cloak and ran through Drahmak's chest. After a split second hesitation, Ran's sword was also at his side and he now swung it a Drahmak's head, cutting it away from his body. Xesca chanted and a beam of white light came from her hand, igniting Drahmak's body.

"Pointless," Xesca said, shaking her head. "Why would the possible ruler of a planet do something so pointless?"

"I don't believe it!" Alexander exclaimed. "You killed Drahmak without even trying! You just killed him!"

"It doesn't make sense Xesca," Gregor said, ignoring his brother. "You're right. What could he have possibly hoped he would be gaining if he killed me? Could I really have been that important?"

"I still think I have heard this all somewhere else before..." Ran trailed off.

"Can we leave this planet?" Gregor asked.

"Defalorn recommended not to." Candace said.

"Defalorn recommended that we not try it on our own," Gregor corrected her. "What if someone native to this planet, therefore native to the arch, slid us off. We've been sliding around since we got here."

"Where did you have in mind?" Xesca asked.

"Ran's home planet."

"Why?" Ran perked up.

"You keep telling us how familiar this all is to you, I want to look up why." Gregor said simply. "Alex, is there anyone on the planet who can do interplanetary slides?"

"It's rumored that people like that exist, but no one is sure who or where they are."

"We need to find one little brother, and we need to find him or her yesterday, get me."

"What about the horde outside the fort walls?" Haley asked.

"Leave that to me," Gregor said, smiling. "Candace, if you can make more of those laser devices, do it. Get everybody up on the wall and ready to fire on my signal." He picked up Drahmak's head where it lay. "I think that this will shock them into submission. Just in case, aim for the worm's riders."

With a wave of his hand, Gregor opened a slide portal. "I'm going to appear in the middle of them and tell them that we've killed their master, it is time for them to retreat. If they don't, take out a few of them with the lasers and stir the worms up. They may cause just the havoc we need."

Candace ran out with five more lasers in her arms, rallying people onto the wall. "What do you want me to do?" Ran asked.

"Go with my brother. Keep him safe, no matter what. I know that you could wash out and that he can't die, but it makes me feel better just the same. Also, when you find the intergalactic slider, you are going to have to help direct them to your home planet."

"You have my word my friend," Ran said, grasping Gregor's hand.

"You just can not help taking charge, can you Gregor?" Xesca asked.

"I'm sorry, I'm doing it again, aren't I?" He said, sheepishly.

"It is quite all right. I am amazed at your ability time and time again. I have no problem with the role of advisor as opposed to operations. What would you like me to do?"

"Well, you could help me get my ass out of trouble if this whole thing about appearing in the middle of the lot of them blows up in my face."

Xesca grinned broadly. "It would be my pleasure."

"You know, we are going to have to have a talk later about what it is you find amusing," Gregor said jokingly.

Xesca smiled back at him, "You are a horrible young man, I believe that I have already pointed that out though?"

They headed toward the portal, "Wait!" Haley called. "I'm coming with you."

"Like Hell"

"Look big brother, nothing can happen to me and we are still working under the veil that even if it did, it won't matter anyways so what," she stood with her hands placed firmly on her hips, "do you think you can stop the queen?"

Xesca's smile grew larger as Gregor's faded. "She does have a point, oh great leader. If I were in charge I think that I may be able to dissuade her, but," she shrugged, "I am uncertain what to do since I am not in charge."

Gregor turned to Xesca, a mixture of amusement and concern on his face, "You really are picking up all of our bad habits, aren't you?"

"The ability to adapt quickly is one of the reasons why I was sent to train at such a young age."

"Yeah, yeah, yeah," Gregor shook his head. "All right, you can come. But, you stay right next to the two of us and you keep your head clear. I don't need a flood of your emotions clouding mine. Got it?"

"Got it."

"Now, can we go?"

"Just lead the way, oh fearless leader," Haley said, making a mock sort of bow.

The three emerged in the midst of a swarm of troglodytes, goblin looking creatures, and creatures that looked like shadows. Gregor held the head of Drahmak up for them all to see, but it was Haley who spoke.

"I am Queen Haley Holden of the Great Eastern States. My warrior protector has slain Lord Drahmak." The crowd gathered around them were amazed at the head of their master. "I lay claim to all that was once his, here and now!"

"How do we know that iss the real head of Drahmak?" one of the troglodytes hissed.

"Here," Gregor thew the head at him, "see for yourself."

"You will all return to Drahmak's keep and begin to dismantle it. I will be along in five days time to oversee that everything is destroyed. Do not fail your queen or suffer the same fate as your former master, is that understood?"

"I am not convinced" the questioning troglodyte said.

Xesca's sword shot out from her cloak and she held it to the neck of the troglodyte. "Perhaps you would feel more honor if you shared the fate of your master?"

The horde around them stirred at the show of aggression. "The shadow bows to no human."

Gregor had his eyes closed, chanting quietly since he threw the head to the troglodyte, holding his arms at his side, palms down. Now he turned his hands palms up and his eyes snapped open. Wind arose around the trio like a funnel cloud, pushing back the monsters around them. Xesca raised her rifle quickly and fired at two worm riders, taking them down quickly. She then drew up a slide portal and grabbed Haley.

"Come quickly," Xesca shouted, "I am unsure as to how long your brother can sustain this wind."

"I didn't even know he could create this wind!"

"Possibly the brother you knew could not do it." Xesca pushed Haley through the portal. She turned to Gregor. The force of his wind was beginning to lift him off of the ground. All around him, creatures of all shapes and sizes that had been caught in the whirlwind were swirling and flying to and fro. "Gregor!" Xesca shouted over the din. "End your spell and come. We have to get out of here!"

But Gregor was locked into the spell and it was getting away from him, as is the case with large spells. Xesca could see the strain beginning to show on his face. The power that he was drawing on to use this geomagic spell was tearing him apart.

Reacting quickly, Xesca closed her hand around the illusion stone in her pocket and reached out with her mind. *Ran, have Alexander bring you back to my location. Gregor is locked in a geomagic spell and cannot break free. You are the only other one of us with the knowledge to help him. Hurry please, the spell is beginning to hurt him.*

Almost instantly, Ran and Alexander where at Xesca's side. Ran turned and pushed Alexander back through his own slide portal before it closed. "Hold that portal darlin'", Ran shouted over the wind, "and get ready!" Ran chanted quickly and rose off the ground, streaking toward Gregor, who was now fifteen feet high and still climbing. When he reached him, Ran quickly wrapped Gregor in his arms and, instead of using counter geomagic, he removed Gregor's bracelet.

Gregor was cut off from all his magic and slumped into Ran's arms. Ran flowed back down to the ground, and quickly ran through the portal with Xesca behind.

"I should have thought to do that," Xesca said, angrily.

"Don't worry yourself over it, I just came up with it as I flew up to him. I could have tried a counter-magic, but that would've hurt the both of us. Don't know about you," Ran said smiling down at Gregor, "but I'm not getting hurt if I can help it this time around."

Back inside the fort, the Holden family circled Gregor with concern on their faces. They barraged the duo with questions.

"He'll be fine," Ran said with a wave. "Just drained him is all. He reached too far, stretched too hard. He's pushing this 'can't be hurt' thing to the limit."

"Is there anything we should do for him?" Haley asked.

"Yeah, don't give him back his bracelet until the three of us have had a chance to yell at him good."

"Ran, perhaps you should resume your search of a way off of this planet?" Xesca said calmly. "I will assist Candace on the wall of this fortress. Please, be as quick as possible."

"Actually, Alex and I have been thinking about that. What if I held the coordinates and he opened the portal? I can't slide anyway, so it wouldn't be like I was using my power."

"Alexander, do you believe yourself up to the task?" Xesca asked. "You have never used your powers to leave a planet before. While similar, there are quite a few large differences."

"We'll just try it," Alexander said. "If it doesn't work, we'll come right back."

"What if you were to slide to a planet where you could not breathe the air? What if the moment the sun of a planet hit you, your skin boiled? Or worse, if you land on a sun? No, this sounds like too much of a risk for us to attempt it at this juncture."

"Please Ms. Xesca, let me try. I think I can do it," Alexander pleaded.

Xesca studied him for a moment longer. "We need a volunteer," she said finally.

"For what?" Ran asked.

"I am not allowing a member of this team to risk washing out over something we were told not to attempt. Also, if we want to attempt again if we fail, Alexander cannot be the one who goes through the portal. We need a volunteer." She turned to the Holden family, "Alexander will hold the portal open. Upon your arrival, you will draw three sharp breaths and move about to make sure that everything is similar to this planet. Then, come back through the portal and report."

"What if we are attacked on the other side and can't get back," Haley asked.

"We will attempt twice. Ran can give coordinates of two very different locales on the same planet. If the first attempt fails, we will get another volunteer for the second. If that attempt fails, even if both times we were on the right planet and the person was just overwhelmed before they could return, we will still discontinue."

"I'll do it," Arthur Holden came forward. He pointed to one of his nephews, "Get me a sword and shield quickly."

"Are you sure Dad?" Alexander asked.

"You just make sure to do your part and I will get home safely," Arthur said confidently. "If it is the right planet, nothing will stop me from getting back and letting you know."

"Here," Ran said, holding out his hand. He gave Arthur a stone. "It's an illusion stone with no illusion but to change your eyes. Hold it in your hand and I can read your thoughts. Get in trouble that we can help you with and you can pitch it through the portal." Ran paused for a moment. "You're a brave man for your family sir. I am sorry if we did not make a good impression of ourselves when this day began."

"You all have fought bravely time and time again. I am sure that when you show me this in your reality, I will stand by you and support you whenever I can." Arthur clasped Ran's hand. "Even if I remember nothing of this, which I still have a hard time believing, you can always remember that at least once the four of you impressed an old man and his family and maybe even saved their world." Turning, Arthur entered the portal. To everyone waiting on the other side, the moments he was out of view seemed to stretch into eons.

Chapter 23

Interlude: Back in the tower 2

Arthur reappeared in less than a minutes time. "The air is safe to breathe, the sun is shining, and a very castle type building was in front of me no more than a jog. It has high corner towers and a drawbridge for no reason because there was no moat that I could see.

"That is my brother's house, the house of the *Culdat* of the land. Our library is in there. Whatever I am remembering, it would be in that , library, I spent a lot of time there when I was growing up."

Gregor opened his mouth to speak. "Very well then," Xesca spoke up, cutting Gregor off, "I think that Gregor and I will stay behind, to take some time to heal. Candace, you and Alexander will accompany Ran to his home planet and see what you can discover of the situation. We will meet back at your home," she motioned to Alexander, "as that will be the easiest spot for you to slide back to when you are finished."

Xesca turned to Arthur, "Do you know of any more soldiers that we can bring to defend the boarders of this land? I would have to believe that the vampires that live here are going to plan a reprisal and perhaps even see opportunity in Drahmak's demise. We should..."

"Wait..." Gregor started. "That won't be necessary. Alexander, close the portal."

"What do you mean Gregor?" Candace asked.

"We are leaving right now. I know what it is we are supposed to learn here."

"Actually, I was about to say that I think I had pieced it all out," Ran joined in. "Let me take a stab at it, will you for a minute Gregor?" Gregor motioned for Ran to continue. "This entire mission, we have looked to save these people. They are Gregor's family and we have to help them. Even when we kept explaining to them that we will leave and everything that we had done for them would vanish, we still try to help them.

"Everything about this arch has kept leading us to want to stay here. Don't you see it, we have a desire to battle on and we keep trying to do anything in our power to stop these monsters."

"That's what we do," Candace cut in. "It is what I want to be Himanoco for. I want to help and defend people who cannot do it alone."

Realization spread across Xesca face while Ran continued, "And therein lies the problem sweetheart. You three have youth on your side as an excuse, but I should have caught on to this on the first day. Honey, sometimes in life, no matter how strong you are or how prepared you can be, you just can't do anything. A true warrior," Ran shook his head, "no, a true Himanoco warrior recognizes that they can do things other people cannot. They can defeat enemies that would crush whole armies, they stand as leaders among the universe. And that means that they sometimes forget that no one person can do everything."

"Ran is right," Xesca said patiently, putting her hand on Candace's shoulder. "We have labored time and time again to help these people, to investigate what was going on, and have even explained to ourselves to not get too attached to them. We have been fooling ourselves."

Suddenly, the doorway of the meeting building that they were all standing in changed to match that of the Himanoco Archways. "You see Candace," Gregor said, standing with some difficulty, "a true warrior knows when it is time to leave the field and accept what he cannot change. It is time for me to leave this family that I love to their own ends and pray that they survive and it is time for all of you to come with."

The arch shimmered and threatened to fade out. "It's just not fair!" Candace shouted. "We should stay here until we find out what we can do to wipe out the vampires from this planet and protect these people!"

"Candace," Haley's face was solemn, "you have to go. You cannot do anything here. By the way you've explained it to me, you could live with us your whole life, die, and it would still be exactly the same result. You are not here now. Don't throw everything you have, everything that you can become, away on us."

Marion stood behind her daughter, "You know what you must do. Please, do not worry."

The arch snapped back into brilliance. "I am so sorry," Candace sniffed, tears in her eyes. She turned and ran through archway.

"Your bravery throughout this mission was an inspiration," Xesca said, addressing everyone in the room. Turning her attention to Alexander, "You, young man, are perhaps too much like your older brother. However, you are also perhaps better than he. Stay strong for your family." She turned and walked through the archway.

Ran's look was even more forlorn than Candace. "You have given me more over the last few days than you can realize. I have been so determined over the last five years, so single minded. You folks gave me something to believe in, something to fight for. Please, stay strong!" He turned and headed through the archway as well.

Left with just his family, Gregor leaned on the wall by the archway to stand up. "You all have been enough like the you that I know from my reality that I am sure that I am like the me you know in this reality. When I leave, to you, I am dead. I know it won't mean anything to you and that you won't remember, but it means something to me, so come here," he motioned toward himself. "I am going to hold you all and tell you that I love you. It's all I have left."

In a crush, his siblings rushed to him and wrap their arms around him, crying. Arthur and Marion are also crying as they hold onto their children, smiles beaming down at Gregor through the tears. "We are very proud of our son, in every reality," Arthur said softly. Letting him go his family watches as Gregor turns and walks into the archway and vanished.

₪

Rubbing their eyes again, Defalorn's voice rings out, "Congratulations, you have all completed the second level and are now on the third and final level to prove worthy of being a Himanoco warrior. Take a moment to collect your thoughts."

"Master, are you absolutely positive about the reality we face not existing outside of the archway and nothing we do inside having any effect?" Gregor asked.

"You wish to share your exploits again?" Defalorn asked.

"I'll write this time Gregor," Ran said quietly. "Go ahead and tell him."

"Sir, it was my home planet, in the present day, but nothing like what I left. The planet was covered in vampires. I was there in that reality and it would have appeared that the me in that reality died the instant that the me standing before you arrived."

Stunned, Defalorn muttered something in a language that none of the others understood. "You are certain?"

"That it was my family?" Gregor asked, watching Defalorn intently. "Of course. Also we are certain that the me in that reality died. The instant thing may have been a little off, but it had to be with moments. Why? What did you just say?"

"It is unimportant," Defalorn shrugged. "You must continue with your training. Here are your journals for the third archway; you can just leave the ones from the second on that bench." He walked to the archway, and it came alive just like the last two. "If you will all pass through, I will see you when you emerge."

"You did not answer my question. Is the archway reality restricted to just the archway?"

"Gregor, no one has been able to substantiate what goes on in the archway. I believe that it does not exist outside of the archway because I have never found it anywhere in this reality. I also believe that everything is returned to the proper place and time without our intervention, because that was how it has been told for generations untold. Proof is impossible though."

Gregor shrugged at Candace and they headed toward the archway. Ran set his journal down and picked up a new one. The rest held on to the ones that they were given in the last archway. "We did not write anything down." Xesca explained as they all passed through and vanished.

₪

This time, when they were gone, Defalorn almost ran to the journal to read it. The contents were written in Ran's steady hand, and Defalorn later copied the entire passage down for his own log.

Jehan, Mart'rishla, and Edsith, thank you all for guiding your lowly servant and showing him what he has been too stubborn to understand. Thank you also for giving me three of the greatest people I have ever known to call friends. Never have I ever deserved such blessings, yet you still deem me worthy. Mayhap someday I will be able to be worthy in my own eyes.

Gregor walked away from everything and everyone he ever loved to continue. Xesca, Candace and I turned our back on people who needed heroes like no one we are ever likely to meet again. I remembered the story that our adventure follows, and although I am sure all of my companions will think that this was mostly Gregor's challenge, it was almost entirely mine.

My father used to scare me with the legend of Arsilan. Arsilan was a legendary hero on my planet said to have fought all kinds of daemon in his lifetime. He battled everything that we faced; vampires, troglodytes, bancth worms, everything. The scary part, and the only time I was ever certain that my father was a man and not a monster, was that so consumed with fighting was Arsilan that he didn't even notice when he became the very thing he despised. So single minded and unrelenting, he never noticed the damage to towns, to families of the men he led to the death, to anything so long as the world was "safe" and evil was dispatched. Cost was never an issue. My father taught me about war, not cost..

So it has been for me. What of the families of the guard that I killed, my onetime friends? I could have continued to expose them to the magih. I could have brought the entire village under my protection on my family lands. We had the land and the entire village wasn't that large. Instead, I leapt at the opportunity to do onto them what I had seen them do. I reveled in anger, death, and destruction, the very things that I despised when I was a part of them. Cruelty, under the guise of justice, is still cruelty.

It was a shame that Gregor's family had to be the model to teach me a lesson. I will carry a mountain of regret that he was forced pain for my pride. May he forgive me my sins as you three gods have chosen to do. I persevere.

Immediately upon finishing copying the passage, he set out to contact all of the Himanoco warriors that he knew were still loyal to the ways of Himanoco and not Kenor. They had to know what was going on and he figured that at Alden Hall was the best place to be. If this cordon survived level three, it was likely that a war would begin that could shake the very fabric of the universe.

Chapter 24

Level 3 begins

When Gregor, Ran, Xesca and Candace emerged from the archway, they found themselves standing in a forest, with no signs of life anywhere.

"So, what now?" Candace asked sarcastically. "We've gone to my home planet in the future, Gregor's home planet in the present," she paused and then raised her voice in mock excitement. "I know, it's Xesca's home planet four thousand years in the past." She sat down on a nearby stump sulkily.

"Candace, you must try and relax and not take everything so, oh what is the expression, 'hard' I think." Xesca said in a smoothing voice. "I know that it does not seem fair to you that we left those people behind, but it was what we had to do. It was what we were meant to do. We had no choice."

"I know you're right, but I don't have to like it."

Ran had been studying the area, along with Gregor. "Ran," Gregor whispered in his ear, "I can't continue right now. I'm still very weak from the spell and from my rapid healing. I need at least a day or two rest."

"It's alright Gregor, haven't you noticed yet?" Gregor looked at Ran, confusion on his face. "No noise at all except wildlife. The first archway was like this but at least we came out on a road. This time, we are deep in the woods and it would seem that no one is around. It's like the archway is allowing us a break in the action."

Gregor grinned. "You just think there is no one here. We had best scout it out to be certain. And," Gregor paused and looked down at his feet, "thanks for all you did for my family."

"You just relax son, we're gonna fix you up good."

"And what are you two gentlemen whispering about over here?" Xesca said, mock anger on her face.

"Just two gentlemen comparing notes as gentlemen are like to do when they get a moment to themselves away from gentle ladies." Ran said, sounding as though his speech was by rote. "Xesca, why don't we get in some relaxation time before we set out to exploring this archway too deeply. I'm sure that you are still somewhat exhausted from the quick healing that you received in the last arch."

"Yes Ran, and thank you for caring. Gregor, are you exhausted as well?"

"Yeah."

"Hey, wait a minute," Candace came striding over, "I'm the only one who hasn't been hurt hardly at all during our trials. I will go out, gather some game to eat, and hunt so that you three can get some rest."

"Are you sure Candace?" Ran asked. "I can do that and you can stay and help conjure us up a camp."

"Why? All your survival skills and you can't just build one?"

"Now, there is no need to get mouthy with me young lady."

"And there is really no need to question me is there?" Candace had her hands on her hips in a defiant stance. "I'll only be gone a little while, maybe three hours at the most. Set up camp and I'll come back and let you know what I found."

"Thanks Candace," Gregor said, breaking the tension. "Have a good time and bring me back a some deer if you can find something like that. I haven't had venison in a long time."

Candace smiled back, "You just sit tight and I will bring in the biggest stag in the woods." With that, she loped off toward the sun.

"So much for worrying about her coming out of her shell and earning the right to be here," Ran muttered. "I'll use my geomagic to start a shelter over here. I'm sure you two have some sort of tactics you want to review."

"Yeah, how to sleep with little disturbance," Gregor said, laughing.

Ran walked away and Xesca turned to Gregor. "Do you really need the rest? Or is there some other motivation that compels us to not continue with our training?"

"A combination. I am tired, there is no denying that. But," Gregor paused while he searched for the words, "don't you think this is odd, how personal everything has been? Defalorn was looking like a scared rabbit and that has nearly unhinged me."

"You are thinking that something other than training is going on here?"

"I don't know exactly what I am thinking. All I do know is that if a Himanoco Master is concerned about what's going on, I'm terrified." Gregor looked at Xesca with a face full of concern and determination. "I just want to be one hundred percent for whatever we are going to face this time around. The situations have been getting more difficult. The arch seems to want to wash us out."

"Gregor, the archway is designed to push us to our fullest potential. You have to know that that will come with injuries and the possibility that some or none of us will finish the task at hand." Xesca eyed him levelly, "You can not take things so personally or assume that a malevolent force is at hand just because the tasks are difficult."

"I don't assume anything m'lady. I observe." Gregor shrugged. "It could all be nothing. It makes little difference one way or the other anyway. We all will come through this arch. I'd bet we will all train as masters as well."

"So we take a small respite to get our bearings, a more traditional strategy. Honestly, I am happy not to be in the middle of a battle shortly after arriving at our destination."

"Well you two," Ran came back, interrupting the conversation, "I've got a lean-to set up for shelter as well as a small pit dug for the fire. I circled it in stones and got some fire wood. Do you think we need anything else?"

"Yes, information." Gregor said. "I'm sure that Candace will do a good job, but I want more. If Candace hunts like I think she will, she'll cut circles on paths to make sure she doesn't get lost. You, I want to head straight in one direction, away from her."

"Anything in particular that you want me to find?"

"A major part of me is hoping that you don't find anything," Gregor said, sighing. "I think that I just want you to head out, half the days walk in a straight line. Clear another area for a camp and we will make short marches in the same direction. We can't be totally stagnant," He looked to Xesca for confirmation, "but I think that we can move fairly slowly. Half the day will give you the other half to get back."

Xesca nodded her approval. "Tomorrow, when you are out, you can set up wards to keep things safe. Today, just head to the next area and create a campsite."

"Sounds fine. I hate standing still anyway."

Ran loped off in the opposite direction as Candace, moving swiftly. Gregor and Xesca watched him leave before settling back into their conversation. "What about what we have faced so far Xesca? Don't you wonder?"

"I wonder about the future, certainly. The last archway was an alternate reality, of that we are as certain as we possibly can be. But what of the future we saw in the first archway? What we did to those people of Baktarus." Xesca sat down on the ground, her legs folded under her. "What if what we saw was not an alternate reality at all but a possible inevitability?"

"That we will become divided and try to fight each other? It is possible I suppose, but I don't think it is very probable anymore. Especially after the last arch."

"Why?"

"Ran mostly. He was always a concern. He wasn't part of the group. He could pull us apart. But since that last challenge, I don't know, he just seems…different."

"Maybe it was your family?" Xesca asked.

"I don't know. All I can say is that he is more...yielding if that makes any sense. I would have never thought that he would have made the realization that we had to leave to succeed. I just assumed that he would battle on for no reason than to battle. He strikes me as the type."

Xesca shrugged. "Maybe he was right. Maybe it is relative to someone's age. Myself, I was ready to battle on, to find out more. I wanted to win, even though I saw how illogical that line of thinking was as soon as Ran explained it.

"Gregor, you have to realize that on Ohlia, Himanoco cut a swath through my people enough to make a river of blood. We were proud of our skills. We had subjugated the entire planet, wiped it clean of anything evil. In so short of time, Himanoco could have wiped us out.

"So, when I was chosen as one of the strongest warriors on the planet and set to the task of becoming a Himanoco disciple, I assumed I would be powerful enough to handle any situation. It was a hard realization that I cannot."

Gregor let a pause stretch out after Xesca finished speaking before he responded. "Xesca, I have a feeling that in many ways, you may be more right than Ran and I were." Xesca looked puzzled and opened her mouth to argue but Gregor cut her off, "Here me out. The archway took us into an impossible situation. Who's to say that we couldn't, the four of us, conquered that entire planet and ruled until we died? How do we know that we can't do that at will with anything that we encounter? We weren't defeated by the vampires. We were defeated by ourselves. Our own training and our own ambition were what caused us to be in that no-win situation. It wasn't that we couldn't win normally, extenuating circumstances caused us to concede."

"And what does that mean, to us?"

"It means that we have a larger responsibility in general than what I had imagined." Gregor replied, somewhat awestruck at his own realization. "I set out to do this just because I wanted to be the best that I could be. I didn't want to be the best in the universe necessarily." He began to pace back and forth. "Now though, even more so if that future scenario was a glimpse into the realm of the possible, we have to be extra careful. We can rule without opposition. Together we can conquer anything."

"But, in the end, what does that really mean?" Xesca asked again. "I have no desire to rule, personally. I do not even really want to be in charge of a group, that is why I will often yield. All I want is to make sure that no one can ever hurt me or my people ever again. I want to be certain that we will be protected. Beyond that I have no aspirations."

"But what of myself and the others?" Gregor prodded.

"How does that measure up to what we have already learned?"

"Xesca, each of us has the desire to defend the weak. I'm sure that is Ran and Candace's motivation as much as it is yours and mine. But just defending our own may no longer be the only option open to us. We may in fact be called upon to protect the entire universe and we may be the only ones who can do it."

"You get ahead of yourself I think Gregor," Xesca said with a half grin. "We are not even Himanoco warriors yet."

"Xesca," Gregor said, his smile broad, "we were Himanoco warriors before we even started this little adventure. I'm going to take my time, but I am willing to bet that I can prove it."

"How?"

"Patience, Xesca, patience. In traditional strategist style, all things revealed in good time."

Laughing, Xesca got up and went over to Gregor, lightly hitting his shoulder, "You are incorrigible Master Holden!"

"Let's see what our scouts report before I make any sort of hard decisions. But, I get the feeling that this could be our shortest stint yet if I want it to be." Gregor turned and headed toward the fire pit that Ran had dug. Pausing, he turned back to Xesca, "I'll ask you to keep whatever you may reason out to yourself and follow my lead."

"You really do think that you know what this mission holds for us after a little more than an hour?"

"Yes m'lady, I'm almost certain that I do. We'll just wait and see if anything is going to prove me wrong."

Away from the group and left to her own thoughts, Candace immediately began to reflect on the events in the last arch. Of all the people, she thought that Gregor would have had the hardest time leaving, yet it was him who reasoned things out at almost the same time as Ran. And it was Candace and not Gregor who had had a hard time admitting the realization that they laid out before her.

After all, she thought to herself, *I have been raised to do this. I have known nothing but Himanoco. Why wouldn't I think that they could fly to the stars and back if they so desired.* She shook her head ruefully.

After a few hundred yards, she began to see signs of wildlife. Pausing for a moment, she conjured a bow and quiver of brightly fletched arrows. Knocking one to the bow-string, she switched her movements from scouting to stalking. Marking a landmark with her sword every few yards so she could find her way back, Candace came up over a ridge to an open field.

A dozen deer-like animals with large, palm-ated antlers roamed on the woodline across from Candace. She started to create a device to climb a tree by her, when she remembered her black Himanoco cloak. Focusing, she levitated up to a branch that would support her weight, drew down, and loosed an arrow into the herd. A large stag fell where her arrow landed and she cheered quietly. Game seemed plentiful and would fall to her and her companions whenever it needed.

Coming down from the tree, Candace conjures a knife and begins to dress the stag. She didn't get too far in her exploration, nor in her reverie, but she is sure that at least her thoughts will be completed on the walk back.

ℶ

Away from the camp, Ran's thoughts strayed not only to what he just finished writing moments ago in the journal, but the events that led up to his realization. He was going to have to explain himself sometime and it seemed that it was going to have to be sooner rather than later now.

Wincing a little as he leapt over a deadfall, Ran realized just how hard the last few days have been on him. Finding out that you might be able to rule at least a planet, if not the entire universe, then moments later coming to the realization that there are some things that are beyond even all of his power. It was all getting to be quite a bit to process. Ran chanted and began to rise above the tree line. *Why am I bothering to run when I can fly?*

Once in the air, Ran began scanning the surrounding area harder. Trees, hills, valleys and a river were all that marked the landscape for as far as his eyes would see. Moving at close to twenty five miles per hour, the trees began to blur under him and Ran had to keep his eyes up to the horizon. If there was something out there, he was bound to find it.

Ran began laughing to himself as he landed in a field. *We are all going to have to fly if I make this our next base camp. You really need to start using your head a little better old man.* He found stones and whistled as he dug another hole for a fire.

Finishing the campsite, he glanced skyward and noticed that telling time was going to be difficult. It seemed that the sun had hardly moved in the entire time that he had left the camp, but he was certain that at least two to two and a half hours had passed. He also noticed that wildlife seemed scarce. He couldn't remember any birds on his flight and he didn't hear anything moving now.

He began to look at the vegetation with the eye of an apothecary. The plants were all fairly basic and common, deciduous trees that he would expect to see in this sort of climate abounded. He looked further, but nothing really stood out to him. He would have to have Candace conjure some medicine for Gregor.

Ran sat down and started a fire. He was going to relax and collect his thoughts before he went back to join the others. He was still a little shook up from everything that happened in the last two archways and we wanted to sort things out before facing any more trials.

Ran had been on the run for five years following the girls beating and his subsequent rampage. No one knew how to find him. Still, he woke up that morning and a small parchment lay by his head telling him that if he could get to the Alden Hall academy, he would be allowed to train in the ways of the Himanoco warrior. No tracks appeared by the parchment and he had no idea how it had been delivered.

His mind wandered back to the events that had led him to this point and time. He remembered his last days on his home planet with the palpable sense of someone who has had something dear snatched from him. A squad of Blue Guardsmen had lined up five people on a wall and skewered them with arrows. They would kill five people every ten minutes until he turned himself over. They were on their third round of people when he arrived.

The guard attacked Ran instantly, and he fought them carefully, injuring but not killing. He would never be allowed this deal if he killed another group of Blues. Finally, the *culdat* of the land came to the battle and called a cease fire. He met with Ran at his castle.

The *culdat* was a pig of a man; short, squat, and uncaring. He did not want to let Ran leave and protested that his guard would have killed Ran if he had not intervened. Calmly, Ran killed all the men around him with his battle magic, drew one of the dead guard's sword, and told the *culdat* that if he did not find a way for Ran to get off of the planet, he would be dead. The *culdat* summoned his personal slider and Ran was gone.

Ran checked the sky. The sun still wasn't moving, but he was sure that another half of an hour had passed. He returned to his thoughts of the ride to Halith after his invitation was met and the weeks spent in the city. The life of a lover still suited him, and court life with a royal was always what he enjoyed best. He passed the time with Vos, and that girl was a firecracker, to be sure. Whoever finally convinced her to settle down was going to have a whole lot fun for the remainder of his life.

He broke his reverie and took to the sky. It was time to get back to his companions and decide what they were going to do in this arch. They also should discuss what they were going to do after this arch; if they were going to go for master training or if they were just going to be warriors. Flying low across the wood line, Ran didn't notice the smoke to his right.

Chapter 25

Revelations

Defalorn's battle room was cramped. It wasn't designed to hold twelve people, but he needed to talk to everyone and this was the most secure place he could think of next to in the Himanoco Tower. Eleven men and one woman were either seated or stood milling around his table.

"I called you all here to bring your attention to a point that I believe is happening right now in the Himanoco Tower with one of my training cordons. Gregor Holden, Candace Orthon, Ran Grastle, and Xesca, Daughter of Queklain are currently on level three of the tower and the archways seem to be taking a personal interest in this group.

"In the first archway, the foursome landed on Baktarus, Orthon's home planet. It was a future where each of them had become Himanoco warriors and warred over the control of the planet. Himanoco himself revealed to them that he had taken over Kenor Anor through the power of the fabled Sword of Himanoco. He had defeated all four of the cordon to gain our interest, and was on his way to train as a follower of his own clan to fool us.

"In the second archway, they were transported to Holden's home planet in the present day. It was a completely alternate reality, with mythical enemies from the stories on Grastle's home planet of Balderia. It was a test to see if they would actually give up and let the people fend for themselves, something that I know I had to face when I was in the arch and a story we are often recounted. What was so interesting was that it chose to use one of the cordon's actual family and events." Defalorn paused for a moment, trying to find the words to phrase what he wanted to say. "The archway, the tower, the world is trying to tell us something. What?"

Mitris Orthon spoke first. "I know that Kenor and his cronies are on Frotnefalt and Kosivo. I think that they are looking for items of the Wolfwarriors. Anything that they can find to help them try to gather the power of the wolves for Kenor's disposal."

"Mitris and I have been working with some of the leaders of the other clans to try to convince them to turn against Kenor. So far as yet, we have only convinced them to not openly support him. They won't stand up to him yet because they don't feel that it is necessary."

"That's good Ty, but it may not be enough," Defalorn continued. "What if this cordon is a legendary one? Will the others be able to sense it?"

"I, for one, am not sure about that," another of the gathered Himanoco spoke. "I could sense it, but I am quite a bit older than all of you."

"Xavier, we are the only ones we can turn to because we are the only ones that the true power of Himanoco has manifested in," Mitris said calmly. "No one suspects that the twelve of us meet in this way, nor that we have found ways to slow our aging process. Kenor is unbelievably powerful, and I think that he could take any of us one on one, maybe even two or three on one." This comment sent a murmur through the group. Many of them shifted uncomfortably.

"Well gentlemen and lady, I think that we really only have one choice," another of the men spoke up, "we have to gather as many of the other clans warriors as we can and attack Kenor and his followers."

"This is Lord Alex's great plan?" Xavier asked, with a mixture of genuine and mock surprise.

"Really Blade," the only woman in the room chided, but only slightly, "I would have thought that you would have had some sort of grand plan other than full out assault. It seems beneath you."

"Sorry Catleen, you know how I hate to disappoint," Blade flashed a smile that quickly became ironic, "but sometimes the only route at your disposal is a direct one and this is the only thing that I can think of us to do."

"Kenor has over thirty thousand Blackwolf who follow him," said Mitris. "Who knows how many of the other clans wolves will fight along side them. What are we going to be able to bring to the table?"

"I would say the remaining ten to twelve thousand wolves not with Kenor and who have professed that they won't get involved," said Catleen. "I'd guess that we could also bring around two hundred thousand other Wolfwarriors, give or take. We all have cultivated an impressive network of supporters over the years."

"Pagen," Mitris said softly, "what are you expecting of these four in the arch?"

"You all know the prophecies. Eventually, a cordon would go in, they would all come out, and together they would form the new Sword of Blackwolf. I swear to all of you that the things that this group have faced are not normal parts of the training. I don't know what to expect, but I do know that it is going to something we need to start preparing for now."

"And how do we prepare for the unknown?" Xavier asked.

"By doing just what we are doing now," Defalorn continued, "meeting, discussing, and planning. We have to be ready for the worst."

"And what would be the worst?" Mitris asked.

"These four come out, either they side with us, they side with Kenor, or they side with themselves. The two latter options are not options. Am I clear?"

"You really think that they will come out with the Sword?" Blade asked.

"I really think that when they come out, your course of action will be the absolutely correct one."

"We need to go, to make our contacts, and to have everyone at the ready for when this war comes."

"Agreed Xavier," Defalorn stood and so did everyone else who was seated. "Good luck to all of you and may the events we fear not come to pass." With that, seven of the gathered left. Mitris, Catleen, Xavier, and Blade stayed behind with Defalorn. Defalorn sat back down and everyone else followed suit. "What do you think?"

"I think that when they left here, those seven went to report to their informants so Kenor should be knocking on our door sometime soon." Xavier said with a shake of his head. "What I find hard to believe was them buying the story that we can prolong our lives, not to mention them seeming to go along with it."

"Ty especially," Catleen agreed, "when he spoke up, then acquiesced with the rest of them, I thought I would be sick."

"I thought that Mitris might tip our hand with his concern over Candace though," Blade smiled again.

"Hey, it wasn't as though I didn't attempt to convince people. It was just a concerned dad coming out."

"But we all agree that Kenor will drive toward war now?" Defalorn asked.

"Oh yeah, he will fall for this easily."

"He hates yours and Mitris' existence as is," Catleen laughed. "The excuse to come after the two of you alone, not to mention Alexander, Xavier, and I will be more than he can bear."

"She is training well, isn't she?" Mitris asked.

"Focus my friend," Xavier put his hand Mitris' shoulder. "Your daughter is training in the tower, away from the trouble that her father has to face. You want to look out for her, when soon she will emerge a Himanoco warrior and be your equal."

"She will never be my equal," Mitris said simply, "she will always be my daughter. Mayhap she will surpass me in every way."

"Mayhap she will," Defalorn consented. "That would be a very large help to us all."

₪

"Brothers and sisters, today is a joyous day," Kenor cried from a balcony that faced his castle's courtyard. He had used his spell to make his voice sound as though he was standing right next to you when he was talking, but he still shouted. He wanted to accentuate his point. "Today is the day that two thirds of all Himanoco recognize that the

Blackwolf has returned to lead them. Today, we stand nearly completely united and ready to take our true place in all of the universe at the head of the table." A roar of ascent rose up from the crowd.

"And what of those who do not stand with us," he continued. "You all know who they are. Many of you know them personally. Those brothers and sisters have lost their way and it is up to us to help them find the correct path. Those brothers and sisters not here today think that I am false, that I make false claims. We know better." Another roar. "They are currently too narrow minded to realize that the time is now and that the future in our grasp. No one, be they Wolfwarrior or simple civilian has ever been able to stand in opposition of us. We shall show those brothers and sisters not standing here today that that truly means no one."

The crowd could no longer contain themselves. The roar could be heard for several yards from the gathering. Kenor threw his hands up and milked the noise out of the throats of all gathered. Finally, putting his arms down and making a quieting motion, the noise began to subside and he spoke again, completing his speech. "Soon, brothers and sisters, we will be ready. Soon we will have the items that will make all of the other wolf clans stand with us in united glory. Once, five warriors and their disciples could control everything that they saw, so shall it be again. The five clans that the disciples sprung forth shall return to the glory that their founders could brag. Under the flag of the once forsaken, all wolves will be united and will flourish as we were always meant to be."

One last wave to the exuberant crowd and Kenor turned inside. Displays like this repelled him almost as much as they stroked his ego. Almost.

He couldn't believe that so many Himanoco warriors followed him. He knew that he had decreed it and he had to admit that his council did their job well. No one was there with him yet to admit it to, which always made Kenor feel better as he hated to praise anyone.

Still, if it had been someone else in the lead, Kenor liked to believe that he would have never stood outside some balcony window and cheered at whoever was silly enough to wave their arms. He had the power, he had the charisma, but he had no artifact naming him Blackwolf. His own clan named him Blackwolf and that would do for now.

He made his way back to his battle room as his council began to arrive in a series of slide portals. Each of them had a confident grin on their faces. Kenor would fix that.

"Sit, all of you, and tell me why I had to work so hard to convince that crowd outside my window to believe in me?" He saw on their faces, especially Piotren's, that they clearly thought that they had done all of the work. Kenor sighed audibly. If they were going to need further enlightenment, he was most glad no one was here moments ago when he was inwardly praising them. "Where is the Sword of Himanoco?

Why do I not wield the Mace of Chaos? Two months have passed and still nothing has been discovered. Unaag?"

Clearing his throat, Unaag looked Kenor right in the eye. "My apologies my liege, but currently there is still nothing. The chronicles that all list the items of the original wolves say nothing of where they may or may not have stored these items. Also, nothing is said of what Malada may have done with them after the wolves were slain by the original Himanoco."

"What you are telling me is that not only do I not possess these items, I should not expect to posses them anytime in the foreseeable future?"

"Quite opposite my lord," Unaag quickly recovered, "in the foreseeable future these items will be in your possession. How far the foreseeable future is from today is a matter for debate."

Kenor laughed, as did some of the others seated at the table. "That was an impressive answer Unaag. I think that that answer may have actually saved your life." Anton had still be chuckling. Kenor deftly drew a dagger from his side and threw it through Anton's throat before anyone seated had time to realize what had happened. "I did not, however, think that you answer was that impressive."

Silence and furtive glances. The fear that he had once commanded with this group was fading. It was time to drive his point home. "This is not pleasing. Find my items, or all of you will dangle in nooses around this keep and I will find replacements. Am I understood?"

"Aye sir." They spoke in unison.

"Get out of my sight."

Each left in turn and Kenor folded his hands into a steeple and rested his chin on his fingertips. *I'm so close now. I can't fail due to the stupidity of others when I am so close now.*

A gong sounded and a man entered. Kenor broke from his reverie. Ty Litwack came into his chamber.

"My lord, Defalron's group has decided that the only course of action is open war. They seek the assistance of the other clans in this endeavor and have already began to approach the Gingee."

"Excellent work Ty. This is quite important news." Ty stood smiling like the cat who got the cream. "You can leave now."

Crestfallen, Ty made a bow and retreated quickly.

At least I'll get to kill Orthon and Defalorn.

₪

Night was beginning to fall and Gregor and Xesca sat by a camp fire. Xesca seemed anxious for her friends to return, Gregor seemed to not even notice at all. In fact, more often than not, when she turned to look at him, she found that he was already looking at her.

"Why do you stare at me?" she asked finally.

"If I don't, you'll disappear."

Xesca laughed. "I promise, I will not leave you alone in the camp."

"Oh, I don't mean that you'll leave. I mean that you'll disappear."

Xesca's brow scrunched. "What are you talking about Gregor?"

"Half the day's walk would have Ran back by now. Candace should have been back an hour or two ago easily. Where are they?"

"I was wondering that myself. I just thought they may be taking their time. Making a thorough investigation of the area."

"They aren't coming back," Gregor said simply.

"What do you mean?"

"I mean, they aren't coming back. They've most likely already tried. They are confused, searching, but they won't find us."

"I still don't understand."

Gregor sighed. "I am telling you all I am certain about this archway and waiting to see if it is enough for us to pass. I doubt it, but we'll see.

"First, challenge us with our future to see if we can overcome. Throw in Candace's home planet and my hero, Kenor Anor. We won. I won first, but we all passed. Next arch, challenge us with the impossible and see if we forget our training to try and save everyone we see. Throw in my family and Ran's memories, try to take me out of the fray. We won again."

"We have had this discussion already today Gregor. There is no malevolent force guiding this training."

"I said nothing about malevolence, did I? There is a force guiding this training though, and it is going for the only option left at it's disposal. Divide and conquer."

Xesca was still confused. "I will ask you again Gregor, what do you mean?"

"We keep winning because we work together. It is time for us to try to work on our own. At least, that is what this archway seems to be thinking."

"So if you break eye contact with me..."

"You'll vanish and I will be left alone. And so will you." Nothing. No archway appeared for them. "I had already guessed that it wouldn't be that easy."

"So what do we do?"

"I was going to wait to see if you came to the same conclusion on your own. Since you asked, I told you. I guess the next thing to ask is if you want to disappear or not?"

"I have the option?"

"We have the option actually. Having diagnosed the problem, for the time being at least, we could take turns staring at eachother. It's tough to disappear if someone else is watching you."

"What good will that do us exactly?"

"Most likely no good at all. It will just tire us out and we will still be no further along than we are right now. I just thought I should throw the option out there, in case you had some other ideas?"

"No, I do not."

"Do you want more time to think about it?"

Xesca actually thought about that for a moment. "No. I think I would like to face whatever is in store for me and get beyond it."

"Fine. I'm going to get some sleep. I suggest that you do the same. I promise, when you wake up, I'll be gone."

"What if you just get up and leave?"

Gregor smiled his best smile and shrugged. "I won't be any less gone, will I?"

"I suppose not."

"Then, let's get this party started."

He turned his attention from Xesca, lay down, and started the drift toward sleep.

Chapter 26

What Archway 3 holds in store

On his way back to the camp, Ran noticed smoke on the horizon.

How did I miss that before?

He took to the air again. Flying low over the trees, he landed well short of the source of the smoke. Moving quickly and agilely, he slinked his way in closer. When he came to where the source of the smoke must be, a camp of five tents, his jaw fell open.

"Mother?"

"Ran my boy, it is so very good to see you again."

"But, what is this about now?" Ran asked.

"What do you mean, my son?" A man stood beside the woman Ran addressed as mother.

"Father? What does this have to do with my training?"

"Training for what?"

"I am training to be a Himanoco warrior."

"Ugh, why would you want to do that?" his mother scoffed. "They are such an ugly group. You should join the local army."

"Yes," his father agreed. "You should join the local army. It would do you go to toughen up some and get rid of all those silly flowers."

"Actually, I like some of his flowers dear."

"This is ridiculous. What could this possibly mean."

"Ran, your disturbing your mother. Calm down."

"Your dead!" Ran raged at them. "Mother, you died years ago from the cold. Father, a bit more recently, but you died of old age five years ago. What are you doing here!"

"Ran!" His father came over and shook him. "What are you talking about? I'm only in my early fifties and your mother is fine."

"Father, I'm in my early forties! How can you be in your early fifties?"

At this, Ran's mother laughed. "A joke. This was all one of your elaborate jokes."

"Joke?" Ran asked, breathless.

"Ran, you have only seen the summer eighteen times. Now, help your brother set up camp and calm down."

Ran felt his face. It was smooth, clean shaven. He looked down and saw that his clothing had changed and his black cloak was gone. "No, this isn't right. I have to find the others." He turned and stopped cold.

The forest that he had just come out of was gone. The camp sat on an open plain.

For the first time in his life, Ran passed out. He wasn't sure for how long. He heard the voices first as he started to come to.

"Is he all right?"

"We'll see. Give him time."

"I never saw anyone so pale."

"Oh, just leave your brother alone Persiphone. He seemed to have some sort of shock. You know how he can daydream."

Ran awoke to find himself on a cot inside one of the tents he saw earlier. There was a full length mirror set up in the corner. He stood up, the tent as large as a room in most houses and taller than he was.

Regarding himself in the mirror, he stroked his chin carefully. *Still young. And Persiphone's voice. That was the voice of a young girl, not the woman that I remember.*

And yet, many memories he could have recounted by rote seemed to be fading the way of dreams. *No!* He raged. *Hold on to your mind, you old goat. It will do you no good to get sucked into this timeframe. You've lived this life. No need to repeat it.*

Pacing inside the tent, Ran tried to decide what was going on. *This has to be some sort of test. I will hold on to that, no matter how hard it tries to fade. I am in the Himanoco training arch at the academy called*

Alden Hall. I am at the highest level that a person can attain before master training.

He began reciting this as a mantra. *In the archway. This is all part of the test. I must figure things out.*

Where are the others, He wondered. Hot on the heels of that thought though, *what others?*

Ran stopped pacing and looked at himself in the mirror. There were others, he was certain of that. Now though, no matter how hard he tried, he couldn't conjure any faces. He wasn't even sure about any names. *There were others, by Jehan above and below! I know that!*

A head popped in through the flaps on the tent. "I thought I heard movement. Mother, Ran is up."

"Leave me alone Athon."

"Oh sure, no problem. Hey, I already put up the whole camp, felled two deer, and gathered wood to keep the fire going, but I'll let you get your beauty sleep. Gods know, you need it."

"Go throw a humping to that new bride of yours and let me be!"

Athon came full in the tent now. "Mayhap you would like to try me, little brother? You may be handy with a sword, but I was your first teacher."

Sword? "You know that you couldn't take me if you wanted to. You're too old and slow."

Athon ducked out of the tent in a flash. "Let's give it a go then, all right little brother?"

"Athon, you're brother isn't well," their mother admonished. "He passed out earlier. Now you want to try to rough him up."

What about a sword? "It's all right Mother," Ran said, coming out of the tent. "The exercise will do me good. Too bad I won't get too much."

Athon threw a sword to Ran. *This isn't my sword.* He was circling, bounding on his heels.

Ran couldn't stop looking at the sword. When Athon stepped forward, he barely swung up in time to fend off the blow. "Wake up little brother. If you don't, I'll put you back to sleep for quite some time."

His younger sister's Persiphone and Gennifer, his older sister Brelain and her husband, Athon's wife, Mother and Father, all were gathered around to watch the two boys spar. *This isn't my sword.*

Ran danced. Athon forced him to turn from time to time, but for the most part, Ran was the superior swordsman by far and both men knew it. Moving from left to right, changing hands, Ran made his movements appear effortless.

"There you go," Athon huffed. "That's better," he complemented Ran as though he were letting Ran win.

Ran threw away the sword and, with a grin, beckoned his brother on. All of his concerns were fading and without that sword in his hands, he felt better. "Maybe I should just fight barehanded? You could use the help."

Athon's face darkened. "Don't add insult to injury son," their mother called.

"Oh, let them have their fun," their father patter her arm. "It's entertaining to see that boy go." He was referring to Ran and Athon's face showed it.

Thrusting forward, Athon began to make his attacks more serious. Ran was still dancing, this time taking opportunities to jab his brother in the ribs or swat at his backside. *He's going to kill me for this.*

Their sisters applauded every time that Ran got a whack in. Even Athon's wife laughed at him. He became more and more ardent with his attacks.

Deftly, when Athon thrust to strike, Ran spun his brothers wrist and Athon's sword flew into the air. Spinning, he landed an elbow to the back of Athon's head, making him stagger forward. Ran caught the sword and as his brother turned around, fists raised to continue fighting, he found a sword point pointed at his neck.

"Enough? Or shall I tie a hand behind my back and we can continue on?"

"Ran, stop it now." Their mother glided over to him, pushing his sword away. "You won. You seem to be feeling better now. Leave your brother be."

"Mayhap we should let him join Himanoco," his father boomed, clapping a hand on Ran's shoulder. "The boy may be too good for our army."

Laughter all around as the group began to turn back to what they were doing before. Ran noticed Athon's wife steal a glance in his direction as she escorted her husband back to their tent. *What is wrong with this?*

"Come on," his mother pulled his arm and Ran turned his head back to her. "You haven't eaten. I'll make you a plate."

"Mother," Ran started as they broke away from the rest of the camp. "I am sorry for what I said earlier."

"It is all right Ran. You always did have a strange sense of humor."

"I'm sorry if I still sound odd. My head is still groggy for some reason. How is it that we come to be camping?"

"Just a family outing," His mother said, smoothing his hair. "You're father wanted us all to get out of the keep and live small for a few days. He says that humility is a sovereign's duty to experience from time to time."

"Father says many things," Ran said laughing around a mouth full of food. "That doesn't make them all true."

"You must be feeling better, you've gotten your normal uncivil tongue back."

"My tongue has been called many things, but uncivil is far and away my least favorite. Especially when it is your tongue giving it an upbraiding."

"You are just too much man for me, my son," she said laughing. "Your wit has always been sharper than your sword." *My sword again. What about a sword?*

"Mother, might I have a few moments with our young victor?"

"All right Yasvey," his mother darkened a little, her smile turning down at the corners. She quickly recovered though. "Just you do not wear him out too. I think that your husband was quite enough excitement for my youngest boy for one day."

"Yes Mother," she smiled and bowed easily. The smile on his mother's face faded again, but she turned and left quickly enough that Ran was sure only he noticed. Yasvey linked an arm through his. "Walk with me Ran."

Strolling out of the camp, Ran and Yasvey reached a ridge and looked down into the valley below. A herd of wild horses were thundering in the valley below, but it was far enough down that the sound would be enough to cover their voices without making it too difficult for them to talk.

"You were incredible against your brother."

"That wasn't much. My brother is a good warrior, but I have trained harder than he has."

"In between romantic conquests?" she chided him easily, her dark eyes looking deeply into his. "Word has spread of the *culdat's* son who can bewitch a girl with his pretty words and pretty smile. I assume it is you, however if it is my husband, I am sure that you would tell me?"

Ran laughed. *Something isn't right with this.* "My brother is hopelessly devoted to you Yasvey. What man wouldn't be; your beauty is a wonder unto itself." *Remember you are being tested.*

Her laugh was rich and loud. *Too loud. She is flirting, hard.* "You do charm, don't you Ran Grastle."

He smiled, but his mind was swirling. *Why don't I remember this happening? Why would I remember this happening?* "It can hardly be considered charm when a man speaks the truth." *Remember the archway!*

"And is it truth you speak?" She was a good five inches shorter than he, but on tiptoe, with her hand on the back of his head forcing him down, she could kiss him easily enough.

When they broke, her chest heaved with her deep breaths. Ran's head exploded in memories. *She did this before? What did I do? What do I do? Remember you're training!*

"Was that all the truth you have for me?"

Behind him. He knew it in an instant, though his eighteen year old self had not developed the abilities as yet. He threw his arm out and a sword appeared as though it had been hidden up his sleeve. He ran his brother through.

"NO!" Yasvey screamed.

Only it wasn't Yasvey anymore. It was another woman. One he didn't entirely recognize, yet he felt he should know who she was. "Damn you Ran Grastle. Damn you and the horse you rode in on."

He was himself again. He could tell without looking. "Who are you, bitch?"

"Ohh, what happened to all of your charm?"

He swung his sword up between her breasts. "Answer the question!"

"Let's just say I run the show around here. You passed again, damn your eyes. But we'll see about your friends." She dissolved before his eyes and Ran was left alone. When he turned, he was back in the woods. He turned back and the archway was before him.

"Take your reward, Himanoco," her voice came from the trees. "Move on."

"I see you again girl, we'll have a few more words to exchange." Ran muttered under his breath. It felt odd to be looking at the archway without his friends. "Good luck my companions."

He walked through.

₪

"This is wrong."

No one was around to hear her except the dead stag she carried across her shoulders. She said it out loud anyway though. It didn't make her feel any better.

Candace had been tracing and retracing her footsteps for the better part of three hours now. Every time that she knew she should be back at the clearing where Xesca and Gregor were, there was nothing there. Just more woods.

Finally, her third trip back to where the campsite should have been, she set the stag down and thought for a moment. Why would they have left without her? Where could they have gone that they didn't leave a trail for her to follow?

Fear gripped her. *Maybe they figured out what this arch wanted us to learn and left. They may have already passed to the next level!*

She got up, her kill forgotten. Moving swiftly, she cut her way through the underbrush as easily as a hot knife through butter. There was a clearing up ahead. *Maybe I just hadn't been going far enough.*

It was a town. Not just any town, it was Tuscaway. She was home?

Candace jogged into town, her friends forgotten. All of the buildings looked the same. Night was making slow work of the day, but it would soon be dark and she thought it best to get home before then. The last thing she needed was her father to be angry with her for being in Tuscaway alone, especially at night.

She continued her jog up to the keep that she and her father called home. Castle Orthon never seemed to loom, like most of its brethren had a tendency to do. It was just there, a friendly reminder that the people were always safe in it's shadow. A horse would have been more practical and she wondered why she hadn't been riding.

She walked into the main hall of the keep and flopped down on one of the large, overstuffed benches that lined the room.

"Well Daughter, you may want to explain where it was you were to me instead of facing your father."

Candace spun at the voice. "Mother?"

"None other." She said simply. "Giselle has already started to prepare our chambers for the evening or else it could have very well been her voice that you heard behind you."

"How can this be?"

"Well, you wanted to go down to the city to pick up some items and I told you not alone. Then you went anyway. Now you're back. Did I leave anything out?"

"Mom, you've been dead for my whole life. You died in child birth."

"Really? Well, I felt a bit chilly. Mayhap it's because I have no body heat." She laughed.

"I'm serious!"

"As am I! If I'm not your mother, who am I? And how did you know my voice if you've never heard it before? Did you hit your head?"

Candace's mind whirled. Visions of her father filled her thoughts, and her mother was always there beside him. *This is wrong.*

"Eliece, have you seen Candace?"

"She's in here Mitris. And she seems a bit off."

Candace's father walked into the hall. *Where's his cloak?* she thought. It was immediately followed by *What cloak?* "What seems to be the trouble, Sweetheart?"

"Dad, didn't Mom die at child birth? I'm not making this up, am I?"

"Well, I suppose that your mother can be a bit frigid from time to time," Mitris said with a grin and Eliece gently slapped his arm. "But no, I think that she is still alive."

"Why aren't you wearing your Himanoco cloak?"

"Himanoco? Why would I have a Himanoco cloak? I hate that clan."

Candace's mouth hung agape. *This is wrong!* "But you have been Himanoco my whole life. Grandpa was one too. I got to start my training because of our name." *Training. What about training?*

"Your grandfather is Malada. I am Malada. Your mother is Malada. You will be one as well." Mitris looked as his daughter carefully. "Did you hit your head or something?"

"No I didn't! Would you two quit asking me about my head!"

"What is all the ruckus?" a voice asked.

A boy. Two, maybe three years younger than her. He had her eyes; her father's eyes. "Who is this supposed to be?"

"Oh yes, I died giving birth to you, so I must have never pushed your brother Paxson from my womb either?"

"Brother?"

"Mitris, I am really beginning to get worried about her now. I don't think that she is faking."

More memories. The typically goings on of brother and sister. *I have no siblings. My mother died. This is wrong!*

"What's wrong Candace? You look like you just saw a spook."

Paxson had a sword fastened to his belt. "You aren't going to be Malada."

"You would be right there. I am going to be Gingee. Did you forget or something?"

"Why do I remember this?" Candace raged as she got up. She started backing away from her family. "It doesn't make sense! It's like I have two sets of memories and this one is trying to impose itself on the ones already there. I don't know you people! My mother died. I am going to be Himanoco!"

What about Himanoco? Why do I keep coming back to that? Why did I notice his sword?

"Candace, maybe you better sit back down," Mitris said, coming to his daughter calmly, hands outstretched. "We'll sort all this out together."

"No!" she yelled. "Stay away from me!"

Candace turned and bolted from the castle. She ran toward the backside, to the training fields. She saw Casgill's cabin and bolted straight to it. When she reached it, she began pounding on the door with both her fists.

"By Jehan!" the voice inside yelled. Casgill jerked the door open and regarded Candace. "My lady? What is it that I can do for you?"

"Get me a sword, now!"

"You are training Malada. Don't you want a dagger?"

"Sword, damn your hide! Get me a sword and get out here!" Candace paced to the corner of the training field. "Bring one for yourself too!"

Casgill came out with two of his training blades. "I am *ahin dak* Candace. You can't beat me."

"Throw me the sword and let's see."

He shrugged and threw her the sword. Her family had caught up with her and were beginning to shout now.

"Candace, what are you doing?"

"Why do you keep saying that I died?"

"Sis, you couldn't take Casgill if you wanted to. Probably not even with magic."

"Quiet! All of you! Let me concentrate, by Jehan!" She gripped the sword in her right hand. *Not right. But not as wrong either.* "Come at me."

"Candace," Casgill said quietly, "this is enough."

"Damn you for a coward if you don't come at me with all of your skill right now you overgrown turnip head!"

Casgill launched with the thoughtless speed of someone doing what they were born to do. He was more astounded by the sound than the resistance he felt at the end of his blade.

Candace had swung up to meet his blow. She had done it instinctively. "That all you've got?"

Moving just as quickly as the *ahin dak*, the two traded blows around the practice field. Candace began to laugh, her moves becoming easier and easier as Casgill labored for breath and fought with all of his skill. "Dance with me Casgill. I want to show you some of the steps that I know."

Candace switched her grip. Instead of holding her sword with the point up, she had her hand over the hilt and the point pointed at the ground. Casgill looked confused, but his body continued the attack where his mind would have thought more about what was going on. Swinging her sword overhand, she followed his to the ground.

Now she stood with her back to him. Elbowing him in the ribs, she jammed her foot down on his instep. Casgill stumbled backward, lifting his leg in pain. Changing her grip back to a more traditional hold, she spun again to face her opponent. Sword up, she knocked Casgill's right out of his hand, knowing instinctively where it would be.

Candace leaped in the air and front kicked Casgill right on the chin. He crumbled in a heap. "Come on little brother. You next!"

Paxson started to draw his sword but Mitris grabbed his wrist. "How did you do that?"

"I told you. I have other memories."

"Paxson, summon your grandfather. Candace is possessed."

Paxson looked from his father to his sister, not sure what to do. Candace saw that her mother was dry washing her hands in concern. Mitris threw what looked like a glowing white ball at her. It opened into a cage that held her quick. "Go!" he called at Paxson.

Candace reached into her mind for any memory that would give her a spell out of this trap. Paxson would get their grandfather, who Candace believed also to be already dead in these alternate memories. She needed to escape. *Your cloak would give you the power.*

Suddenly she remembered where she should have been. The stag. The forest. *This is wrong!* Reaching out with her mind again, she drew on all her strength and broke free.

"You are not real! This is a test by the archway! I am Himanoco and you will be too once I am out of this damn tower!"

"Auuuugh!" her mother cried in anguish. It wasn't her mother anymore though. A different woman stood in her place. "Why did you resist? This was everything you ever wanted. A mother, a family! How could you fight all this?"

"I want those things, but not at the cost of Himanoco. I have worked too long!"

"Eighteen years is too long? Try living for centuries and then come to me about too long!"

"You will not plague me anymore. I am leaving this. Now." She shot her sword out from her cloak.

"You can go, I suppose. I would take another try at you, but it wouldn't be fair and he would just interfere anyway." The woman was vanishing before her eyes. "I warn you though, do not think too much of your accomplishment against me. I will remember you well Candace Orthon. If we meet again, things may turn out differently."

"I will remember you too woman, whatever your name may have been. If we meet again, you can count on things turning out differently."

She could see the glow of the archway from behind her. When she turned around, the forest was back and the shimmer was almost blinding. *Mother. Brother. This has cost me so much. Gregor's family we couldn't save. I might kill my planet. Why is it so difficult to get what I want?*

"Why! Why is it so difficult to get what I want!" Tears flow unbidden down Candace's cheek. "I will make whoever is doing this to me pay! I swear by all that I am! Someone will pay for making me cry!"

ת

Gregor awoke quietly. He surveyed the area, trying not to betray too much awareness in case someone was watching him. It looked just like the camp that he had fallen asleep in.

When he turned over, he could not stop his jaw from going slack with shock. Xesca lay on her side, just as she had been when he had fallen asleep. More ever, Candace and Ran were back and were laying around the campfires dying embers.

Gregor bound to his feet. He felt well rested and overall a lot better than he had the past couple of days. His heart hammered with nerves though. "What are all of you doing here?"

Candace yawned and stretched. "What do you mean Gregor?"

"Yeah," Ran said, stifling a yawn of his own. "You were asleep when we came in so we just decided not to wake you."

"When was that?"

"Pretty late. I go sidetracked, coming across some signs of an old roadway and Candace had a tough time finding any game to down."

"Are you hungry Gregor?" Xesca was up now. "We could prepare something for you if you'd like?"

Gregor smiled. "How long would you like me to play along?"

"What do you mean?" Xesca asked.

"Just what I said. How long would you like me to play along?"

"Gregor, you were wrong about that theory that we were being separated. It's not anything to be ashamed about." Xesca smiled and shrugged. "It was feasible right up until those two came back into the camp last night."

"I wasn't wrong Xesca."

"Than what am I still doing here? Where did Candace and Ran reappear from?"

"It isn't you." Gregor said, confidently.

"How can I not be me Gregor? I feel like me."

"I am sure you do Xesca, but I have spent what has felt like close to three weeks with you training in this archway. At the very least, it's been the equivalent of ten days. I have heard you speak the whole time," his eyes gleamed with triumph, "and you haven't used a contraction once. Your grammar is too clipped for 'you'd' and 'it's'. It was a good effort though."

Xesca smiled and changed into a woman that Gregor recognized. "You knew before we even started. I knew that it would be no fun to try this prank on you."

"How are the others doing, fair Malada?"

"Figured that out too have you?" Malada put her hands on her hips and smiled. "Cagey little warrior aren't you. What else do you know?"

"The first belonged to Gingee. In the second, the vampire looked an awful lot like how they describe Kivkavzed. Here you are in the third. Too bad that the fourth level is voluntary. Would Bayer be waiting to try his luck if we go through?"

"What makes you think that it was Gingee and not Himanoco in the first arch?"

"You would let Himanoco in?"

"He is the Blackwolf, as much as I am the Redwolf. These are his archways, not mine. We draw straws."

Gregor laughed at this. "Straws?"

"Himanoco was building these before he destroyed the Wolves. He asked us to add our personas at the time to his creation. We did. Then, he designed the archway so that when it is activated, we awaken. Three out of five to pass. Four out of five to be considered a master acolyte. That is the provision."

"So, Himanoco, Kivkavzed, and you are out of the way," Gregor mused.

"Leaves just the Bluewolf and Brownwolf to deal with. I knew that you were too powerful for me. Honestly, I thought that Greenwolf had you. He's creative and always does a good job when he is anything but the first to go. I am the best lead off test."

"What really happened? What were you five really like?"

"I didn't ask you what you wanted to know, cagey warrior. I asked you what else you knew. It would appear that we have reached the extent of your knowledge. We had decided that it was forbidden to directly interfere in the training with our true selves, but Himanoco pushed that in the first archway. I won't wait around to see if I can find some way of pushing it in this challenge." Malada pointed at the appearance of the archway to the next level and looked at Gregor pointedly.

"I would have enjoyed a longer conversation with you."

"I am sorry, but I am not here for your enjoyment. I am here to challenge you. You pass. Good luck."

₪

Xesca awoke and Gregor was standing over her. "Seems as though you were wrong my friend."

"So it would seem," Gregor said with a shrug. He offered her some venison and Xesca realized it was that smell that had caused her to rouse. "Candace made it back shortly after we both fell asleep it seems. She said that she had had to range out pretty far before she came across any game. Still no word from Ran."

Xesca sat up and looked around. "Where is Candace now?"

"Out scouting a spot for our next campsite. She seems really concerned about Ran and hasn't really wanted to rest at all."

"She went in the same direction as Ran did last night?"

"Yes."

Xesca looked at Gregor thoughtfully, but did not speak the next thought in her mind. *Poor strategy to send a lone warrior to hunt for a missing lone warrior. Not to mention that I think that we would both agree that anything that would detain Ran would most certainly capture Candace.*

Xesca ate her breakfast in quiet contemplation and Gregor did not prompt her for any conversation. Finally, when she was mostly finished, she spoke up again. "How do you feel this morning?"

"Much better. Well rested and ready to go."

"Perhaps we should start after Candace and see if she uncovered anything in regards to Ran's apparent disappearance?"

"I told Candace to return by the time the sun reaches it's apex. Give her time to scout the area and see what she can do on her own."

"This is not just a challenge for her, it is a challenge for all of us," Xesca admonished. "I think that it would be best if we did not wait."

"Xesca, be patient. Everything will be fine."

Xesca regarded Gregor more closely. She reached out with her cloak to sense if there was any illusion present on him, now that she had had more exposure to it's usage.

"What are you doing?" Gregor asked, startled.

"Checking to see how your healing has progressed."

"You did a fine job on me, I'll be fine."

Xesca drew her sword. "I did nothing to you. I am not a healer." She took a ready stance. "Reveal yourself to me or face me in open combat."

Gregor seemed to shimmer slightly with light and was replaced by an attractive woman who appeared to be human and youngish, no older than Gregor himself. "Damn you all and the way that you pay attention to detail. I cannot remember the last time a more suspicious group of trainees entered my task."

"What did you do with my companions?"

"Nothing. They are fine, and so are you. I may have shaken Candace up a bit, but she'll recover just fine." The woman motioned with her hands and the archway appeared behind Xesca. "You have passed this trial. You are free to attend to the next."

Xesca looked at the archway and then back at the woman. "I should not enter the archway until I know that my companions are all safe."

"Well, you won't know until you enter the archway," the woman said, snidely, "since all of your companions have already passed and are ready to come out on the next level."

"Who are you?" Xesca asked.

"Don't you know yet, Xesca, daughter of Queklian? Have you not deduced?"

"Malada?"

"The one and only."

"But," Xesca made her sword vanish and came forward. "how can that be?"

"I already took the liberty of explaining all that I intend to explain to your friend Gregor. Ask him for details. Take your prize and leave me in peace."

Xesca headed to the arch, then stopped. She was not ready to go quite yet. "Why did you send Himanoco to our planet?"

"I did nothing of the sort. The real Malada may have had a hand in it, I am uncertain."

"How can you be Malada and call someone else 'the real Malada'?"

Malada sighed deeply with impatience. "I am Malada as she saw herself at the time of the creation of this particular set of arches. People have been passing through this archway for centuries and we are always here. They have told me that I was supposed to be dead, so I naturally assume that the me that existed in changeable time and space has ceased to be. Does this make sense to you?"

"Some what." Xesca said truthfully.

"I have all the knowledge of Malada up until the time of the making of this tower, as well as all the knowledge that I have personally amassed by testing Blackwolf trainees low these centuries. The event that you speak of, 'sending Himanoco to a planet', if there were more green skin people like you on this planet, I have no knowledge of it. I have never seen one of your kind before this moment."

"You would tell me if you knew?"

"My dear, there is precious little to enjoy in a life of servitude that will never end unless this tower is destroyed. Even if the tower were destroyed and my quasi life were ended, I would have no knowledge of it, no flash of memories, no last second words to take down. I tell you with all candidness that I was not a nice person then and have soured over the years, so if I could torture you with the reason, it would be so much more fun than to torture you with fact that I just do not know."

Xesca was truly flabbergasted and had no notion of what she should possibly say. So, without a single word more, she turned and ran straight through the archway.

Chapter 27

Interlude: Back in the tower 3

Each of the foursome came out of the archway, each had prepared for the shock of the different level of light and already had their hands shading their eyes. "Congratulations, you have all completed the third level and are now Himanoco warriors. It is now time to decide if you would like to become Himanoco masters."

"Save your breath, Master Defalorn," Gregor said, "we all are going to go on."

"You speak for the cordon?" Defalorn asked.

"Yes, he does," Xesca said with a note of finality in her voice. "He has almost the whole time."

"Before we go on though," Candace interjected, "can we talk amongst ourselves for a few minutes?"

"About?"

"The last archway separated us and made us face it alone," Gregor explained. "I'm guessing that the challenge was harder on Candace and Ran because they did not know it was going to do that like Xesca and I did."

"How did you know what it was going to do?" Ran asked.

"It made sense, based on what the other trials had been like. You two not returning to camp was what had solidified it for me."

"It gave me my mother!" Candace cried out. "I had a brother! A bitch of a woman played an awful trick and I want to hurt her more than anyone I've ever met!"

Xesca took her hand gently. "That 'bitch' was Malada."

"Malada?" Ran and Defalorn said at the same time.

"Just as it was Himanoco in the first archway and Kivkavzed in the second. Only Gingee and Bayer remain and it's a crap shoot to see which one we'll get."

"Gregor, what nonsense is this?" Defalorn said, obviously not believing a word.

"Have the arches never revealed themselves to you Master?" Xesca asked.

"The Wolves are dead," Defalorn said simply. "Pass through the last archway for confirmation."

"The Wolves *are* dead," Gregor interjected, "but that doesn't mean some portion of them doesn't still exist. The clans are living proof. You said yourself that the arches are mysterious in origin and usage."

"You seem to think that you have solved the mystery." Defalorn said, still unable to hide a thunderstruck look on his face.

"Malada told us who she was," Xesca explained simply, still rubbing Candace's back slowly, soothingly. "She explained many things."

"And you think that, because the archway told you that it was projecting the original Wolfwarriors, it is true?"

"Master, it makes too much sense not to be true," Ran said, quietly. All eyes fixed on him, since he had said so little. "I'm older than these companions of mine, and I have heard more tales. We are forming a vergeance. Powers are flowing here that even you don't fully grasp. Step aside and let us surpass you."

Defalorn had no response. His jaw worked as though he were talking, but no sound came out. Candace dried her eyes and stood up proud. "There is nothing left for you to give to us Master," Gregor said. "We'll face this challenge and we will be back just as quickly as we can."

Chapter 28

Master Training Begins

The foursome walked through the archway in the Himanoco Tower and emerged in a large room. The walls were made of stone and mortar, and the feel was of a common room or foyer of a castle. Each wall sported an ornate tapestry of different colors and designs.

"No windows," Xesca remarked.

"That's significant to you?" Candace asked.

"Buildings on my planet do not have windows."

"No door either," Ran said.

Gregor drew his sword. The others followed suit. "Stand ready."

The pattern on the tapestry to the right of the group began to swirl. They spread out in the foyer so that each of the four could get a clear shot at the tapestry, should an attack be coming. Gregor kept his eyes on the rest of the room, while Ran chanted softly to release a battle magic blast.

A man walked out from the tapestry. "I have conferred with the others. I know what you know and what they have striven to teach. My name is Gingee."

"What is it that you will teach us, oh mighty Bluewolf?" Xesca asked reverently.

"Don't give him too much credit dear," Ran said, his right hand glowing white. He balled it into a fist, "I don't think we should revere any of these Wolves anymore."

"All too true," Gingee said simply. "Himanoco broke the rules when he showed you that he could come back into existence. For his part, Kivkavzed played it straight. Malada explained far too much in her test. Now you have me.

"I have no love of you or what you stand for, I'll tell you that much. However," a sadness entered Gingee's face and voice, "you will leave this portal and I will not. Therefore, it is best that we get a few things taught to you." He motioned and all the tapestries on the remaining walls began to swirl like the first. "For my test, I too will separate you. And, since so many other taboos have already been revealed, so now shall I follow suit.

"Each of the four tapestries will show you what you need to know, based on the things you've asked and the actions that you've taken.

The beauty of the Malada Archway, and these are her design, even if Himanoco made some modifications, is that it can show a user all of the possible outcomes of their actions, allowing you to test several strategies in real time situations. Malada's Archway could be programmed to reflect the 'real world'. Himanoco's Archway draws the essence of everyone that passes through it into itself and we then can create tasks based on the 'real world'.

"I need you to know what has been going on these past three months while you have been toiling here in the training tower. I will need you to prepare for what could possibly come. Most of all, I need you to help all the Wolfwarrior clans, as sour a taste that thought leaves in my mouth."

"You aren't supposed to be able to do magic." Candace said simply

"It is a misconception of the universe that I have no magical prowess. The same with Bayer. We could use magic, we chose not to out of a purity of clan and power."

"What is so important that we have to see things separately? Why can't we all experience the four tapestries together?"

"Because, Prince Holden," Gingee smiled mischievously, "I say so."

"And if we refuse?" Candace asked.

"I know how you battled my acolytes while waiting to enter this training," Gingee shot her a withering glance. "Of all the people that I have to help, the fact that you are involved irks me the most."

Candace reddened slightly but didn't back down. "So why do it then? You're so high and mighty, how do we know you aren't just playing with us? How do we know that anything you say or anything that we see be taken seriously?"

"The lass has a valid point," Ran said, still ready to attack. "Everyone else has been setting us up to fail. Why don't you seem to be?"

"Fine," Gingee sighed, "I'll tell you more. But then, you should really begin working on this.

"As you are already aware of, each of us had our own, personal weapons, armor, shields, and such. Even Bayer, the fist. These items have been imbued with our essence, our very souls, if you want to use the word. Gathered together, wielded by a true acolyte, we can overtake their essence with our own and are effectively reborn.

"Much of the universe has changed and four out of the five of us believe that there is no room for us anymore. The fifth, Bayer, drew the right to this test and the other four of us held him back so that I could come. We want you four to find a way to stop us from returning by gathering all of our items and keeping them in safer places. This is the task that we are here to teach you. This is what will make you masters.

And I despise the fact that the forsaken's acolytes are the chosen ones, but what can I do? For all of his shortcomings, he was still the best.

"Now," he finished, motioning again, "will the four of you get on with it already."

"Move to the center of the room, so we can all back into the tapestries and still keep our eye on you," Gregor commanded.

Still smiling, Gingee bowed to acknowledge the request and backed slowly to the center of the room, his hands held out in a submissive way. Each of the four of them held their swords trained on him incase he decided to make a move.

"Everyone, on three," Gregor called.

"Good luck everyone," Xesca said.

"One…Two…Now!" Gregor shouted.

All four backed into their respective tapestries and vanished.

Chapter 29

Candace Alone

Candace emerged back in the same room that she had just left. "What in Jehan is this?"

"I'm not sure," Gregor said, looking just as surprised.

The room had changed slightly so that all the tapestries were gone and now a door appeared. Ran and Xesca were standing with the same confused looks upon their faces. Gingee still stood in the middle of the room, the same smile on his face.

"You really are dense aren't you." He didn't make it a question. "Did I not just get through explaining how you were facing the four possible futures separately, yet you would each be making choices based on the probability? I will be sorely disappointed if I had to explain this to all four of you each time one of you emerges from my tapestries."

"You really are an evil man," Xesca said simply. "Why do you chastise us for asking questions about our situation?"

"Because I think that the questions that you ask are beneath both you and I. Use your brains for the love of Jehan."

"Can I kill him please?" Ran asked.

"Bloodthirsty, isn't he?" Gingee said to Xesca.

"And I would not provoke him further if I were you," Xesca said pointedly.

"My my," he chuckled, "it would appear that your companions attitude has started to rub on you Xesca."

"Just let us out of here," Candace said.

"Just a moment now," Gingee held up a hand in apology. "There are some more things that you should know.

"First, unlike the first three archways, you can not wash out of this. By accepting my invitation, you are masters. The reason for this is we want you to try to succeed with no qualms about your own death. We know that sometimes sentimentality overcomes a human and they will sacrifice themselves for the greater good.

"Second, it is very important to pay attention to everything that happens. If you ever hope to change things, or if you want things to go the way they went in this archway, you need observe and act. Since things are individualized, and Candace, this is your tapestry, bear in mind your responsibility to this expedition." Gingee moved out of the way and motioned to the door. "Good luck."

Xesca fired a beam of battle magic that caught Gingee in the right leg, about mid-calf. He screamed in pain. "Xesca!" Candace exclaimed.

"I could not abide his smugness anymore. He will not remain hurt after we leave in any case."

Ran laughed heartily and even Gregor cracked a smile. Candace was still a little shaken we she said, "Come on you three, we need to get started."

They exited the only door in the tower room and emerged in an open field. They were surrounded by what looked to be ten thousand fellow Blackwolf warriors. Across the field, approximately three hundred yards, were another batch of Blackwolf warriors and it looked as though these two groups were ready to fight.

"Where are we?" Candace asked.

"Frotnefalt," Xesca said, with a certain amount of awe. "Believed to be the birthplace of Malada herself."

"You still sound reverent to these Wolves," Ran said. "I think that we may have misplaced our admiration over the years. Good warriors they may have been, but they seem morally bankrupt."

"Can we claim otherwise?" Gregor asked. "If we are as powerful as we seem, even amongst our own clan, how long until that absolute power corrupts absolutely?"

"Is this the place that we should be discussing this?" Candace asked. "What is happening?"

"War," Mitris said simply. Candace gasped as her father stood before her. "Clan war. We are the last and we stand now on Frotnefalt praying that the Malada will come to our aid and not Kenor's."

"How did we get to war?" Candace asked

"What are we supposed to learn?" Xesca asked

"I know..." Gregor said quietly. They all looked at him and his eyes began to roll in his head. "I know it all." He thrust his sword arm out in front of him, and the others felt compelled to form a ring around him. They each put their arm out in similar fashion and between them, their swords appeared. Each of their sword points touched and in the center where all points came together, another sword appeared.

"By Jehan above and below," Mitris cursed softly, "you can actually call the Sword of Himanoco."

"Candace, this is your challenge," Gregor said softly, sounding more like the voice of Gingee than his own, "take the sword and see what you can do."

Candace put her sword away in a swirl of cloak and took the Sword of Himanoco in her hand. Thoughts flooded her mind, making her breathe rapidly. So many battles, this sword had drank so much blood over it's lifetime. She felt a longing for use, a desire to kill oozing from the hilt of the blade.

"This is horrible," Candace said staring at the sword as if it were the most disgusting thing in the universe. "It can think."

"What can think?" Gregor asked. He seemed to be coming out of a dream and his voice was a little wispy.

"The sword." Candace shuddered. "It wants to kill. It likes it."

"Himanoco liked power," Xesca said, "and the sword likes to kill. Perhaps Gingee was wrong and it is not their own spirits that will come through the weapons, but their own desires?"

"But Himanoco in the first archway?" Ran protested.

"That was his version of events he thought would happen. Just as this is Gingee's. But do they know? Did they ever try to posses someone through their weapons and armor?"

"So here, even in Gingee's little 'test', the sword can't act like anything but the way it is supposed to," Gregor mused, "or is Gingee protecting you from experiencing the full effect of the sword?"

"What are all of you talking about?" Mitris asked. "They are about to charge!"

Candace swung her attention and saw that most of the company around them were standing with the same awestruck looks that her father wore. Across the field, the other group of Himanoco were beginning to stir in their ranks.

Candace felt her way through the sword, testing it to see if their was some sort of presence inside, someone she could converse with. All she felt was a general malevolence and desire to hurt something. That feeling she could supress, she thought.

She also felt the memories again. Past battles, strategies, spells and power were their at her beckon call. If she opened her mind, they would rush in with the information that she would need.

If I open my mind, she thought, *then the sword will take me over. Is that how it can control it's user, by forcing them to rely heavily on what it knows? Well, not me. Jehan give my the strength to control my own mind when I ask you now, cursed sword, what can you do?*

As if a voice whispered softly in her ear, *I can do any task your will sets before me. Have I not shown you that already?*

Candace closed her eyes and grasped the sword tightly in both hands, *Give me mass spells of protection for my companions.*

Protection, the sword scoffed, *I am a weapon, not armor. Why would you waste my abilities on protection?*

Just do it, you evil little thing.

Very well. The sword used her own voice, and Candace heard herself chanting in a language she had never known, a spell she had never heard.

When she finished, she opened her eyes and could see that everyone within the sound of her voice had a light blue hue surrounding them.

What did you do?

A spell of protection. Their skin will turn three death blows from a solid weapon. I don't know any protection against magic, so please don't ask me.

"They charge!" Gregor called.

Candace looked around frantically. "Gregor?"

"I don't know if we are supposed to be taking someone's lead or not, personally, I don't care," Gregor said loudly. "Ran, Xesca, lay us down some battle magic to beat the band. Candace, whip up a laser or two to try and slow these mother's down." Gregor chanted under his breath and began to kick up a wind.

We need more than lasers and wind, we need a spell.

Then ask me and I shall deliver.

No! Candace screamed in her head. *I do not invite you in. You are just a sword!*

And Himanoco was just a warrior. What do you think it is that makes you all so great. Inborn skill and leaned talents make a warrior good. A good weapon makes a warrior great.

"No!" Candace shouted. She threw the sword point down in the ground. "I will not!"

"Candace," Mitris called out, "the sword!" He came over and grabbed the Sword of Himanoco.

"Father no!"

Mitris' eyes turned from their normal playful blue to a steel gray. "The power..." he whispered. "How could you ever have given this up?"

"Father, please, don't. The sword will take you over."

"But we will destroy them all!" Mitris roared. He pointed the sword as Kenor's troops hit their lines with full force. Streams of power, to rival any battle magic anyone had ever seen, spewed forth into the battle. Bodies of both sides were disintegrated everywhere that the beam touched.

"Mitris," Gregor called, breaking his spell, "you are hurting your own! Don't use the sword if you don't have better control than that!"

But if Mitris could hear Gregor's cries, he gave no sign. He just kept the sword pointed into clusters of battling Himanoco and fired the beams of energy.

"Ran," Gregor yelled, "Xesca, we have to take Mitris down and get the sword away from him."

"Don't hurt my father!"

"Candace!" Ran roared. "He's hurting us!"

I can still feel you in my mind sword. Why?

I only serve the one who calls me forth. It takes all four of you to call to me, but you were the one that wielded me this time. I serve you until you put me away. If someone else uses me, I take them over until you come back to claim me. This one is an acolyte, like you, but not as powerful. He is easy to overcome.

Return to my hand, now!

And if I refuse?

NOW!

The Sword of Himanoco flew out of Mitris' hand and straight into Candace's. *What would you have of me now?*

Same spell, but better control. I can distinguish which warriors I want you to hit. Feed off of them.

Feed? You will allow me to feed?

Do what I ask and I reward you. Deal?

Yes!

Candace opened her eyes and the sword began to dance in her hand. She rushed forward into the thick of the battle, her companions on her flank. As the sword bit into flesh, smaller, more precise beams of battle magic shot in all directions and felled each of their targets.

They saw him. Standing tall and battling ferociously was Kenor Anor. He had some light wounds on his person and the sword showed Candace how those wounds were healing so quickly that soon they would all be gone. *Himanoco's Armor.*

You know this?

I served the same warrior with it for over four centuries. We know each other.

You can pierce it?

The sword laughed. *Allow me to find out. Please!*

Candace screamed. "Stay back, all of you. Kenor is mine!"

She rushed forward. *I am not the best sword. I am not the best magic user. Gregor should be meeting this challenge. Ran. Xesca. Anyone but me.*

You have me and you have yourself. The sword's attitude actually seemed to be softening. *You called me forth. We can win.*

Why the sudden change in attitude?

I am full on the blood of warriors. I am challenging a suit of armor that is as strong as I am. This is what I enjoy most in my existence and you have given these things to me. Why would I not be pleased and try to help you?

What does the armor feed on? Another four steps and their swords would ring out.

Life. I feed on death, the mace on suffering, and the armor on life.

He wasn't wearing it in the murals, Candace remembered as Kenor swung his sword up to meet her. *Pictures of his greatest battles and he didn't have his own armor on?*

Himanoco rarely wore the armor when he knew that the battle would be long and hard. It would weaken him as much as it would sustain.

They danced. Feinting, thrusting, parrying and dodging, Candace and Kenor were fighting to the death. *So small wounds?*

Better in the long run than a death blow. He might still be strong enough to draw the power from the armor and keep himself alive.

Magic then, in small sparks every time that the swords meet. Shower him with burns.

Good plan.

The battle was epic. Most of the other, smaller skirmishes began to stop so people could form a ring around the two combatants. Every time that their swords struck each other, Kenor would be showered in sparks that were burning into his arms as well as the armor.

The armor is vain, the sword spoke in Candace's mind. *It will draw his strength to heal itself if he doesn't direct it. Keep him occupied and I will focus my attacks on the armor itself, making it look like I am trying to find a way through it.*

Candace changed her approach. Her mind flashed to another one on one battle where she (he) had to get through another powerful defense. She (he) remembered using a spell to strike the defense time and time again. *Don't put thoughts in my mind unless I ask! I am fighting for my life here!*

I'm just trying to help. Don't get so angry.

She struck with battle magic that she didn't know she could call a moment ago. Kenor laughed as the beam hit the armor full on and caused just a small amount of damage.

"Stick to the sword, foolish girl," he said, pressing her back with his blows. "Your magic is nothing against Himanoco's Armor."

The sparks were getting into the damaged part of the armor, causing more damage. "Magic will be your undoing, Kenor," Candace said, panting. "You've forgotten that Himanoco controls both."

"What do you think that this armor is, silly girl? It's magic has healed all the damage that you have done, as well as protected itself."

Candace spun and pivoted and caught Kenor in the high thigh with a slicing blow. He fell back a little, stunned. The blow was not deep though, and the armor went to work at once. Another blast of battle magic rocked Kenor off his feet and damaged the repaired armor.

If he uses his magic, I can block it.

I thought you couldn't protect me against magic?

I know of no mass spells that defend against magic, but nothing can hurt me. I taught Himanoco that spell, as well as the spell of belonging, so all of the acolytes could perform it.

Can you break the armor now?

Soon. He's weakening; slowing. It won't be long now and an opening will appear and we will slice through.

Kenor was on his feet in a flash. Rushing forward, he and Candace continued the dance. Time ticked on and all other skirmishes had halted. The entire field watched to see which side of Himanoco's clan would gain supremacy. Candace noticed some Malada markings in the gathering crowd. They were just as confused about what to do and awestruck at the awesome battle as the Himanoco.

Now Candace, the sword rang in her mind. *NOW!*

Again, she pressed forward. The blade sought entrance eagerly and Candace could feel it's desire pressing upon her as when she first picked it up. It wanted to prove that it was the stronger of Himanoco's items. It wanted to taste this adversary's blood. And, to her surprise, Candace found that she wanted nothing more than to give the sword what it wanted.

Kenor's parry slipped. It seemed that his arms had gotten too heavy to lift. Candace ran him through, the Sword of Himanoco cutting through Himanoco's Armor like it was paper. Kenor's face was a portrait of pain and surprise. He slumped to his knees as she pulled her blade back out.

We must remove the armor. It clasps on the shoulders.

Candace hit both clasps with magic from the sword and the armor opened as Kenor fell on his face in the dirt. His back was blood soaked from the sword's exit wound.

Gregor, Ran, and Xesca came forward as the circle tried to decide what it should do. It was Gregor's voice that rang out on the wings of the wind.

"No one challenges. Malada's clan is recognized for coming to the aid of Himanoco, but now is excused. Blackwolf warriors will not bite their brothers and sisters anymore. This cordon holds both the Sword of Himanoco and Himanoco's Armor. We wield where others falter." Some sidelong glances were taken at Mitris and he hung his head in shame. "All of Kenor Anor's decrees are naught. All who followed him shall not be chastised for their actions. They were not disloyal to Blackwolf, for all they knew his claim was true. They are admitted back by their own forsaken brethren and the clan is once again whole."

He is better suited for the armor. It will enjoy him.

What do you mean, enjoy?

That one stands for justice, if not for adventure. He is patient and forgiving. He will not kill unless provoked. You will kill to bargin. I am better suited for you.

What about Ran and Xesca?

The Ohalian is not suited for any of us. Too much logic. The Balderian is more suited for the Mace. It will come to us without having to search like the dead man did.

Why?

Silly girl, we would respond to any true acolyte. You just have to know how to call, with a cordon. Four are trained, one to anchor, one to fight, one to protect, and one destroy. When all four come forth together, they can call the items of Himanoco forth just as they can their own weapons and cloaks.

So, to be a true acolyte, you have to be shown this. Why haven't others learned this?

What makes you think that no others have?

Candace saw the faces of the former owners of the sword, all the way back to Himanoco himself. *You've been busy.*

Give him the armor, the Earthling. It will bind the rest of the clan to us.

Us?

I am you partner if you want me Candace. I will not use you. Much.

That is so much more reassuring.

What can I say? Do you want reassurance or do you want to win?

"Gregor," she said, "put on the armor. The sword wants you to."

Gregor looked down at the bloodstained ground. He bent down to put the armor on when suddenly, to Candace's shock, the entire world froze.

Gingee walked among the frozen faces toward Candace. "Excellent job Miss Orthon. I am quite pleased."

"What are you so happy about?"

"The sword chose you. It chose out who should use what in your cordon. I must say that I was uncertain if you or one of your companions would be able to wield the sword so fluently. It will modify the other tapestries. Gregor is next, I think."

"But, what did I learn that was so important?"

"By Jehan, don't you realize that this is all about to happen?" Gingee was livid. "As soon as you come out of the Master's archway, Defalorn is going to usher you to this very field. Kenor will be standing across from you, wearing that very armor." He surveyed the area. "The only thing that I would do different is make sure that the sword never falls into your fathers hands. He is far to willing."

"This is all about to happen..." Candace stammered.

"And you want it to happen. You can try to call the armor like you did the sword, that was brilliant, I must say."

"Call the armor?"

"Like the sword said," Gingee smiled in spite of everything, "and no, I didn't modify that. That is how the Sword of Himanoco really is, because Himanoco's memories are a part of this."

"So, is that all?"

Instead of an answer, Gingee bowed deeply and the archway appeared behind him. It sucked her through without a word.

Chapter 30

Gregor Alone

Gregor emerged back in the same room that he had just left. Ran, Candace, and Xesca all looked at him uncertainly. "Nice touch."

"What do you mean, 'nice touch'?" Candace asked with concern.

"He's making this as real as he can by taking us right back to where we were," Gregor motioned to Gingee. "And since he said that our decisions were what he wanted, it stands to reason that you all are here too."

"Excellent work Master Holden," Gingee lauded. "I am quite pleased that at least you deduced what was going on. Now, a brief explanation.

"First, unlike the first three archways, you can not wash out of this. By accepting my invitation, you are masters. The reason for this is we want you to try to succeed with no qualms about your own death. This is the second challenge faced and I was quite pleased with the results of the first.

"Second, it is very important to pay attention to everything that happens. If you ever hope to change things, or if you want things to go the way they went in this archway, you need observe and act. Gregor, this is your tapestry, so it has fallen on you to make sure that everything goes well with this particular challenge." Gingee motioned to the door. "Good luck in your endeavors."

Ran regarded Gingee threateningly as they left. "Leave him alone Ran," Gregor said softly, "it won't accomplish anything."

"Fine," Ran growled and they all went out.

The scene immediately changed to one Gregor was completely unfamiliar with. A lone ranch house stood off in the distance. A small knoll rolled out behind it to a line of deciduous trees. Cicadas and crickets sang in the night.

"By Jehan," Candace muttered softly, "is that Himanoco that just came out of the wood line?"

They all looked as a man dressed in black emerged, walking slowly but surely toward the house. What little light was there shone on his silver gauntlets. The sigil, black on black and in low light was still unmistakable.

"It is Himanoco," Xesca whispered. "Where are we?"

"I know this legend," Ran said under his breath. "This is the night that he kills his brother wolves."

"I've heard that," Gregor spoke up. "'A lone ranch house wearing night's mask. A small table did they fill. They would sit and decide a task. Until the night that three were killed.'"

"Not a perfect rhyme," Xesca said.

"Easy there teach," Gregor laughed, "I didn't make it up."

"He's going in," Candace hissed. "Should we follow."

"Let's get closer at least," Gregor motioned. As they got up to the house, keeping in the shadows, they noticed a window into a kitchen with a small kitchen table. "Do any of you guys know some sort of spell that they might not notice but will still let us listen in?"

"Amazingly enough, I do," a voice said from behind them.

They all whirled, swords at the ready, not caring who saw. Malada stood before them. "I am as surprised to see you all as you are to see me. I do ask however that you keep your voices down. This is educational."

"What the hell is this for? We can't change anything!"

"Quite right Gregor. But you need to know these things."

"How do you know us?" Candace asked. "You didn't know who we were in this time."

"Silly girl, you no more exist in this time than I do."

"I just don't understand this stuff."

"Candace, what she means is that this is not the time frame that Himanoco killed the other male wolves, it is a copy of that," Xesca said patiently, putting her sword away. "And since we are still in the tower, in the archway were she has already met us, of course she knows who we are."

"If anything, the question is simply this," Gregor looked at Malada. "You stood outside and watched this happen?"

"Yes."

"Why? They were your companions."

"They were more than that. They were my family. They were my *only* companions. I don't know how this is going to sound to you, and I apologize to whoever Gingee chose to see this, because you are getting cheated, but I'll do what I can.

"You already know that this is my creation that Himanoco modified. But, what you may or may not realize is that if this was my creation, don't you think that I had been using them all along? I found all four of my brothers. I recruited them. They were the family that I built."

"You recruited them?" Ran asked.

"I recruited them. I explored far and wide in my archways. More lifetimes of information than a human would normally have acquired. I found these four warriors every time I tried to subjugate the universe. One of them would stand in my way unless I convinced them to join me. The only one I wasn't sure about Himanoco.

"Gingee was first. We were lovers, he and I. Closer than all the others, we worked together on most everything. I thought that together we could take Himanoco, but it would be better to have him join us like the others had. Gingee said no at first, but I convinced him otherwise.

"Himanoco found out how to prolong our lives. We were in our three and four hundreds when the event that you could turn and witness happened. Gingee thought he had been wrong and that it was right and good that we had Himanoco join. I knew otherwise. I knew that he was planning to turn."

"And still," Candace cried out and the others hissed at her to be quiet. "And still you did nothing!"

"What would you have me do?" Malada threw her hands in the air in exasperation. "Kill him for what might have happened? Warn them? You don't think I warned them to be careful with him? I didn't live long enough in the archway to see what would happen when he joined. I didn't know he would turn until he was already a member of our clan!"

"Look," Ran whispered.

They turned back to the scene. Three men lay dead at the table and the fourth, Himanoco, was looking at them out the window. In a flash he had a portal open behind him. In another flash, he appeared outside the house, right in front of the group.

"Malada? You were here?"

"Of course I was. Did you think that I didn't know what you would do? Malada the gentile, who always seemed to know exactly what to do and when to do it? I showed you this creation, when I showed no one else. You think that I didn't use it?"

"You didn't stop me."

"I will. I will kill you in three months time. You would have known that if you had any imagination in you, but I knew that you wouldn't use my archways in that matter. What I had never guessed and didn't find out until just now was how little the universe would remember the story.

"So enlighten your followers, my dear Himanoco. Give them reason to an otherwise disjointed story. Tell them why you did what you did, they are dying to know."

Himanoco turned to face Gregor, "You don't know do you. You didn't know before when you faced me in the first archway."

"No one knows."

"Simply put, I didn't want to battle anymore. After three hundred years, I was exhausted. Then, ravaging the Ohlian home world because of a task that Gingee, Bayer, and Kivkavzed agreed should be done, I was disheartened."

"That is why you do not know who I am," Xesca said, turning to Malada. "You did not vote on the mission to my planet."

363

"I knew that they were going there, but I knew nothing about the inhabitants," Malada agreed.

"Bayer had stumbled across them and thought that their longevity may be a threat to us," Himanoco continued. "He convinced Kivkavzed and they convinced Gingee. He didn't want to consult you. I was chosen to go, since I was becoming the one with the largest number of acolytes. The people of the planet were peaceable. They were unprepared. My acolytes and I routed them. I felt horrible. I wanted to be done.

"But you know how it is Malada," Himanoco looked at her, almost sheepishly, "you would have never let me go. If I had left, the four remaining wolves would have hunted me down and killed me. I had hoped that you and I could reach an agreement."

There was a pause where no one was exactly sure what to say. "This isn't the story that I want to know," Gregor said finally.

"What do you want to know Gregor?" Himanoco asked.

"I want to know why Malada disappeared instead of rebuilding the wolf clans."

"That isn't a question that I can answer," Malada said simply. "I don't know where my reality self went."

"You have a theory though."

Malada looked at Gregor shrewdly. "You're right, I do. I don't think I went anywhere at all. I think that I am still alive and have been so for the past several millennia. Much like Himanoco, I was becoming exhausted with war. Gingee had become so bloodthirsty and Bayer distrusted everything." She looked over at Candace. "Yet another reason that I did not stop him, mistress Orthon, was that I wanted out as much as he did."

"You still killed him." Candace spat.

"I wanted out. It didn't mean I had to forgive."

"Who would you be in our reality?" Ran asked.

"Hard to say really. I know how I felt at the time I joined with this archway. I know how I felt when I had found out what the real Himanoco had done, just as he knows how he felt. I would guess that I would still be a member of my clan, and a high ranking one."

"Do you have any ideas on how we can flush you out?" Gregor asked.

"Only that I will want to reveal myself. I hate not having the attention of the truly powerful. Show that you are truly powerful and I will come to you."

"I can't believe that you did that," Gingee said from behind them all.

Himanoco and Malada were the quickest. They both attempted to attack him with battle magic, but it passed right through. Himanoco drew his sword, but Gingee was quicker and instead of attacking, Himanoco was on the defensive.

"We were a clan!" Gingee raged, forcing Himanoco back. Everyone else was looking at each other, not really sure what to do. "We were lovers! You could have stopped him!"

"I couldn't stop him and you know it," Malada had drawn a dagger that no one had seen and had almost stabbed Gingee in the throat. He had moved at the last minute and she ended up leaving a large gash down his neck. Gingee quickly waved his arms for the archway to appear and a wind sucked Gregor through it in an instant.

Chapter 31

Xesca Alone

Xesca emerged in the same chamber that she had just left. Candace was regarding her, a confused look on her face. "It is fine Candace. This is my tapestry. He has used the archway trick to make sub arches out of the tapestries that he had us enter. Unique."

"Two out of three so far," Gingee said with a bow. "I submit to your deductive reasoning."

"Just get on with it," Ran growled. "I don't like this at all."

"Touchy," Gingee teased. "Now then, to explain. You can not wash out of this archway, even if you are killed. Since you entered into the tapestry that I provided for you, you are considered a master. The reason for this is we want you to try to succeed with no qualms about your own death. This is the third challenge faced and I will let you know that your predecessors set the bar high.

"Secondly and more important is to be aware of everything that happens. Pay close attention, because I am going to throw you into a projected future. This is your opportunity to experiment with the archway's powers." Gingee bowed again and motioned them to the door.

"Who have you tested so far?" Gregor asked.

"Not a concern."

"It is to me."

"Gregor, what does it matter. You will all be done soon enough."

"Because," Xesca interjected, "decisions we have already made will affect the decisions that we are going to make. It would be quite helpful to know who has already been deciding things for us. Even more helpful would be to know what they have decided."

Gingee sighed. "So far, I have seen the results from Candace and Gregor's tapestry. I won't tell you what they did for fear the it will cloud what you do in this test."

"Very well. Gregor, Candace, Ran, let us go." The foursome headed out through the door and emerged at the Alden Hall campus. Ran, Candace and Gregor all showed signs of having aged. Xesca estimated that it had been approximately fifteen to twenty years.

"We're older," Ran said, his voice more raspy and less playful than it had been moments ago.

"Sixteen years," Gregor said. "I know that. I don't know why I know that, but I do know that."

"Why are we back at Alden Hall?" Candace asked.

"You work here," Ran noticed. Candace's clothing had change to match what Defalorn had been wearing when they went into the archway. "You are apparently the Himanoco instructor here."

"And look at how many other changes," Gregor commented. All around them, students bustled to and fro. To their eyes, it appeared that one in every five was bearing the Blackwolf pin. "You see all these Himanoco trainees?"

"Seven hundred twenty six this year," Candace said by rote, then caught herself. "Seven hundred twenty six? There were only twenty sixteen years ago when we tested."

"Seems to me that we are the flavor of the week," Gregor said, astounded.

"There are more dormitories, more classrooms, more everything." Xesca had found a map of the grounds posted nearby. "This academy has started training Blackwolf warriors from the onset, instead of just letting them gather skills and then come here to finish."

"We did this," Ran said quietly. "It just came to me. We had a battle. It was a large one. People heard that we had the power of the Blackwolf. We told the story. The clan isn't nearly as forsaken as it used to be."

"Students started coming," Gregor continued. "We started teaching swordskill and magical disciplines. We aren't full time members here but still teach from time to time. All but you Candace. You took over Defalorn's job."

"This is all interesting, but not anything that we had to know," Xesca said. "What is it that this is supposed to be showing us?"

"Mistress Orthon! Mistress Orthon!" A Himanoco student was running in the foursome's direction. "The other master's are here in your ready room off of your office."

"Thank you, young Adept. That will be all." He saluted and left quickly.

"Adept?" Ran asked.

"It's the next level up from Trainee. Then Partisan. Then they can take the Arch trials." Candace was astounded again. "How do I know all of this?"

"We created that too?" Gregor smiled. "Leave it to us to revolutionize an entire system of learning that had been going on for thousands of years. We are a vain bunch, aren't we?"

"We had better get going and find out what it is that people are gathering for."

The four moved across the campus in a sea of saluting students. Finally, they reached Alden Hall and went up the stairs to Himanoco

Master's office. The mural and illusionary hallway was still in place. "Good to see we didn't change everything," Ran joked.

They went into Candace's office and through to the ready room. Six Himanoco warriors, four men and two women were seated around a table. That left one chair and Candace took it, her friends standing around her.

"Candace, I didn't think that the rest of your cordon would be here," one of the men said nervously.

"Do you fear the cordon?"

"No, of course not."

"What about you, Professor Blade?" Gregor asked.

"Gregor, we have been equals for years now. You don't have to call me 'Professor'. And no, I think that it is good that you are all together. We need to discuss things."

"The Bayer clan is demanding that we turn over Bayer's Gauntlets," one of the woman said "They claim that, no matter what strides we have made to redeem the clan, Himanoco is still forsaken and has no call to the items of the Brownwolf."

"If we refuse?" Ran said quietly.

"They will attack," the other woman said. "It will be a clan war! The Bayer clan outnumbers us five to one and they are quite capable. Our ranks have swelled, but there is still no way we could stand a full on clan war."

"Why do we not just give gauntlets to them?" Xesca asked.

"It was your own urging Xesca," Blade said simply. "You were who found them and you said that it wasn't advisable as the gauntlets function similar to the Sword of Himanoco." He motioned to Gregor, "They nearly destroyed your friend Chase Park."

"Chase?" Gregor was confused. He couldn't remember anyone named Chase. He recovered quickly though. "Why doesn't Chase tell his clan what happened?"

"He did. Other contacts did as well. But they all think that their relationship to you clouds their judgment."

"My friends," Ran said, "if it comes down to a clan war, than that is what it will be. I have no fear of the Bayer. And the Malada has proven to be our ally in many things. I think that it would actually behoove us to put the Bayer in their place."

One of the woman gasped and another of the men jumped to his feet. "Not all of us are as powerful as the Himanoco Cordon, Master Grastle." He spat the last with contempt. "We would be risking many lives over something that doesn't belong to us."

"Gingee and Kivkavzed have both agreed to our control over their founders items," Xesca said. "Why should Bayer be different?"

Ran pulled out the Mace of Chaos. The table let out an audible gasp. All but Blade. "I say we let them come."

"And I say," Candace stood up, the Sword of Himanoco in her hand, "that we strike first. Had it not been for us, no one would have cared about their clan items. We find them. We catalog them. We protect them. If that isn't good enough for them, they can feel the wrath of Himanoco!"

"I guess that this is what we are here for," Gregor whispered into Xesca's ear. "What do you think that we should do?"

"I honestly do not know. Memories are flitting through my head and I am uncertain what information I should work with. Everything is clouded by the fact that there is a sixteen year gap."

"Maybe we should just play along with the war then?"

"Excuse me Xesca, Gregor," Blade said with a clearing of his throat. "But is there something you would like to share?"

"You take that tone and wonder why I still refer to you as Professor Blade?" Gregor teased easily. Blade chuckled. He was the only one. "We were planning where the first strike should attack and how large a force it should encompass."

"Unless this collective would like to challenge the will of the Himanoco Cordon?" Xesca asked. There were worried glances, but no one spoke up. "Very well, I shall get together my Partisan's and my Warriors. We shall strike at Thom on as the noon sun shines on Kosivo. I shall expect all of you to be there as well." A murmur of "Aye" went round the table. "I think that is all that I have to add. Anyone else?"

No one said anything and most of the others left. One of the women and Blade stayed behind with the foursome. "Are you sure that this is wise?" the woman asked.

"Andretta," Blade interrupted, "I don't think that they want to hear that question. I think that what question we should ask is what do they already know?"

"What do you mean?" Xesca asked.

"It is never coincidence when you four are together that trouble is sure to follow. Everyone knows that you built the first new academy in five thousand years, complete with another Himanoco Tower and arches to test the students. We also know that you tend to use those arches to test theory and usually know just what people will say before they say it. So, I ask again, what do you already know?"

"Malada Arches?" Candace asked. She turned to Xesca. "You can make Malada Arches?"

"So it would appear." Xesca stoked her chin thoughtfully. "I honestly have not prepared for this Professor. I think that I can safely say that we will all be as surprised to see what happens as you all will be." The Blackwolf master named Andretta fainted dead away.

"Rally the troops," Ran said to her, the mace still in his hand. "We will meet you there."

"Aye."

Xesca opened a slide portal to coordinates she would have been uncertain of just a few moments before. She stood before a campus that she was both familiar and unfamiliar with. Moving quickly to her office, she found two students to act as pages, "You, gather all of the Partisan's to the field behind the tower as fast as you can. You, gather as many Blackwolves as you can and have them meet us at the birthplace of the Brownwolf. Go now, both of you."

She moved about her office for a few moments after the two pages left. *My office,* she thought to herself, *in my academy on my planet. This is what the future holds for me. I accomplished everything that I set out to do. I am preparing a new race to never be worried about the wolves again. And now I agreed to frighten the universe again by sending the Blackwolf snarling and biting his brown brother. Must it always be this way?*

Then Xesca remembered. This was all at her disposal to change. If things did not work out well, if this plan for this situation was a bust, she still had a chance to do things differently. If this situation came around again, she could work from this experience. It made her feel better.

She moved quickly across the campus to where her students were gathered. "We go to war against the Bayer clan to protect the Bayer Gauntlets. I realize that you are all still students, but you train hard and it is time to earn the field experience that those who aspire to bear the name Himanoco should have."

"Aye!"

Xesca opened a slide portal so large that even she marveled at it. *How powerful are we?* They rushed through and came out in the town of Thom. "Squads of twenty," Xesca called out, "you will be assigned to a master as soon as they arrive. Engage the enemy as soon as you see them."

"Aye!"

"So, you're taking command of this one, my lovely green skinned lady?"

"Ran, it feels like years since you called me that."

"I'll make sure that I do it more frequently then." He smiled at the double meaning.

"Take a twenty and use them how you like."

"Aye ma'am."

She assigned all of the masters, including Gregor and Candace in a similar fashion, taking the last three squads for herself. Skirmishes had started almost immediately, and she noticed several Gingee and Kivkavzed soldiers fighting alongside the Bayer. She had used a telepathy that she knew she now had to advise all of the master's to subdue the other clansmen but not kill when at all possible. This fight was with Bayer and it would be too poetic if the Blackwolf warriors started killing off Green, Blue, and Brownwolves.

Slicing through the crowds of soldiers, the Blackwolves pressed on. The resistance they met felt token by nature. It seemed, in fact, that nothing the other clans could throw at them was even going to slow them down. *Gregor, shall we hold?*

We can. This is a walk.

"Ran!"

Xesca spun where she heard Candace yell. Ran had fallen. By the time Xesca had gotten to him, he was dead. "No!" She raised her sword to order the push for victory.

A hand clasped her sword hand. "Xesca stop. The plan doesn't change because Ran is down."

"They killed him!"

"This is war! People die! You can't avenge every death!"

Her chest heaved. Her head spun. Still, Xesca reached out with her mind and gave the order to stop fighting. "I will not avenge, but I will not forgive either."

With her mind and the power in her cloak, she sent one simple message, *We will always prevail. Do not try to prevent us from what we will do.*

She looked around her and to her shock, no one was moving at all. Time itself seemed to have stopped everyone but her. She suddenly spotted Gingee, moving amongst the ranks toward her. "Excellent battle Xesca."

"I lost an ally."

"And gained the knowledge that you needed."

"And what was that exactly?"

"Oh, you disappoint me," Gingee said, full of scorn. "You have so much power, you could rule the universe. You got a glimpse of that in the first arch with Himanoco and Candace's planet. Now you see that if you work together, you can control everything.

"And yet, you wouldn't even have tried if not for this not being in the dimension that you consider to be reality. Now that you have seen what could happen, that you lose one of your new closest friends, you most likely won't try again. But I tell you this, if you do search for the clan items, which your group has every indication of doing, then the other clans will turn against you. It is unavoidable."

"Not if we give them the items."

"Then you may have to deal with the wolves incarnate. I tell you with all certainty that if I am reborn because of my items and can not subvert you, I will try to destroy not only you but as many of your clan I can until I have control of them."

"So, we should turn away from searching for the clan items?"

"You should do whatever you think that you should do. I wanted to gauge your strengths. I have. This has been quite enlightening, as have the other experiences. I am very pleased and can hardly wait for the last one." Gingee waved a hand and the archway in Himanoco Tower appeared. A gust of wind drew her through it and she was gone.

Chapter 32

Ran Alone

Ran emerged in the same room he had just stepped through. "This is getting ridiculous!"

"What?" Candace asked, confused.

"This damnable hopping from one archway to the next, bouncing around from place to place, staying in the same place...augh!"

"Calm down Ran," Gregor said.

"No, you calm down," Ran spun and drew his sword in one deft motion. He leveled the point at Gingee's heart. "I'm going to kill this bastard right now."

"Now now Ran, no need to get violent," Gingee wore a nervous smile. "This is not meant to enrage you, just educate."

"By Jehan's own voice if you utter one more word I will cleave your tongue from your head!"

Gingee had his own sword out and batted Ran's away from his neck. "Do you really want to do this disciple? If I could defeat your master, what in the universe gives you the impression that I could not beat you?"

Ran's growl was nearly feral as he drew his sword back. "You tread thin Gingee."

"And I do not care. This is not entirely for you Ran, no matter how important you think that you are. I have some things that I would like to find out as well and I am going to pay for this insurrection when you four are gone."

"You know, I hear your appeals and rationalizations and I still don't care. Keep pushing me Gingee and we'll test what thousands of years in evolution have taught me!"

"All right, all right," Gingee put his sword away and held up his hands. "This is the last tapestry. When you finish, you four will emerge back in you precious Himanoco Tower as masters. I say when you finish, because it doesn't matter whether you survive or die, you are a master for accepting my challenge.

"Ran, I have something a little different planned for you, especially after this little outburst. Pay close attention to detail, because the things that you are about to see and hear are possible courses that your lives could take and you will be the only one who can remember what happened." Gingee bowed deeply, mockingly. "Good luck."

Ran and his friends went directly to the door without another word. On the other side, Ran could feel his age, more acutely.

"Ran, you've gotten older," Candace exclaimed, then heard her own voice.

"We've all gotten older," Gregor said. "I'd say somewhere in the neighborhood of thirty years older."

"Thirty two long years since we trained together in the tower," Ran said, sounding old even to himself. It stood to reason though, thirty two years into the future would make him seventy-five.

They surveyed where they were. A large manor house was in front of them. The house sat on the top of a knoll, looking over a small valley. Grapes grew in the valley below. "Is this someone's home?" Xesca asked.

"This is my home," Ran said, "I don't know how I know that it's my home, but it is. And, by Jehan above and below..." he trailed off.

"What?" Candace asked.

"That's my wife at the window. My children, hardly children anymore, should be here shortly to visit. I am expecting them."

They all looked at the woman waving at them from the window. "That's Giselle! She's the headmistress of my families house!"

"Not anymore Candace," Ran smiled serenly, a look that confused the other three. "She's been my wife for the past twenty-four years. We did meet through you though, at your wedding."

"My wedding," Candace sputtered.

"Father!" A man's voice called from behind them. A strapping young man, broad of shoulders and quite well muscled bounded up the walk-way toward the house, a blushing girl in tow.

"Gelder!" Ran exclaimed, bounding toward his son. Even though the man was quite large looking, especially next to Ran's older, leaner body, Ran wrapped him in a vise like embrace. "And your wife Sirrah," he broke the embrace on his son, just to lift up the young lady and spin her around.

"Father Ran, please," she said, laughing, "you'll hurt yourself."

"Not my father!" Gelder laughed. "He will never lose his strength until his last breath is out of him." They took note of the other three smiling faces in the group. Gelder shook Gregor's hand and embraced Xesca and Candace in turn, referring to each as either 'uncle' or 'aunt'.

"When is your sister going to arrive?" Ran asked.

Gelder's look immediately changed from jovial to one of consternation. "Father, Bonilla won't be coming."

"By Jehan why not?"

"Yes brother, why wouldn't I be coming to this joyous day?" A strikingly beautiful young woman appeared behind them. She was dressed in blue, wearing the marks of Gingee. "Am I no longer invited to my parents home?"

Gelder moved in front of Sirrah. Ran was unsure what was going on, and it was Gregor who noticed first. "She carries Gingee's Sword. She is the hand of Gingee."

"What?"

"Don't you remember Father?" Bonilla's voice hung heavy with sarcasm and contempt. "It was you who made this all possible. You and the high and mighty Himanoco Cordon who found all of the Wolf Items. You and your cordon who tried to keep them out of the hands of true acolytes." She brandished the sword menacingly. "Now though, Gingee's Sword is back where it belongs, in the hands of a true Bluewolf. Perhaps it will get to drink of Himanoco blood after all."

"Bonilla," Ran started. He couldn't say anything else but the name over and over again.

Gelder on the other hand, was more prepared. He is Kivkavzed and transforms into a mixture of a man and a tiger. "Softly, little sister," the words were difficult to discern, sounding half growl and half speech. "You want to be careful with me."

"Oh? And why is that big brother?"

Gelder's chest gave off a small glow. A medallion worked it's way out from under his shirt to hang in clear view. "Because I wear the Heart of Kivkavzed. Gingee may be powerful, but Kivkavzed and Himanoco together are more than a match."

"You would stand with this traitorous bunch?" Bonilla waved her hand. "Your blood betrayed you. The only reason you have the Heart is because they didn't know about it. How long do you think it would have been before they take it away? Or, more appropriately, how long do you think it will be?"

Candace drew the Sword of Himanoco. "This is gone on long enough, my young *dhalion*. The Gingee Sword in your hands is no match for the Sword of Himanoco in mine."

"No!" Ran shouted. "There will be no blood shed today." Giselle had come out of the house and joined in the commotion. "None that I don't administer anyway."

In a flash, Ran switched his stance and drew his own sword from his cloak. Bonilla just got her sword up in time to deflect the blow. "You want to dance with me Father?"

"Little girl, I taught you most of your dance steps. The better question is if you want to dance with me?"

Their swords rang in a small volley of clanging metal. Giselle screamed out "No!" but Ran waved his hand and Xesca held her arm. Ran and Bonilla were astounding to watch, each feinting and slashing, coming close but not getting one or the other off balance.

"You are fifty years my senior," Bonilla said, beginning to pant from the strain. "How long do you think that you can keep this up?"

But Ran just laughed. His strength may have waned over the years, but not his skill. And his body, while not capable of large showings of power, was still more than durable enough to duel.

Gelder had transformed back into a full human. He was standing by Gregor. "What is Father thinking? He can't match Bonilla."

But Gregor was smiling broadly. "Your Father doesn't realize how old he is. He thinks that this is training in the Himanoco Tower."

"What? You four trained in the tower over thirty years ago!"

"My sworn son," Gregor put his hand on Gelder's shoulder, "sometimes it feels like eons ago. Sometimes, it feels like we never left. Trust in these four old wolves," he grinned again and Gelder felt a little more at ease. "We aren't ready to die yet."

Bonilla was pressing. Ran's chest was heaving, his heart pounding. "Oh, my sweet Bonilla, it is time that we end this."

"I will end you soon, my poisonous father."

It happened in a flash. Ran had dropped his sword just before a vicious downward slash from Bonilla. He sidestepped and Bonilla was unprepared, the momentum from her blow carrying her and the sword forward toward the ground. As she stepped forward to regain her balance, Ran drew the belt dagger that he had given her for her twelfth birthday from the hip he knew that she wore it on. As she straightened, he spun behind her, pulling the blade up to her throat.

"Ran! If you kill our daughter, I will never forgive you!" Giselle cried in anguish and Candace helped Xesca to restrain her.

"See the man your husband is Mother?"

"See the daughter you have Giselle?" Ran retorted. "She betrayed her flesh. If I do not kill her, she will kill me."

"You are right old man," Bonilla spat. "I won't hesitate."

"You won't have the chance."

Everyone turned to the voice that spoke those words. Another young woman, just a little older than Bonilla was standing behind them. She was of the Himanoco clan. "She will be persecuted by her own clan for the crimes of tampering with the Wolf Items."

"Kendall," Gregor said softly.

"Don't worry Father," she said, walking over to him. "I can handle my cousin."

"I am no blood of yours!" Bonilla spat.

"I won't hold that against you," Kendall said lightly. Bonilla raged, struggling in her fathers grip and lightly cutting herself on her own blade. "I can handle her Uncle Ran. Let her go."

"Do not turn me over to this bitch!"

Ran let her go and Kendall waved her arms. A shining cell formed around Bonilla. "She can't break free. Bonilla was never much on magic."

"Is this the future that I am force to face?" Ran raged. "My own daughter is swayed by this power!"

The scene froze. No one and nothing moved. "Possibly." Gingee's voice came from Ran's right. "So many things are possible.

"But you see these two? Your son Gelder is an upstanding member of the Kivkavzed clan. He uses the Heart of Kivkavzed for good. And this one," he motions to Kendall, "is a member of a multi-clan team that you four formed. Based on finding our items, you four decided that it was best to give the appropriate item to the appropriate clan. After that, to make sure that the item's power wasn't abused, you formed that consortium. Kendall is the head of the Blackwolf members."

"What happens to my daughter?" Ran asked.

"What ever you want to happen to your daughter. That was always the difficulty with studying the future, especially the distant future, so many things can change. You never know, now that you know that this is a possible future, what you may do or say that will change this event."

"Then why did you torture me with this?" Ran raged.

"Because you threatened me in the tower. I warned you to tread soft."

"You lousy, contemptible, slime!"

"Enough! You need no more!" Gingee waved his hand and the archway appeared behind him. Before Ran could react, the archway sucked him through.

Chapter 33

Training is concluded

"You did it!"

"Now that," Candace said, breathless, "was intense!"

"I would like to give you a moment to catch you breath, but" Defalorn started but Candace cut him off.

"And we are going to take that moment and more Master. If you will excuse us, we will be along shortly to Frotnefalt to help you battle Kenor. Just give us a few moments to collect ourselves and discuss what happened."

The rest of the group hid their surprise at Candace's statements. Defalorn, however, was aghast. "How could you possibly have known what was happening while you were in the archway?"

"It is too long to explain and you may have a difficult time believing anyway. Just trust that we will trot along shortly."

Defalorn's jaw worked soundlessly. Finally, without another word, he turned and left the tower.

"Candace," Gregor asked, "what was that all about?"

"I don't think that I have a whole lot of time to explain and I am sure that you all would love to tell what happened to you. Unfortunately, save it for another day.

"Kenor has been splitting the clan while we've been in the tower. In fact, most of the clan sides with him. My father is against him, and so am I. He has been searching for the Himanoco Items to convince people that he is the Blackwolf incarnate. He has the armor. I know a way that we can get it away from him and use it for ourselves."

"How?" Xesca asked.

"Everyone, form a circle. Now, step back and call for your sword," Candace stuck out her sword hand and her sword came streaking forward. The others followed suit, so that the four points were touching "And we call to the Sword of Himanoco just like this."

They all did as she directed. The sword appeared in the circle before them. "Outstanding!" Ran exclaimed. "I think our young Candace may have gotten the best of Gingee's little tour."

"You haven't heard my story yet," Gregor said, marveling at the sword. "Opinions may vary."

"We will have to save that for another day," Xesca said. She opened a portal to Frotnefalt. "Come. Candace, are you handling the sword?'"

"Yes. It is for me."

"Than you seem to know what is going to happen. You take the lead."

The four charged through the portal that Xesca had opened onto the field of battle. An army of Himanoco warriors stared across a field at a larger army of the same. Candace found her father quickly, with Defalorn already explaining why they weren't there.

"Father, I need you and your friends, or whoever is charge, to divide up the army into small groups and wait for the enemy to rush us. We can not engage the attack first."

"Candace," Defalorn stared, "is that the Sword of Himanoco?"

"Yes it is."

You have called me forth. Do you know how many centuries it has been since I have been called forth? The sword whispered in Candace's mind.

I know you sword. The archways showed me your mind and your heart. I know all about what you are and what you can do. I am your mistress now and you will just have to get used to that.

It has been years since I have had a master of any kind. I relish the opportunity to serve.

And I know why that is, so don't try to fool or seduce me. I seduce you. Prepare yourself.

Candace thought in her mind what she knew that the sword could already do. *You do know me* the sword said to her, excitedly.

"Ran, Gregor, you will each call the other items in the same fashion in just a moment. Xesca, I am sorry, but in my vision there was no item for you."

"Do not apologize Candace. I do not believe that I would want to wield an actual item of the original Himanoco. It has been a difficult enough course to follow in his footsteps.'"

"Fair enough. Gregor, the armor is yours. Ran, the mace."

"But Candace, you said that Kenor already is wearing the armor."

"Yes, but he didn't summon it, he found it lying around. It will respond to us better. First though, I want to meet and face him. To stand against him, item to item. It will help bind the rest of the clan back together."

Candace strode forward, the sword out in front of her. The army had broken from a large mass into tightly formed lines. Eyes followed the sword wherever it went. The army moved to follow her.

Kenor Anor stood at the front of his army. The Himanoco Armor shone brightly. He started forward to meet Candace, his army surging behind him. Once he was within earshot of Candace, he stopped. "I wear Himanoco's Armor. I am the Blackwolf incarnate and all who stand against me stand against their clan."

"You are nothing Kenor. I hold the Sword of Himanoco. My cordon is the Blackwolf Cordon and we are the proctors of the clan."

Murmurs ran through both armies. Two items of the original Himanoco? No one had seen these items in millennia and now two of them were together?

"How do we know that is the real sword?" Kenor asked haughtily. Both armies began to ring the two, neither of them attacking each other. Kenor was churning inside. *This is not what is supposed to happen!*

Candace leveled the sword point at Kenor. Two bolts fired, one at each shoulder. The clasps that held the armor together sprang free and it fell off of Kenor. "Gregor, call to it now!" In a flash, the armor was on Gregor's body. "Ran, the Mace." The Mace of Chaos appeared in Ran's hands. Candace turned and addressed the crowd. "See how the items of the master favor the true disciples of Himanoco? Do you see now that no one person could be what one person was? We are all the Blackwolf incarnate! We are his disciples. He flows through us all!"

Gregor continued. "Those who followed the wrong path are not at fault. They saw one of their brothers claim something and saw that he had the power and an item to prove it. Now you see that he was misguided and so were you."

"Never should Himanoco clansmen ever stand on opposites sides of each other," Ran's voice carried over.

"And let the followers of the forsaken son show the universe that he wishes to make amends," Xesca concluded.

Kenor howled in rage. "How did you do that? How did you take my armor from me? I am the Blackwolf incarnate! The armor told me!"

"The items lie," Candace said simply, "to those who wish to hear those lies."

"No! This is not possible!" Kenor drew his own sword. "I will kill you all and take back what is rightfully mine."

Candace started to step forward and Xesca stopped her. "You wish to claim the title of Blackwolf? Fine. Today, an Ohlian shall stand to make you pay for your crimes."

Xesca leaped at Kenor. Their swords clanged and sparked. Twisting and turning, they moved fluidly. "You are no match for me, Ohlian."

"You overestimate yourself Kenor." Xesca spun her sword quickly and used her free hand to fire a bolt of battle magic with the power of her cloak. The beam burned a whole right through Kenor's stomach.

The look of surprise on his face made Xesca feel sad. "Alas, Blackwolf, it would appear that today your student has surpassed you. I almost regret the fact that this lesson cost you your life." She walked forward and cut his head from his body. "Almost."

A roar ran through the gathered crowd. "The war is over!" "Long live Himanoco!" and "Forever Blackwolf!" were some of the things that were chanted.

"Go back to your lives," Gregor called out.

Slide portals began to open almost immediately. After forty minutes of people leaving the field, all that were left with the cordon was Mitris, Defalorn, Alexander Blade, Catleen, and Xavier.

"So," Mitris cleared his throat, "will someone tell me what just happened?"

"How did you get the Himanoco Items?" Catleen asked.

"How did you know what was going to happen?" Defalorn asked.

"Enough." Gregor said gently, holding up his hands. "Peace, please. I'll explain."

"No, you won't." Ran said.

"Oh?"

"We are masters now, same as them. In fact, we appear to be more powerful than them. If we want to explain things, we might eventually. Right now though, I have been away from my home for the past four months. I would like to get back to it."

"You can't just leave without telling us what happened." Blade protested.

"Sorry Professor," Xesca said, "but this has been a long journey and we are worn out."

"Tell you guys what though," Gregor said, "I promise that we will meet up over the next month and write all down."

"For now though," Candace put away the Sword of Himanoco. She turned to her friends. "I love you my friends."

"I'll second that," Ran said with a smile.

"I, too, love all of you very much." Xesca said, tears in her eyes.

"I feel the same about all of you," Gregor pulled them together in a group embrace. "This has been the adventure of a lifetime."

"I have the feeling children," the look in Ran's eyes was devilish, "that this is just the beginning."

Laughing and crying together, they went their separate ways, back to the waiting arms of their families and friends.

ABOUT THE AUTHOR:

Bryan Foster is a native Michigander, born in the greater Detroit area but spending the majority of his life in the Northern portions of the state. This is his first book, a project he admits he "never really expected to finish", and it became the first of a series he plans to write.

Bryan's a bachelor and an only child with two incredibly supportive parents without whom this book wouldn't have been possible. When he isn't writing or spending time with his family, you can visit him at his day job, the last downtown hotel in Petoskey. In fact, he encourages it. He's always excited to meet new people.

Printed in the United States
54748LVS00002B/121-123